Melissa Lucashenko is a Goorie (Aboriginal) author of Bundjalung and European heritage. Her first novel was published in 1997 and since then her work has received acclaim in many literary awards. *Hard Yards* was shortlisted for the *Courier-Mail* Book of the Year Award. Her sixth novel, *Too Much Lip*, won the 2019 Miles Franklin Literary Award and the Queensland Premier's Award for a work of State Significance. It was also shortlisted for the Prime Minister's Literary Award for Fiction, the Stella Prize, two Victorian Premier's Literary Awards, two Queensland Literary Awards and two NSW Premier's Literary Awards. Melissa is a Walkley Award winner for her non-fiction, and a founding member of human rights organisation Sisters Inside. She writes about ordinary Australians and the extraordinary lives they lead. Her latest book is *Edenglassie*.

Also by Melissa Lucashenko

MELISSA LUCASHENKO

HARD YARDS

UQP

First published 1999 by University of Queensland Press
PO Box 6042, St Lucia, Queensland 4067 Australia

This edition published 2023

University of Queensland Press (UQP) acknowledges the Traditional Owners
and their custodianship of the lands on which UQP operates. We pay our
respects to their Ancestors and their descendants, who continue cultural and
spiritual connections to Country. We recognise their valuable contributions to
Australian and global society.

uqp.com.au
reception@uqp.com.au

Cover design by Jenna Lee
Author photograph by LaVonne Bobongie Photography
Typeset in 11.5/15 pt Bembo by Post Pre-press Group, Brisbane
Printed in Australia by McPherson's Printing Group

  University of Queensland Press is supported by the
Queensland Government through Arts Queensland.

 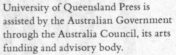 University of Queensland Press is
assisted by the Australian Government
through the Australia Council, its arts
funding and advisory body.

A catalogue record for this book is available from the National Library of
Australia.

ISBN 978 0 7022 6608 9 (pbk)
ISBN 978 0 7022 6403 0 (epdf)
ISBN 978 0 7022 6759 8 (epub)

University of Queensland Press uses papers that are natural, renewable and
recyclable products made from wood grown in well-managed forests and other
controlled sources. The logging and manufacturing processes conform to the
environmental regulations of the country of origin.

MIX
Paper | Supporting
responsible forestry
FSC® C001695

'It was genocide.'

—Sir Ronald Wilson,
Report of the *Inquiry into the Removal of Aboriginal Children*

PROLOGUE

It took the boy a long time to go over to the hooded phone booth.

When he finally got there, hesitant and afraid, he noticed that the front bit of the *White Pages* had been ripped off. There was a greasy ruffle of torn paper edges, smudgy with soft black ink, where the As and Bs should have been. When you looked at the front of the book, you saw the C and some numbers written in lipstick, pen, pencil. Meaningless messages from other lives – *charlie 3345 9860* or *Bruce Carpets 3231 0099* – crap like that. Taxi numbers, a lot of em, because of it being the Transit Centre. But it wouldn't have mattered to Roo where he was ringing from, here or the moon, because he was packing it, eh.

He braced his shoulder against the clear wall of the phone booth and searched through what remained of the phone book with wavering hands. Just lucky it starts with M, eh, he thought, as he thrust two silver coins into the phone and dialled. Blood pulsed inside his skin like he'd sprinted six blocks, when all he'd really done was push away his coffee cup, the last brown drops of liquid streaking down the white styrofoam, and then walk a few strides on a hard lino floor that reflected the glare of them big overhead lights back at him.

As he waited for the phone to answer, Roo was suddenly overcome by a wave of dizzying nausea. He choked on stuff that was trying to make its way up his throat. If a bloke didn't know better, he thought when the retching had passed, you'd think all them things they say about being scared was just words. But its true, eh, that's the funny thing. Your hands really *do* shake. You really *do* go blank. He used the edge of a twenty-cent coin to try and chisel some of the metallic paint off the phone as he waited.

Someone's picked it up. O God O God, what now?

'Is Graeme Madden there, please?' Roo croaked.

'The Maddens haven't lived here for twelve months. Sorry.' The woman hung up.

He stood, breathing hard, lost. Hadn't counted on that. So what now? Another smoke, fuck yeah, a durrie. He shivered with satisfaction at the first lungful, then dug out his coins and tried the next number in the book. It wasn't as bad the second time round, not with the possibility of wrong numbers lined up beside the other terrifying option.

'Can I, um, speak to Graeme Madden please?' Breathe out a stream of white that slowly, slowly dissipates into nothing. Hope the security guards don't come. Tap tap tap with a coin on the box.

'Ah, there's no Graeme Madden here. There's a Glenda Madden, but she's at work, is that who ya mean?'

'Nuh, wrong number.' Now it was Roo's turn to hang up. Two down, two to go. He stomped his feet on the hard white floor in a brief agitated dance, and then reached into his pocket once more.

'Is Graeme Madden there?' Say yes, fuck ya. He kicked at the booth's perspex wall with the toe of his basketball boot. It was pretty solid; you'd have to really boot it hard to crack the cunt.

'Graeme? You mean Garth ... Hey, Garth, phone mate—' Clunk.

Wanker. If I said Graeme, then I fucken meant Graeme, din' I? Roo looked at the last number, guts tightening with anxiety. On the Russian roulette principle, this was gonna be the one. A Mount Gravatt address. He counted his little remaining change; there was still enough. Don't wuss out now, he told himself, just do it, okay? He noticed himself sweating.

The ringing of the phone. An answering machine. A man' voice, slow and deliberate: *You have called Graeme and Faith Madden. We are unable to take your call at the present moment, so leave a message after the beep and we will endeavour to get back to you as soon as possible ... BEEEEEEEEEP.*

Roo stood dumbly holding the phone. Blood thrummed wildly in his ears. A group of Taiwanese went past, loud in their tourist excitement as they trailed enormous suitcases behind them. Trains groaned and swooshed on the floor below him. For fully half a minute Roo found he couldn't move, couldn't think. Then in slow motion he pressed the little phone doovers down to break the connection, and straightaway rang the number again. *You have called ...*

Hear that? Six ta four on, that's yer old man. Faith must be his wife, eh. Roo ripped the page out of the phone book, pocketed it and stepped out into Roma Street. He noted the tall pig standing outside, and then took off in the direction of the Myer Centre. His problem had changed; the question buzzing in Roo's slightly dizzy head now was how best to get to Mount Gravatt, ten kilometres from the city, when the sum of his worldly wealth was sitting in the cash box of a very public phone.

PART ONE

DARKNESS KINDLED

CHAPTER ONE

The morning of Stanley's funeral dawned clear and hot.

'Get the TV and the video, and the CD ... take them discs too Darryl, they'll go if we leave 'em,' ordered Mrs King from the lounge where she sat in frantic grief. 'And the glasses, that thievin' gin always wanted them, yeah and the camera. Nah, hang on, we'll need it to take photers, leave it, eh, put it in me handbag, Daz. Zat it?'

She lit another cigarette and drew down hard on it. Dell King was a short black woman, forty-eight years old. Today she was going to bury her youngest son, the third dead of nine. You couldn't easily read about this story in her dark eyes. If the deaths and the life that went with them showed at all it was in a heaviness of movement, a kind of silent pessimism that weighed her body down. There was something about Dell King that reminded you of rock. Her opinions were longstanding ones, and it was a long time since she'd seen fit to revise any of them. In others this might have been rigidity, but in Mum King it had become a kind of stolid wisdom which had saved her. Red-eyed and gaunt with suffering, she hadn't quite succumbed to despair, not yet, though it was knocking hard at the door this morning. How could she give up, with Leena and the twins to worry about? You'd love nothing more than to stop the world and get off, but there was just too much to do to indulge ya'self, with that little luxury. Things happened that ya couldn't stand, and ya just stood them, thassall, and then life went on.

'What about?' Darryl held up his late brother's treasured Broncos cap and jacket.

'Yeah.' Mum began to cry again. She held her palms to her eyes. 'Put 'em in the car.' Then the phone rang for the millionth time since last Saturday.

'Muu-um! Legal Service,' called a female voice from the kitchen. Mum got grimly to her feet and, hoping that there would be no more terrible delays, no more talk of autopsies and head injuries and blood alcohol levels, went to talk to the fella.

Darryl's scowl hardened as he took the jacket and cap outside and laid them gently on the back seat of the van. A couple of weeks ago he'd gone and gotten the cap back special from Todd's place, so Stanley could wear it getting outa John Oxley. Today, since no one had rung to say this was all some stupid migloo mistake – because no one (incredibly) had come knocking to admit that, oh sorry, brother was really alright after all and still locked up waiting for his weekly visit – today the jacket and cap were going to be buried with him. Darryl couldn't tell anyone, but ever since they got the bad news he'd had the absurd feeling that if he hadn't gone and got the cap and jacket, hadn't tempted fate like that, then Stanley would still be alive. It was his fault Stanley was dead. Why did he always have to do too much? Why was he always, in the end, so very wrong no matter how hard he tried? It was just no good.

Darryl climbed in and sat on the back seat of the van where no one could see his shame. He doubled over and held the jacket against his face, wracked with silent bewildered sobs. He was twenty-one and sposed to be tough, sposed to be hardheaded like a blackfella gets early on to protect himself. Darryl was twenty-one, but he was the oldest of the Kings, and if Stanley was the only regular jailbird of the family, if Leena knew she had an uncle to call on when she needed to, and if the twins were still at school and lookin like they just might stay on, they had Darryl to thank as much as Mum. Floundering in the aftermath of Stanley's death, though, Darryl could do nothing but hold on to the fierce shards of his world and hope that the chaos he felt inside would stay hidden there. He couldn't write notes to teachers or administer hidings to fix this up; the luxury of his omnipotence had ended.

Everyone was kept busy all that morning following Mum King's instructions. Everyone except for Jimmy, that is, who was still charged. The other boys had had the good grace to sober up for the service, but then Jimmy never did know when to stop. One in every family. They reckon.

'My bruvver,' he howled softly to himself at the kitchen table, 'My lil' bruvver ...' till Mum finally

9

couldn't stand it any more and told him to fucken shut up or fuck off. He raised a bleary, wounded profile to her. 'My bruvver ...' A brown arm wobbled in the air, the hand desperately clutching a half-size bottle of bourbon.

'Ah, what'd I do ta deserve you? Ain't you got no shame?' The woman abused him tiredly. It would have to have been Stanley we lost, my baby. An immense tide of anger rocked beneath her words. Hold it in, woman. A lifetime holding it in, what can another day do? Just for today. Like that time she went with Joe to the AA, one day at a time. Oh, she laughed, eh. Worked that one out for herself long ago.

'Oh yeah, my lil' bruvver's gone and if I wanna drink, I'll fucken drink. So fuck you and fuck—' Jimmy began to drag himself to his feet in affront.

Mum swung round and silenced him with a savage look. Enraged, she seized the bottle and hurled it out the open door. It smashed on the concrete path. Pieces of glass glittered evilly in the grass. Shocked, Jimmy was silent. Mum blew her breath out noisily, signalling her anger. 'Ah shit, Darryl, get some coffee inta him, willya? What's the time? Christ! Where's Leena? Didja lock the bikes in the shed?'

'Yeah. Don't worry Mum, it's all done now. Shaleena be here dreckly she said.' Darryl looked around the living room. All that was left was the oldest lounge, long consigned to the dogs, and a worthless chipboard cabinet. Everything of value had been lodged with the Wheelers next door, away from the grasping criminal hands of Stanley's father's family. It was safe, now, to go to the chapel.

★

Roo squatted in the scrub, watching the street through a fringe of wattle branches. A light rain fell. In the last hour his jeans had gone from the palest washed-out sky blue to a dark cobalt; now as the sun lowered itself onto the distant hills he was feeling cold and damp. He shifted his heels uneasily on the wet grass and craved a cigarette, a cone, a charge. Something.

A short distance from his vantage point on the side of the mountain, the Madden house sat at the top of a steep concrete driveway. It was no bigger or smaller than the other ordinary brick houses close by, but being on high ground, it drew the eye. Its height gave the house a slight air of importance. You could tell it'd be the place the neighbours would sit around talking about at night, the one they'd be wishing they'd bought instead. Peering through the wet yellow blossoms, Roo could see the driveway and the front patio that was enclosed with fat white stumpy railings meant to give the house a mock-Italian look. There were potted plants – umbrella trees – on the patio, and a well-tended garden. A couple of gums in the front yard, some little trees flowering along the fenceline and shrubs up against the lower walls. The lawn was mowed. There were no toys or kids stuff laying around, and after carefully watching for an hour Roo was sure no one was home. A weldmesh fence surrounded the lot, and a Doberman bitch was lying on her bed under the patio overhang, shivering as the rain whipped up under the eaves. Poor thing.

He considered breaking in and having a durrie while they were out, but the dog put him off. Not too keen on dogs. It was too late now anyway. Five-twenty. If

Graeme Madden worked office hours there was every chance he'd be home soon. You stupid bastard, Roo told himself, why'ntya think of it sooner? Too eager to get a look at the man, he'd missed his chance to check his life out first, see if he even wanted to be any part of it. Just the whisper of the idea – *Father* – and he'd taken off from the adoption mob, made the call, hoiked out to the southern suburbs. And for what? Roo sat in the bush, feeling wet and foolish.

He took a long, measured look at the house. From that patio you'd be able to see for a real long way over Holland Park, probably into the Gabba and towards town. Not right into the city, of course, but a long way. So, his Dad mightn't be full-on rich, but he must have a bit of money. A job, anyway – it wasn't no dole house. So far, so good. Mount Gravatt was an ordinary suburb for ordinary people. A few Murries lived out this way, not heaps but some. Wouldn't be none in this street but, not with brand-new Magnas and two-year old Pajeros in the driveways. The blacks lived more on the other side of Logan Road, further away from the bush that was conveniently hiding his skinny white face from this fella – this mysterious prick – who'd dropped him into the welfare system seventeen years ago and walked away without a second thought.

The low hum of a car engine a block away turned quickly into a silver Commodore coming up the street. Roo caught a glimpse of the man driving it, a biggish bloke with light brown hair. The car accelerated towards the house to make it up the steep driveway, then came to a stop just out of Roo's sight. He craned his neck as far out of the bush as he could without being seen. The car door banged shut, and Roo saw the man walk away towards the house, hunched over and holding a black folder above his head because of the rain. He looked, oh, old, eh. Forty or something. Fit though, pretty tall and big in the shoulders like a footy player, but dressed flash in a business shirt and trousers. Must be some sorta desk jockey then. Solicitor, maybe – that'd be handy. From a distance he didn't look a lot like Roo, but then he didn't *not* look like him either. He didn't have two heads or nothin. It was hard to say. Roo breathed out hard. That – that there – hurrying into the house, could be his father.

He rocked back on his heels and drew his hands down his wet face. Now what? Should he go up to the gate and wait for the dog to bark? One thing for sure, if he waited here getting wet much longer he was gunna miss the memorial service and Shaleena'd bore it right up him, the stompy little cow. He could hear her voice raised in anger at him already. He stood up, still undecided about exactly what to do, and stepped out of the bush as though he was a casual jogger. The bitumen gleamed black and wet, a river of tar running down the slope to the crossroads. He stood a minute at the edge of the road, then, aware of more time passing and more water dripping down his back, reluctantly began jogging past the house back to the shops. Fuck it. It was a stupid gammon idea anyway. Tomorrow he could—

'Hey!'

Roo spun on his heel. The man was standing at the front of the house, gripping the railing in both wide-apart hands. The dog stood alert by his side, ears pricked. He was fit alright. The muscles in his arms were hard and ridged and he had very little flab around the waist. He wasn't all that tall, a few centimetres more than him, but heaps heavier. And he wasn't only older, bigger and probably tougher, but he was hostile as well. If Roo was a dog, the hair on his back'd be up. He started to get jumpy in anticipation of that generic activity that his probation officer called Trouble.

When the man spoke, it was in a slow, lazily offensive tone that said *I'm in charge here, buddy.*

'What were ya doing in there, pal?' The male voice of authority got Roo's back up straightaway. As if he owns the bloody mountain, the migloo prick.

'Oh, and who the fuck are you?' he snorted without thinking. Then remembered oddly, that's what I'm here to find out. The man didn't blink or move. A hard case.

'Oh, bit of a toughnut are ya? Never mind who I am, sonny. If I catch ya hanging round my house again I'll kick ya little arse for ya, got that? Taking little smartarse cunts like you apart's my favourite occupation.' This bloke talked just like the coppers in the mall. Like he hated ya even if he didn't know ya. Like the very idea of ya was offensive. Roo stared at him angrily. The man had a broken nose from his footy playing, and a flat mean eye. I'll fix you, Roo thought. *Are you my father?* But he couldn't say it.

'Well, what're ya lookin at, shitfabrains?' the man demanded.

Still Roo said nothing. The man shook his head, oozing sarcasm.

'Are you some kinda fucken moron?' The last two words clear and slow for his benefit, with a finger to show him the way. 'Piss off.'

Roo hesitated one last time. He was way overdue at the funeral, but he'd come all this way. This hardheaded bastard could be his father, for Chrissake. He had to know. He searched desperately for a way to say it but his mouth was full of cotton wool. He vainly tried to swallow his spit.

'Right.' The man vaulted the railing to sort him out.

'Are you Graeme Madden?' Roo suddenly said, backing quickly away in a panic, his feet wanting to be several blocks away.

That stopped him. The man squinted aggressively at Roo's earrings and tats. How did this little cockroach know his name, and what did he want with it?

'What?'

'Are you Graeme Madden?' Roo repeated shakily. The man looked at him. Only the wire fence stood between them. Both of them were getting rained on. A dribble of cold water found its way under Roo's collar and set a course for his navel. He shivered but kept his gaze on the man.

'Who wants ta know?' The mouth was a thin straight line under flinty eyes. Roo couldn't say it. It was in his mind to say it but he just couldn't get it out, eh. What if he didn't believe him? What if he said, *So what*?

The man sighed and rolled his eyes. This kid was obviously not the full quid. He spoke slowly again. 'What's your name, sonny? What are you hanging around here for?'

Roo gave him a strange look. 'Reuben, Reuben Glover … I'm lookin for Graeme Madden.'

'Well, let's say for the sake of argument that you've found him. Whaddya fucken want? You think I got nothing better to do than stand around in the rain?'

The man's twisted face made Roo think of wounds. The rain had wet his sandy hair enough to make it stick down flat to his scalp, showing what Mum King called a slightly advancing forehead. His hand was pushed through the top of the weldmesh and he was a thread away from jumping the fence. This bloke hates me, Roo thought without surprise, so why am I here? Stupidly, what came into his head was something out of *The Cat in the Hat*. Something Leena read to the twins at night when they couldn't sleep.

Put Me Down, said the Fish, I do Not wish to Fall!
Put Me Down, said the Fish, this is No Fun at All!

Roo swallowed the huge lump in his throat. This was no fun at all. This was terrible, heaps worse than court. Looking at the man's grim grey eyes and hard-chiselled face Roo could tell that the man didn't really want to know. He breathed out with extreme precision and felt his heart free-falling down, down, down. The worm of loathing began turning inside him again. For his *stupid* hoping, after he'd told himself over and over to wise up. For dreaming again of someone who might properly … ah fuck, ya shoulda known. It was the same old story of the big world – his promises to himself broken, his lies to others upheld. Roo sucked the fragments of his heart together with a sharp indrawn breath then spat out the bitter words which were already half true. 'Nothin. Forget it.' He turned and jogged heavily away into the rain.

Graeme Madden went back inside and slammed the door. Kid standing around in the rain like a bloody drongo. What was *that* all about?

By the time the hearse pulled into the yard of the chapel, the heat of the day had finally turned to darkness and solid sheeting rain. Hardly anyone had thought to bring umbrellas, so they stood awkwardly under the inadequate protection of the chapel eaves, pretending that they didn't mind getting wet, not with Stanley lying there cold, and Aunty Della King gone pale with the strain. Talk about bad luck, eh. That woman had the worst luck in the world, even for blackfellas.

Everything had already been pretty much said at the community meeting on Saturday morning. The men clumped together in silence and looked at the ground. Pairs and threes of shattered women spoke softly to each other. (Whose son next? Whose nephew? Which, in ten years, of the baby boys now being nursed in the steamed-up cars by their mothers, whose casual love was today briefly replaced by a close-hugging and a cossetting of the bemused tots; by refusals to pass bubba on to Aunty, or even Nan.)

The teenage girls shivered in inappropriate sexy black evening dresses, the rain sliding in silver droplets down their bare arms and backs. Other than Darryl, who was constantly beside his mother, the dazed young men stood on the fringes of the group, their anger building as they smoked and swore. Tonight their families would cop it, and any strangers who carelessly wandered into their orbit. They would punch their love of poor dead Stanley onto the bodies of others. No one could say they didn't care then, no one could ignore them and the horror of their loss. For now though, they cursed the police, the screws, the doctors, the migs, the whole white world. They kicked at grass and car tyres, bowed their heads and folded their arms against the rain.

Just as the coffin had been borne inside, a late arrival – a taxi – pulled up a little away from the group. Roo burst out of the passenger door and walked quickly up to take his place next to Shaleena and Darryl, ignoring the curious looks he got for being both late and white. He gave Darryl a hard angry hug, then leaned across to grasp Jimmy's shoulder, but Jimmy swung away in contempt. Roo knew what he was thinking. The mig again. Who invited this white cunt to Stanley's funeral? Why'd Darryl let Shaleena go with a mig in the first place? Roo stood stockstill. Let it go. He didn't really expect anything better, not today of all days. Darryl motioned with his head. Forget it, man, come over here, you'll be right.

Roo stood, seething, for a beat of three, then shifted.

'You took ya good time,' Shaleena accused him after he'd taken her five-dollar note over to the taxi. 'Everyone was asking where ya were. Sayin ya got no respect.'

Roo shrugged off this invitation to an argument. A series of stress-fractures were running through his life, and he was having to concentrate just so he didn't spin right out, eh. His fingers were doing that tingling shit they did when he was about to spin. Cos Stanley was dead (*dead!*). His probable father was a mean, hard prick who didn't give a shit. Shaleena was always on his fucken case. Behind in his training. Never any money for escaping this life. Roo stared at the length of the shining hearse, blanking out. After a moment, Darryl put his arm around Mum's heaving shoulders and then they filed inside. Roo, too. White or not, screwup or not, it was time to say goodbye to buddaboy.

Inside, dull rectangles of light showed where the stained-glass windows were being lashed with rain. At the front of the church, Uncle Eddie was conducting some business with a smoking bucket of gum leaves. Mum went to the old man and cried on his shoulder. Then Darryl ushered her along the front row and sat himself down beside her without removing his arm. Rock of Ages. The rest of the family took up the opposite and second aisles, and community members sat in descending order of importance or self-importance behind them. There was little talk, just the sad quiet sound of the congregation brushing rain off themselves and preparing to mourn among their own.

Roo had a better grip on himself now, but he could have almost wept when he saw the preacher step up to the front near the altar thing. Fucken hell. The man could talk the leg off an iron pot. Off a fossilised pot. No wonder he became a preacher. Well that way he got a captive audience, didn't he? He could talk underwater with a mouth full of wet cement, he could, truegod. Uncle Eddie retreated, taking his bucket outside. His job was finished, for now.

'Dearly beloved,' the preacher began, 'it has fallen to me on this tragic occasion to say a few words …' And on and on he droned. A few words, Roo thought hysterically after fifteen minutes, more like a few million. After what seemed like a thousand 'O Lord's' and ten thousand 'Christ in whose name we are redeemed', the man drew his sermon to a long and trailing close. He looked up from behind his glasses as if he was about to recall some vital point he'd accidentally failed to cover, but Darryl stalled him by standing and pulling a single sheet of paper from his shirt pocket. He strode up and the preacher, displaced, reluctantly stood aside, hands behind his back.

Tall and stern in a borrowed suit, Darryl looked out over the patchwork of faces, their undivided attention turned back on him. Somewhere stranded in the middle sat three women, two of them white, dressed in the pale blue uniform of the Queensland Police; the seats beside them were glaringly empty. The silence of the crowd held as Darryl fought for composure. He was well-liked, well-respected by those who knew him, and those who didn't were hushed by the circumstances of Stanley's death and by the name King. Darryl smoothed the paper in front of him on the podium. A lightbulb flashed from the back of the room, prompting a brief angry murmur which subsided as Darryl started the eulogy for his cousinbrother.

'Brisbane Elders,' he began strongly. 'Visitors from the Kombumerri, Waka Waka, Kabi Kabi and Muninjali tribes. Minister Jackson, Uncles, Aunties, brothers 'n sisters, I hafta welcome you here today on behalf of the family. We're here today to say goodbye to … to a special young Murri fella who was took before his time. Our brother, Stanley—' and here Darryl's voice broke into a harsh rasping. He straightened himself up with such obvious physical effort that it turned Roo's heart to water. Others in the audience were pushing back the swelling tears with the back of their hands. Wet faces gleamed in front of the speaker.

He went on: 'Stanley used to say that for Murries hard times come easy. Before young brother was taken from us, I used to think that he meant Murries're always getting into trouble, and that it wasn't ever hard for us mob to find hard times. That we didn't have to look too far for em. Now all of us here who knew my brother, knew he wasn't no angel. He'd seen the inside of a lockup more than once; he done wrong by some people, including some people here today, and I hope he knew it, too. But Stanley didn't deserve to die the way he did. He was a young one, just a child of seventeen.' Darryl paused, and he abandoned the paper in front of him. 'I been thinkin ever since it happened, ya know, thinkin that maybe what Stanley meant when he said that hard times come easy was that when you see enough hard times, you get sorta good at it, if that's not a silly thing to say. How many times've we seen each other at the funerals of young ones, young fellas, this year? And what about last year? Or the year before that? We need to, we need to stick up for each other, not always be knockin each other, or lettin each other just … go. There's too many of us going. We been here too long to give up now ... forty thousand years this ground's been trod by blackfellas jinung. Fifty thousand! More ... you, and you, and you –' pointing to wide-eyed young men, '– you gonna be next? Or you?' Darryl shook his head in sorrow, muttering under his breath that he didn't know, he didn't know. Then he spoke up again.

'Anyway, I don't know much 'bout politics, so I'm not gonna say nothin' much about that side of it. I wanna tell youse about Stanley, anyway that's what we're here for, eh. I wanna remember the good stuff, happy times. One good thing I remember, me 'n Stanley went 'long last year to that show at South Bank, you know that one from up North with them paintings. We had a bit of a look around at em and then we talked to that old fella that come down from the Cape. He was real quiet, eh, he only said a few words to us, but I never forgot what he said, talkin about his Country up there. Said he was real homesick goin away from his people and his sites; his grandfather dreaming was waiting there for him to go back and finish up there. Said it, just like that. He didn't look sick to me, just old, but then about a coupla months later someone told me, sure enough, he went back and passed away there in the first week he was home. He knew. He *knew*. And you know what it was he told us, me and Stanley? He liked Stanley, see, took a shine to 'im cos he was such a deadly didge player, and he said, don't go thinking you lost your Country, boy. Said it was still there waiting, said the spirits are all 'round, daytime, nighttime, allatime, and they very patient. Two hundred years!' Darryl spat the words in the policewomen's direction. 'What's that to fifty, sixty, seventy thousand? Nothin. That old fella he took us over an' showed us somethin in one of them pictures, this crocodile dreaming it was, and he reckons, "When you know your Country proper way, it grows into you, grows through your heart and your blood and then they can't never take it away from you cos there's no difference between it and you." That's what he said — they can't never take it away.' Darryl glared at the crowd.

'That old fella was talking about finishing up and he sounded real happy, you know. I think maybe ... maybe he was trying to tell us something that day, maybe he seen more than his own future there. Anyway. He gorn now. Stanley was our brother, our son and our cousin, and he's gorn too. He part of our Country, ere la.' Darryl had by now accepted the wetness running down from the corners of his eyes, and his words were punctuated with gasps and sniffs. 'Stanley wouldna been happy 'bout finishin up, specially not this way, but I know one thing, his Country's took 'im back. They can hate us, and they can even kill us, but they can't do nothin 'bout that, we belong ere. And so long it's here wif all of us, so's he. Youse wanna remember that when ya hear them white fellas talk 'bout him on TV and that.'

Darryl looked up bleakly and in a gesture that came from nowhere cut the air with his right hand. 'Okay, thassall now.' He went and sat down again as the preacher organised everyone to sing 'Amazing Grace'. Tears ran from his tightly shut eyes. Jimmy and Mum King clutched at Darryl from both sides, weeping. Roo reached forward from the row behind and grabbed the man's shoulder with his pale hand. Darryl's hand came back and covered Roo's as the two of them looked down at the floorboards. As his mate sobbed his heart out, it was all Roo could do to stop himself from crying. Yer just a weak cunt, he told himself. But the tears didn't go anywhere in a hurry.

CHAPTER TWO

Graeme Madden checked the time showing on the microwave. It'd be an hour later in Sydney, eight-thirty, so Faith'd still be at home. Or rather: should still be home. He didn't know where the bloody hell she was half the time these days. A spasm of irritation passed across his face at the thought. Scrabbling with one hand for his lighter, Graeme used the other to dial the number that was written in Faith's neat hand on the pad beside the phone. A woman answered.

'Faith?' He lit a fag to calm himself.

'No, it's Margaret. Is that you Graeme?' His sister-in-law sounded exhausted.

'Yeah. How are ya?' For politeness' sake, as if he gave a shit. Poor bloody bitch, but he didn't want her howling down the phone at him, that was Faith's department. He didn't know how females stood hearing each other's problems all the time. Gabfest, no thanks.

'Yeah, well ... he's had a bad night ... I'll get Faith for ya, hang on.'

Graeme suppressed a tiny shudder. Not that you could

catch it over the phone, of course, but still. The Big C. And Pete only three years older than him.

He heard two women's voices in the background, then Faith coming towards the phone, saying to her sister, 'I think they're on the big bed, or else still in the dryer ... Hi, love, it's me.'

'Hi. How is he, I mean how're you?'

'Oh,' hesitating, 'okay. He's not too good, he was vomiting all night again. Marg's just about had it. We're going in again this morning and I think the doctors are going to make him stay in this time ...' Faith trailed off.

Graeme grunted in sympathy and said, 'Well, at least that'll take the strain off you two. He shoulda been in hospital weeks ago if he's that crook.'

'... and the kids are crying all the time, you know, and Claire's saying she won't go to school so Margaret doesn't know what to do with her. What can she do?'

'Kick her arse, that's what,' Graeme replied tightly. Twelve years old and 'won't'. He'd show her 'won't' if he was there. He blew a stream of smoke out the kitchen window flyscreen towards the bush. 'So when're ya coming back?'

'Oh, Christ, Grae,' said Faith helplessly. 'They're saying it's only a matter of time. Might only be a week or two ...'

'They've been saying that since Christmas.' Graeme's voice was flat, not quite hiding his anger.

'I know you've been patient, love, you've been great, but it's ... it won't be much longer. And it's my *family*.'

'So what does that make me?' he complained.

There was aggrieved silence from the other end. As

26

if she wouldn't actually come out and say it: two adults trapped in a stale marriage don't add up to a family. And, fucken hell, it wasn't as if he hadn't tried, for Chrissake. He'd been more happy for her to go and stay with Margaret, help her out when Peter got worse at New Year's. Forked out for the ticket without a second thought, and that was nearly four hundred bucks. But she was *his* wife, not Peter's. Two months was a long time for a bloke like him to live on his own, he reminded her. Peter had his own family to cry over him; Faith's place was with her husband. Specially now, when he was looking down the barrel of a gun. Surely that wasn't difficult to understand?

'Look,' he said, trying to sound more diplomatic than he felt, 'I know its hard for Margie, eh. But I just want to know how long its gonna be, luv. I mean, don't you think you should be here with me, luv, helping *me*? They're gonna start up the investigation again, and I mean, Jesus, I'm starting to think you're never coming home.'

'What do you mean, investigation? I thought that was all settled.' Faith was alarmed.

'Tell that to the marines.' Faint traces of fear began to seep into Graeme's voice. 'The politically correct brigade are gonna have a departmental inquiry into the fucken thing, they've got the IIU onto it now, so just get your arse on a plane by next week, alright? Margaret'll be alright, she's a big girl. Ya can't hold her hand forever, ya know.'

'Well … I don't know, Grae,' whispering, 'she's not too good – she's popping Seros like it's going out of fashion. And Peter's getting weaker every day.'

Graeme's strained patience finally snapped. 'Okay, okay then, alright. That's lovely that is. Piss off for two months to take care of your brother-in-law and then when your husband's got fucken problems of his own … I must say you've got your priorities right. Thanks for nothin.' Graeme hung up on his wife, knowing that his last words would seal her decision. She knew right from wrong, even if she did go off the rails occasionally.

Shaking her head with tiredness and anger, Faith carefully replaced the phone on its base. The lousy bastard. He acted as if she was here by choice, as if she preferred being down here watching her sister go round the twist, wiping Peter's backside and watching a young man turn old in front of her eyes. Was that why he sounded so strange? Not just pissed off, but *odd*. An unease followed her that day that she couldn't put down to simple guilt over neglecting Graeme. Something was out of place somewhere but she just couldn't put a name to it.

At work, Graeme threw his squash bag in the corner of his small office and grabbed a coffee cup printed with a homily on the nature of stress. When he'd filled it up in the tearoom and said g'day to the other early birds, he came back inside and sat at his computer. Reuben Glover, eh. He entered the name into the system and nodded with satisfaction as the stats came up in glowing green and black. It figured. If he couldn't pick a crim after fifteen years, and ten of those years long aggravating ones in uniform, there was something wrong. Reuben John Glover, a.k.a. John Samuel Glover, d.o.b. 31 March

28

1979. He'd been picked up the first time at thirteen for shoplifting down the Gold Coast. Stayed off the system for nearly a year, then got pinched by the dog squad at the Gabba pool hall trying to flog a hot video. Hmm, that sounded like he might be a smackie, but he was wearing a surfie shirt the other day, clean arms and was too healthy anyway, carrying too much weight, so rule that out. Graeme's cop brain started to creak into action, searching for patterns and connections that would escape a civilian. Why the Gold Coast, for instance? What would keep a young white kid hanging around the Gabba? Who dealt out of the pool hall? Who bought hot gear in the inner south that he could talk to?

He scrolled further down Reuben's record – the usual smalltime stuff. Break and enters. Assault on a security guard at the Hyperdome. Well looky here, the little shit can fight, look at that ... Broke his jaw in two places. Did eight months in John Oxley cos he was still sixteen, got good behaviour and paroled, then picked up again for another b and e six weeks later, locked up for five months ... It was a wonder he hadn't run in to this kid around the traps, Graeme mused. Funny record though, really, it was all over the place. You wouldn't expect a young kid tough enough to bash a security guard to ever get good behaviour, for one thing. Unless he *was* a druggie after all, off his face, and the guard couldn't drop him cos he was sky high, and not feeling the hits.

And now Reuben John Glover had been out of trouble since last September. Almost half a year with no charges and no parole violations. That didn't ring true either. There was something funny here, but what was it?

Glover, the man worried at the name like a terrier, *Glover*. After a few minutes he gave up. He was sure he'd never heard of him.

'Hey, Ellen,' Graeme called out to the big room outside, 'c'mere for a sec, will ya?'

The woman came in and stood next to him, looking at the screen. Graeme resisted the automatic urge to goose her glorious arse in its tight navy skirt. She was Bill's root, not his. 'Reuben John Glover. Mean anything to you?'

She thought a moment, tilting her head, then said, 'Name rings a bell, but I can't ... Nup, sorry. I know the name but I've never pinched him. Ask Bill, he might know.'

'Okay, ta. Where is he, d'ya know?'

'Off with the Fat Controller. Had to see him at nine.'

'Righto. Ask him when he gets back for me, will ya?'

Graeme leaned back in his chair, sipping the percolated coffee that kept the whole division rolling. They all drank too much of it, jug after hot black caffeinated jug. Then wondered why they couldn't relax. Well, fuck it, what did cops need to relax for? You could relax when you were dead.

'Going to pick him up for his birthday, are ya?' Ellen joked on her way out of the room.

Graeme glanced after her quizzically and then turned back to the screen – d.o.b. 31 March 1979. The funny feeling clicked into place. Ah ha. Of course. That was it – it was his own son's birth date, coming up in a couple of weeks, only it'd slipped his mind this year, what with Faith being away. Graeme raised his eyebrows and pushed his bottom lip out in surprise, then nodded to himself. This little Glover shit was the same age exactly. Ah, well, that was what had been nagging in the back of his mind as he read the screen. Pleased at solving the problem, he drained his coffee cup, leaned forward again and keyed his way into the normal workday format. It was a full minute before it occurred to Graeme what the date might mean.

The big man froze where he sat in front of the computer, horrified, then spent the next quarter hour trying to picture Roo's face beneath the Whitesox baseball cap in the rain. He couldn't get much closer than dark-ringed hazel eyes and brown hair clipped short with a number-two blade. Tattoos on his left forearm, chinky stuff. He remembered thinking that the kid wouldn't have been bad looking if he took out those stupid fucking earrings and cleaned himself up a bit. Average height, good build. A bit more solid than your usual 19-year-old petty crim, enough to make him think twice about kicking his arse straight off. But certainly Reuben John Glover was no carbon copy of Graeme Walter Madden. The big man folded his arms, staring out for a long time at the Roma Street traffic, wondering.

Late on Tuesday morning Shaleena and Jimmy got out of a cab and stood in the hot sun outside the medical centre. A handful of dark kids yahooed in the big flash playground, littlies chucking pine bark at each other while the bigger ones sprinted around the slides and swings. Bleary and grogsick, Jimmy suddenly came to life as he saw a fella he knew down at the end of the street. He raised an almost straight arm to him, fingers splayed, head tilted down. Seeing Jimmy, the man raised his own arm and jerked his chin, an invitation to the pub.

'Well, you comin in or what?' Shaleena said to her brother, with little hope.

Jimmy muttered something out of the corner of his mouth and headed down to the hotel. Shaleena looked at his disappearing back sourly, but without surprise – it was pension week. 'Well don't think ya gonna come running ta me for a lift tonight!' she yelled at his back, then pushed open the door of the clinic and got ready to wait.

Forty-five minutes later Shaleena looked quizzically at the nurse.

'See?' The Murri sister pointed to the strip of paper which was turning dark red. And even pink would've been confirmation enough. 'You're pregnant alright. So, is it good news?'

Shaleena put her hands on her puku. A baby.

'Christ, I dunno. Not sure, eh.' She laughed nervously. A baby.

Sister Johnson smiled a tired smile. 'Well, now what you need to do is make sure you look after Baby, and yourself, okay? Is the father around?'

Shaleena nodded.

'Not a rough one is he, like that?' Sister pursed her lips in the direction of the hospital. Max, she meant, and the time Shaleena went to the PA for a fortnight. So many jahjams lost through domestics; so many hysterical women crying in the waiting room come Monday morning.

'Nah, fuck that, he's good, eh, real gentle one. Migloo one. You seen him, eh – at that rally!'

'So ya gonna have a little pale fella, eh?' Sister said. And thought, but didn't say it, new bubba'll bring back Stanley, luv, and give poor Aunty Della something to smile about again.

Shaleena was only sixteen, but it could have been worse. She had her head screwed on, and wasn't as wild as some of them young ones. Them what followed the football around, drinking and partying and all but forgetting they were mothers. And as far as anyone knew, Shaleena didn't go crazy for the yandy like some of 'em did. Sister pulled out her pamphlets on nutrition and smoking, and began her usual lecture, this time with a molecule of hope that she wasn't wasting her breath.

At home Roo swung around from the incestuous couple spilling their guts on *Donahue*. His jaw dropped in time-honoured imitation of all new fathers.

'Yer fucken what?'

'Knocked up. Yer gonna be a father.' At least, I think you are, Shaleena thought. And if it comes out dark like Max, well, too bad. Just say my Murri blood came out on top, he won't know the difference.

Roo crossed his arms – couldn't help a shiver. What did this mean? He stood and looked at his girlfriend's stomach. Flat as a tack.

'How far along?' he asked, putting a nervous hand on her.

She grinned as she answered. 'Two 'n a half months.'

Two and a half months, that was ten weeks.

'D'ya want it?' Roo asked. He felt the soft brush of a noose against his throat. This was his year to make the state squad and get himself noticed in time for Sydney 2000. If there was anything he didn't need ...

Shaleena made a face. Want it, don't want it ... what difference did that make? It was here, wasn't it? Where was Mum? She'd know what to do. 'Yeah, 'spose so. Do you?'

Roo looked at the TV, not answering.

Shaleena frowned. 'Roo?'

He shrugged awkwardly. 'Two months' not too late, if you ...' He left the suggestion trailing in the air.

'Ah, Jesus! You don't want it!' she cried, hurt.

Roo began to swear under his breath. 'Christ, Leena, I've got one kid already! I've been through all this,' he said defensively. 'The fucken things cry all night, whinge all fucken day, cost a fortune.' And you can kiss your sex life goodbye, he thought, and once that goes, whaddya got? Nappies and bottles, that's what. Who wants to be tied down to one chick with a howling babyshaped anchor, anyway? He had training to think of, and he was sick of fightin allatime. He felt like packing up and just pissing off to the nearest caravan park most mornings. And that was without a bloody baby to make things worse. The noose got tighter. Roo developed trouble breathing. Babies began multiplying in his imagination. He didn't know what to say. Even when they argued he still loved

34

Leena. But babies! Jesus! He hated the little bastards with their puke and their shit. Babies ruined everything.

'So ya don't want it?' she insisted.

Roo tossed his head around. 'Ah, I don't wanta talk about it, okay? It's up to you.'

'Whaddya mean, ya don't wanta talk about it! I'm pregnant. We've gotta talk about it!' Shaleena was getting proper pissed off with him now. White cunt thinks he can waltz in and—

'Look,' he said, swinging angrily around on her and raising his voice. 'How d'ya know it's mine, eh? How d'ya know it ain't fucken Max's?'

Shaleena stared at him, nonplussed.

'I just know, alright,' she said finally.

Roo snorted. 'Oh, that's very reassuring. Not.'

'You calling me a liar?' Shaleena spat. 'It can't be his, you dumb mothafucka, it's gotta be yours!'

'Yeah, and I bet if he wasn't locked up for the next two years it'd be his all of a sudden, too, eh, ya—' Roo bit the jealous accusations back. They'd been through all this, time and time again. It still hurt, but.

'You don't believe me, do ya? Max's been locked up for weeks! I know it's yours ...'

'How many weeks?'

'Seven. Or maybe eight. No, ten.' Shaleena snapped, rapidly revising as she spoke.

'Yeah, well, maybe it's someone else's then.' Roo ignored the hurt in her face. 'So, you want it, keep it. I don't wanna know nothin about babies, they *shit* me, okay? It's your decision. I've got one kid, and I don't want no more.'

'So you don't want it! You get me pregnant and then tell me ya don't want it!' Shaleena cried furiously.

'No, I don't want it.' Roo became sarcastic as well as loud. 'Read my lips – I Don't Want A Baby. Specially not some other black prick's. Okay, that clear enough? So now ya know. If ya wanna get rid of it, fine. Otherwise it's up to you – is that clear enough?'

'Perfectly clear, ya white arsehole, so why'nt ya fuck off and die, ya using cunt!'

'Don't want what?' Darryl asked, still half-asleep in the hallway with a towel around him. I dunno, he thought, these two, always bloody bluin. 'Whaddya have to bloody yell and wake a bloke up for?' he demanded. 'What's going on?'

Mum called out from the loo, 'What're youse lot on about?'

'I'm pregnant!' Shaleena yelled, 'and now he wants me ta have an abortion. Scared it might be too black for him, I spose.'

Darryl frowned sleepily at that. Abortions were a real migloo thing. Murries kept their kids. That's why they had so bloody many, eh. Shaleena didn't wanna go and—

'Oh, Jesus, I didn't say nothin about that!' Roo hurled at her. 'I just said I don't need any more kids ...' He tried to explain to Darryl. 'I've gotta chance at the state squad this year, I can't be up all night with bloody babies and shit ...'

Mum appeared, pulling frantically at her tracksuit pants which clung around her muscular thighs.

'Well, if she's pregnant, man, what else does that

mean 'cept getting rid of it?' Darryl asked. 'S'not gunna spontaneously fucken disappear, is it?'

Roo shrugged hopelessly and raised his open hands, gesturing *I'm harmless, I don't wanna fight ya, man.* 'Oh, Christ, I'm fucked if I know. Look, I'm late for training. I'm outta here.' He went to get his bag with his spikes and shorts from the bedroom. Just a few things to put in it, he'd go and stay … where? Somewhere'd turn up.

'Yeah, well if you fucken go now you can stay gone, ya white cunt,' Shaleena spat at Roo's back. 'Nice type, eh,' she told her brother. 'Knocks me up and has his pleasure and then won't cop the consequences. Ya should knock his fucken block off.'

Darryl rubbed his sleepy head. This was a nice turn-up for the books. What was Roo doing runnin out on her? Darryl blinked, trying to wake himself up, then wished he hadn't when he remembered: Stanley. A wave of grief poured into him. His muscles felt weak from the crippling realisation that buddaboy was dead and gone. He sagged visibly in the hall, thinking, how can these two fight when he's only been dead a week? Where's their respect, where's the love? They're like bloody animals or something. Irritation caught in his throat.

'Whaddya you say?' Mum asked Shaleena heavily. 'Did I hear ya say what I think ya said?'

Her daughter looked shamefaced at her and nodded.

'And Roo wants her to get rid of it,' Darryl added quickly over her shoulder, making Shaleena squeal with anger.

Roo returned and began to remonstrate with him, but Mum was standing in the way. 'Shut it, you,' she snarled at the white boy. 'Fucken carryon in my house when there's just bin a fucken tragedy. What do you lot know 'bout babies anyway?' She grabbed Shaleena tight by the arm. 'Babies *woman* business, so you two can fuck right off outta it now. Bloody men bigfuckenotin emselves! She wants ta have it, she'll have it! She wants ta do somepin else, youse can get the fuck out of er way. S'nothin ta do with no men.'

'Good,' said Roo with cheery sarcasm as he walked away. 'That's what I told her in the first place.'

Seeing that Darryl wasn't going to act, Shaleena suddenly ran in to the bedroom and started throwing things at Roo. Cheeky white cunt. You – flying rubbish basket – *fucken cunt* – china ornament that smashed in a shower of sharp white chips – *you fucken wanker of a migloo* – sports bag – *prick with ya fucken 'I love ya Leena, I'll never leave ya Leena' and now ya fucken* – three stilettos in quick succession – *run out on me. I shoulda listened to Jimmy in the first fucken place*—

Roo watched Leena's rage as though it belonged in another place and time. As if it wasn't him she was talking to. Was this his woman? Was this what they called love? No, it was the power of babies again. The word had hardly been mentioned and already things were disintegrating around him, just like before, in Newcastle.

Roo felt tears coming to the surface, but he pushed them down, ducked the missiles, and pushed the furious girl sideways onto the bed. He fought down the beserker inside himself that wanted to fist the walls and door, and yes, Leena too. He put a finger in her face and spoke through his teeth.

'Listen to Jimmy if ya want. If that's what ya want ... but don't pretend ya so bloody innocent. You know how babies're made, even if it is mine, which I doubt.' His eyes blazed at her saying what his mouth wouldn't – *slut, two-timer* – and Shaleena glared back at him, tearless and mute.

To avoid any immediate decision about whether he was obliged to have a go at Roo, Darryl went for a piss. By the time he came out, Roo, who was an old hand at getting out when the going was good, had grabbed his things and left. Relieved of his brotherly responsibilities, Darryl went and had his breakfast. After ten confused and headachey minutes in front of a bowl of cornflakes he decided he didn't know what to think about Roo's clearing out. He was doing the wrong thing by Leena, for sure, but then – to face the unpleasant truth – a bloke wouldn't be too sure if the kid was his, would he? Ah, shit, if he run into Roo he'd probably be obliged to job him, but he wouldn't go lookin for it.

He was a tough little bastard, with the highly desirable talents of being able to fight and run like the clappers.

CHAPTER THREE

His muscles stretched and loose, Roo stood in his Nikes and looked dreamily at the red rubber track. He was surrounded by the coloured seats of the ANZ Stadium. White lines curved with beautiful taut precision around the four-hundred-metre circuit, and if only you could put your feet past 'em quick enough, well ... glory was yours, eh. He lifted his knees quickly in a bam-bam-bam rhythm to test his hamstrings, imagining that the stands were full of adoring fans. What must it feel like to be Cathy Freeman or Michael Johnson? To walk out on the track and hear that animal roar that said you were loved?

One day ... Roo grimaced, knowing that his dream was everyone else's as well.

He flexed a leg. The two fists of his quads stood out above his knee; his hammie was a round belly of power. He dug a forefinger into his calf, testing. It was like rock, tapering down into a fine razor-edged Achilles tendon. He bounced on the balls of his feet, feeling the rubber track spring underneath his weight. Seventy-two kilos of human steak, that's what I am, he thought, prime rib.

Physically he was close to ready. There was more to running than muscle though, there was balance and rhythm and style and confidence. There was that spark that fired your feet when it all went right, that made it feel like someone else was doing the running. He was in okay shape. Just so long as this babyshit business could be avoided, things would be alright, Roo thought. His brow creased remembering Leena's anger. Fucken women. Always a drama somewhere. If it's got tits or wheels it's trouble and ain't that the fucken truth. Soberly, he pulled both his feet up against his bum in turn, stretching the quads, then refocused as the coach blew his whistle.

'Slow shuffle, 800' came the order, and the pack of fifteen athletes moved off for two steady laps before the hard work began. Roo kept up with everyone during the hour and a half training and the coach seemed satisfied when he said he'd been at a funeral the other day. Sympathetic even.

'Who died?' he asked kindly.

'Me girlfriend's cousin,' Roo said, not adding the details that had put the death on the front page of the paper. Another blackfella dead in custody, another cop on suspicion, as if there was any question that the cunts had gotten into Stanley at the watchhouse.

'What was it, a car accident or something?'

'Yeah,' Roo lied.

'Oh, sorry. But you better not miss any more training before Easter, eh.'

Roo nodded. Coach was trying to help, he knew. It was an ambiguous comment, a warning that wouldn't have been made if he had no chance of making the squad.

'How's the leg?'

'Fine, heaps better.' A nagging tendonitis had finally cleared up.

'Okay, you can knock off now. Get yourself a shower, slugger.'

Roo shaped up comically, and poked a slow fist at the older man, who ducked and weaved in a poor imitation of a boxer. 'Dead meat.' Roo condemned him with a grin.

'Fast meat,' the coach corrected. 'Faster than you if you don't work a bit harder.'

'Oh, dream!' Roo threw over his shoulder at the thirty-year-old, but the coach's attention had already shifted to the hurdlers.

When Roo came dripping out of the shower he found to his surprise that Darryl was waiting for him in the changeroom. Leena and Jimmy were in the car, he said. Roo stood, slowly towelling himself off, seeing his naked reflection in the wall mirror out of the corner of his eye. An athlete with a familiar face was engrossed in strapping his leg in one corner. There were only the three of them in the room. First off Roo tried to move the whole show, talk Darryl into taking the argument outside, but it was a no go. Leena's cousinbrother folded his dark arms and put his head down like a bull. His black eyes glittered under a red headband. Now that Leena had shamed him into this he'd put all thoughts of friendship away and would go through with it, come what may.

'So are ya coming back home with us or not? Ya can't just fucken run out on Leena like that with no warning, mate. You got a responsibility to her. And to yer kid.'

The threat was implied, not stated; the high-jumper with the injured leg didn't twig. Oh why don't ya piss off, mate, Roo begged the other athlete silently, already feeling the shame if Coach caught him fighting. One place in my life where I'm straight, he thought, and they have to come and fuck that up too. At the same time, he was sussing the room for weapons and sharp edges. There was an old bit of chair-frame within easy reach of Darryl's left hand, but nothing close for Roo to pick up. He casually went over and sat on the wooden slatted bench that ran the length of the room, a manoeuvre that halved the distance from him to the door. He stretched his arms to each side, bracing himself in case he needed to leap up suddenly.

'Ah, c'mon, look Darryl,' he began lightly.

But Darryl didn't want to look, or listen. A couple of cans sucked down fast in the car took priority. Listening to Roo wasn't what this was about. He raised his voice. 'Nah, you look! You better fucken come home with us now, or else you can fuck off for good, geddit? Think Leena can't do no better than you, eh?' A genuine anger rose in Darryl, fuelled by the knowledge that he had been manipulated into this confrontation. When Jimmy got home, charged, he had taunted him mercilessly about his migloo friend running out on Leen, and hadn't been slow to mention Stanley's murder. He didn't have to spell out the connection. Part of Darryl knew that it was bullshit, was perfectly capable of making distinctions between whitefellas. But goaded by Jimmy's expert barbs, and with the image of Stanley's coffin agonisingly fresh in his mind's eye, Darryl was just about ready to lump Roo in with the rest of them.

Roo told himself he was embarrassed in front of the high-jumper, that was all that was wrong. Fucken shamejob, eh. This little scene wouldn't be a problem if it'd happened in private. He pushed aside the reality. A line had been drawn by the Kings while he wasn't looking and now he was on the wrong side of it. Roo suddenly knew, as Darryl knew, and Jimmy and Leena no doubt knew, there was no way he was gonna walk out of there Darryl's mate. It might not have happened this way before, there might have been a chance even with the baby, but not now. Not after Stanley. Feeling the jaws of the trap, Roo exploded. Fucken mongrels. Why'd I do it? Why'd I let myself believe … Why'd Stanley hafta go and … He stood up looking murderous, jaw set.

'Who the fuck d'ya think you are, eh, coming in here where ya not invited and giving me ultimatums, eh? Geez, me knees are knockin Darryl.' Christ, anyone'd think it was him that had the kickboxing trophies, not Roo. Dutch courage, in buckets. Roo could flog Darryl sober, let alone pissed, an idea which was becoming more and more appealing. Just say the word, brother. Then remembering the coach, Roo corrected his stance so he wasn't actually inviting him to knock his head off.

The Murri man wavered in his duty, knowing Roo could punch on like nobody's business.

'Nice type, aren't ya?' Darryl scowled from where he stood. 'Fucken migs, ya all the same. Well, if I see anything more of ya around me sista, mate, you'll regret it. I'm tellin ya now, I'll fucken drive ya, ya white cunt.'

The high-jumper stood up quickly and, glancing in alarm at Roo, left the room. That's torn it, Roo thought, someone'll be here any minute. Get caught in a blue here they're liable to kick me outta the team. Gotta get him out. Play it cool … don't ignore him or he'll flare, but don't overdo it either. Roo folded his arms – an aggro stance but also one that said he wasn't about to start throwing punches.

'Ah, look, just fucken forget it, willya, Darryl. I'm not about to come back to someone else's screaming kid, okay, ya can tell her that. You know she'd rather be with friggin Max than me if he weren't locked up.' He said this in a calm voice, hoping the reference to Leena's mixed feelings for him might work.

He stood still for a few moments, then took the chance and turned his back, pretending to pack his bag. All the while listening for the scud of Darryl's front foot coming closer. Nothing. And then heard him taking the opening and going, thank Christ, with a few more general threats of what he was going to do to him. Yeah, right, dream on, pal …

Roo stood up, threw his damp head back and breathed out tension. There were tears accumulating in him somewhere deep. Tears for lost … something. He didn't have a word for what him and Darryl had. Lost laughs, maybe. Mates, for a few weeks or a few months. But ya couldn't do it, it was too hard. Black and white, what could you expect? Roo put those tears in a little box and put it away in his back pocket. Fuck Darryl. Fuck him. And Leena. He'd kiss the lot of 'em goodbye, that's what he'd do.

He'd thought when he got with Leena that maybe things were gonna be alright at last, surrounded by this mob of mixed-up blackfellas. Thought the Kings' was a place he could maybe be himself, fit in, without people screaming in his ear all his life that he was bad, bad, bad.

You'll come to a bad end, Roo Glover.

You want to listen to your Elders and betters, boy.

You'll end up Prime Minister or in jail, Reuben Glover.

Get outta here, you're not wanted round here, piss off, piss off …

At the Kings', it was solid, there was good stuff along with the bad. He thought it mighta been a home or something. And now this. The dogs. They weren't no different to all of them white cunts that'd fucked him over for years. Well, fuck that for a joke, eh. He'd look out for number one from now on. Smarten up and get on with his life. Screw 'em.

That decision made, the idea of freedom began to wash through Roo's system, and the noose of fatherhood fell away from his neck at last. He began to dress. Then the coach poked his head in, concerned. 'You okay? Someone said there was a black dude in here abusing you.'

Roo innocently smiled and shook his head even as his legs were trembling with emotion. 'Nah, they musta been pulling ya leg, Coach.' When he left, Roo wiped his brow. Fucken Shaleena woulda put Darryl up to it, the stroppy bloody gin. Well, she could kiss his white arse. He wasn't about to jump back into that fray. What fucken for? Plenty more fish in the sea and fish what weren't always moody and knocked-up to boot. Fish what wouldn't drag his colour up every fight they had, fish that never even thought about him being white cos they were too. Fuck her. He was a free man, and about time too.

Roo hoisted his bag onto his well-developed shoulder and went out to the bus stop on Mains Road. The bus to Todd's place went past here, and it'd be as good a place to crash as anywhere else. Only when the blue and gold City Council bus actually wheezed past the street backing onto the mountain did Roo realise that at Todd's he'd be staying within spitting distance of Graeme Madden's place.

'Yeah, course ya can mate, no wuckers. Dad's not back till tomorrow.' From the front veranda Todd was ripped and expansive in his hospitality. 'Grab the lounge if ya want, or else there's an old mattress downstairs I think, eh? Ya wanna cone? I'm just waiting for Sooger to ring up.'

'Yeah, fucken oath. I split up with Leena again this arv.'

'Dead set?' Todd was sympathetic in a fuzzy, wasted fashion. 'That sux, eh.'

'Yeah, maybe. There's some beer there.' Roo threw the grog to his mate, put his training gear in the corner of the room and went to retrieve the mattress out of the garage. Then him and Todd settled down to get well and truly blasted in front of *Roy and HG*.

At five to ten the phone rang. There was a band happening down at the pub, and a bit of a party afterwards, was Todd interested?

'Whaddya reckon?' he asked Roo. 'Do we wanna be in it?'

Roo was feeling high and reckless and single. Hadn't gone feral for a while either, weeks. He stood up and stretched himself towards the ceiling before going julabai. 'Yeah, man, why not?'

'Yo, man. You swing past dreckly n'give us a ride, eh?' Todd said to the phone. 'Ah, come on, s'just up the road ... Why not? Come on ... Ah fuck ya then, ya weak cunt! Oh, true, whaffor? DUI? Yeah, rightio. See ya down there.' He was laughing as he turned to Roo. 'All set. Sooger can't pick us up cos he's lost his licence, but this party should go off, eh, there's all these fucken mad musos from Sydney. They'll have yandy, smack, trips, everythin,' he promised.

But how were they going to get into town, then, Roo asked. Todd winked, and Roo's heart sank.

The two-way phone in Car Eight crackled to life, and the other thirty-nine police cars on Brisbane's roads heard: 'Eight to base, can you give us bona fides on a Timothy Alexander Hall, d.o.b. 8/1/79, and a John Samuel Glover, d.o.b. 31/3/80?'

The two lads sat in the back with their heads down, saying nothing. Roo was frantically trying to calculate how long he'd get, and if he had any chance of making up the lost training in time. He doubted it. It'd probably be fucken Easter before he even fronted Court. Trapped, he stared blankly at the grey carpet on the floor of the car, flicking his lighter over and over again.

'Got any smokes?' Todd whispered. Roo threw one at him. The overwhelming fuck-up he'd made of his life didn't seem possible, but it was all too true. Stanley was dead, Shaleena was pregnant, Darryl had wiped him on behalf of the rest of the family and now, to top it all off, the cherry on the friggin cake, he was sitting in the back of a cop car having fucked-up yet again. You fucken loser, he told himself in dazed disbelief, you stupid fucken good-for-nothing loser.

In the city, Graeme Madden pulled his unmarked Commodore over and turned the police radio up: *John Samuel Glover.* Had he heard right, or was he overdoing this working late business and starting to imagine things? Stress did funny things to a bloke, sometimes ... Thinking furiously, he radioed the operations centre for a location on Car Eight, did a fast left off Herschel Street and hit the pedal. If he made it to Holland Park in time, he could ... what? Get Reuben John Glover (a.k.a.)'s story, for one thing. Find out who the fuck he really was.

Hoping whoever he found at the scene was amenable, Madden screamed down the freeway. When he got there, he saw with relief that Car Eight was being driven by an old mate. There was a uniformed kid there too, a seventeen-week wonder from the Academy, but he knew how to deal with that lot. Yeah, it was the kid alright, sitting with a sleazy wog mate beside him. A hotted-up yellow Hyundai was parked at an outrageous angle behind the cop car.

'Graeme,' Col said in surprise. 'To what do I owe this unexpected pleasure?'

They shook hands. 'This is Alex Little.' Graeme nodded to the probationer, then gestured Col aside.

'Look, mate, would it be alright if I have a word with that young bloke? Glover?'

Col raised his eyebrows. 'Yeah … go for ya life. Watch he doesn't do a runner, but. He's a little hard case.'

'Yeah, I know. What'd ya pick him up for – the car?'

'Yeah. His mate was driving. DUI too.' Col was curious, but he was also enough of an old hand not to ask what Graeme wanted.

Graeme went over to the car and opened the back door. 'Good evening, Mr Glover,' he said.

Roo raised his head and stared at him.

'Shut your mouth, son, a fly'll get in. Jump out, I wanna word with ya.'

John Samuel Glover mechanically shut his mouth and shakily got out to stand on the footpath. Todd made to follow, but Madden shut the door on him, Todd snatching his hand away just in time. Arsehole.

'Floggin cars now, are ya?' Graeme said, deliberately casual as he lit a fag. 'That's a new one.'

Roo goggled at him in shock. What was Graeme Madden doing here? How did he know the pig that'd picked them up? How did he know … *What was happening?* 'What are you doing here?' he asked incredulously.

'It might just be your lucky day, son,' Graeme said, then almost choked on the "son". 'I'm a police officer and …'

Roo's head spun some more. He looked at Madden as if he'd climbed out of a spaceship. A cop. His father, a fucken cop! If there was a God, he had a friggin funny sense of humour, eh.

'... and your real name's Reuben John Madden, is it?'

Roo glanced warily at Col where he stood ten metres away and then nodded, excitement blossoming in him underneath the massive confusion. Somehow Graeme Madden had found out.

'And you were adopted?' Graeme asked in a quiet voice. His face was a hard mask hiding his real feelings. Roo nodded again, flushing red this time.

'Do you know what they called you when you were born?'

'John Walter,' Roo gasped.

Madden examined the boy's face. Hazel eyes, brown hair. Could easily be. A girl's brown face flitted across his mind. Easily. But ... he dropped his eyelids. 'If I find out you're bullshittin me, pal, I'll give ya the drum — you'll wish you were never fucken born.'

Roo stared back, finally knowing the man to be his father. But a cop ... 'It's true, that's what they called me. I went to Births, Deaths and Marriages last month. They said I was born in the Royal Women's.'

'Just wait here.' Graeme went back over to Colin who was drumming his fingers on the car bonnet. 'Look, mate, he's no angel but the kid's a friend of the family ... whaddya reckon, can ya help us out?'

Colin folded his arms and sucked thoughtfully at his bottom lip. Him and Graeme went back a long way. 'Booked him already, mate. Tell ya what, I might be able to see Marko tomorrow and make it illegal use. That's the best I can do ...'

Graeme nodded in relief. He almost felt like crying. Or yelling, or something. 'Yeah, great. Appreciate it, mate, I owe ya one. Ya taking him up to Holland Park?'

'Mmm. You wanna bail him?'

'Yeah, I better.'

Graeme told Roo he'd see him up at the station, then got back into his Commodore. He sat looking blankly at the steering wheel with the lion rampant embossed into it. Graeme sat trying, and failing, to remember the young man he'd been twenty years ago. Tried to remember a time when people were just people, and an encounter with a brown-skinned girl had ended with her knocking on his door and finding Faith there instead, shocked and outraged. What he did remember was the tears, the arguments.

The pained confession that made Faith go and scrub herself over and over and over. A furtive phone call to the welfare. And then a slow fading over the years until he scarcely remembered a thing. Then nothing. Until now, outta nowhere – this kid. His son. His *son*. After nineteen years.

Questions battered at him. What was this going to mean? And could he straighten him out? Why had he turned into a crim – was it his fault for giving up? Was it in the blood? And what was Faith going to say about a long-lost prodigal son that wasn't her own? Madden shook his dazed head. It was messy, it was difficult, and Reuben was a little crim to boot. But it didn't really matter. Nothing that couldn't be fixed. Graeme's face lit up. He'd found his *son*.

Chapter Four

Circle Street, Mount Gravatt. Madden switched off the ignition of the Commodore and waved his right hand. 'Well, this is it. Be it ever so humble ...' The man was glad all of a sudden that he'd taken out that bit extra on the mortgage. The house sat on a hill ablaze with security lights on a timing system. Madden got out, averting his eyes from what lay beyond in the awful night. He unchained the Dobie bitch. She walked around on stiff legs and sniffed at Roo, smelling Jimmy's pigdog Nigga on him.

'What's her name?' Roo asked, backing away. Not too fussed on strange dogs.

'Wimpy. It's okay, girl, leave him alone. C'mere.' He took her by the collar.

'She's gonna go me?' Roo was ready to kick out if he had to.

'Not once she knows you. They're very intelligent, Dobermans.' Madden stroked the sleek wiggling animal.

Dope-wary and with all his outraged senses screaming for explanations, Roo stepped into his father's house.

It was enough to make ya spin right out, eh. Picked up and then ya father rocks up and then he's a cop of all things. Roo looked around him. From the outside the house looked ordinary. Inside, though, it was big and luxurious. A cut-glass ashtray sat on top of a dark wooden table in the kitchen; it was clean, like everything else, but the smell of cigarette smoke lingered, making the house fusty.

Madden led Roo through into the lounge. The boy's eyes bulged. An enormous picture window looked out over the other houses in Mount Gravatt Heights. The dotted lights of the cars on the freeway snaked away silently to the left. A huge television and complicated sound system sat in an expensive cabinet; a fishtank with the usual neons and Angelfish was illuminated opposite. There were footy trophies in the cabinet next to the television – well I got that much right, thought Roo wryly. Can't pick a copper from three feet away, but footy players – let me tell ya … A newspaper lay neatly folded next to the armchair with the TV remote control on top of it. After the Kings', this place was like the Hilton.

'Pull up a pew,' Graeme gestured, and Roo collapsed into the lounge, knowing he looked wrong – was wrong – in his tats, black jeans and muddy Nikes. Graeme offered the kid beer and cigarettes. Anything to break the ice. Roo lit up a fag, but refused the beer. Graeme cracked one for himself anyway. He needed it, and how. Finding your long lost son on top of the interview that the Internal Investigation Unit had inflicted on him that morning would be enough for any man. He was careful not to let his bewilderment show though. A kid doesn't want to find out his father's halfway to being a bloody headcase. Then again, a bloke doesn't want to find his kid in the back of a fucken patrol car, either, does he?

'So ...' Graeme said, wondering where the hell to start, 'I know a bit about ya – I looked ya up on our computers after you were hanging around the other day. I know you've been locked up on and off for the last couple of years, and that you've got a record as long's me arm. And that it's not gonna get any shorter if ya keep on the way yer going.' Roo sat stiffly, listening unwillingly if at all. Being Sergeant Madden obviously wasn't working. Graeme got a grip and shifted tack. 'But be that as it may ... how'd you find me anyway?'

Roo moved around awkwardly on the lounge. Lying to cops was a hard habit to break, that's assuming you even wanted to. He prevaricated. 'I, ah, went and checked out me birth certificate when I got out of John Oxley last time, cos there's this psych in there reckons criminality's inherited, and I wanted to see if my old man was a crim, see?' He grinned cheekily at Madden, who snorted and forced a small smile onto his concrete face.

'Well, he got that wrong.'

'She. It was this chick ... and so I found out about this adoption mob, but they didn't wanna know me, cos you hadn't registered with them, but I—'

'Oh, yeah, Faith and me talked about it once, but we didn't ever get around to doing it.'

Roo glanced fast and deep at his father, and risked it. 'So the other day I went into their office after hours and looked meself up on their records. And then I found ya in the phone book.' He paused. 'Who's me mother? Is that her, is it your wife, on the answering machine? Faith?'

'No!' said Madden hastily. 'Nah. She was ...' He paused as the brown face came back. 'Um, is, I mean, um, just a girl I went with from school. Old girlfriend, Angela Templeton. I was nineteen and she was sixteen, and her parents made her adopt the kid out. They always hated me, even before—'

'Have you got any photos of her?' Roo interrupted.

Graeme stopped and thought. 'Nah. Faith chucked a lot of my old photos out when we got married. I only had a couple anyway. She looked a bit like you. She was skinny with big,' Madden caught himself. 'She was ... she was pretty.'

'So she looked like me, did she?' Roo was rapt.

'Oh, well, yeah, she had brown hair and brown eyes. Wog father, see, Maltese he was.' Graeme invented as he went along. 'You got lucky, looks like ya took after her and not me,' he ended.

There was a short silence while the boy digested this. There had been much talk in the King household that he might be a Murri, what with his brown hair and eyes, and being adopted and everything. One of the stolen generation. It was one of the pluses that had helped him fit in, diluting his whiteness and his anonymity. There goes that theory, Roo thought in bitter disappointment – I'm white.

'If she was a wog, what are you?' he asked Graeme.

'Just Australian. Oh, you mean originally? Ah, me old man was half English and half Irish, and Mum's side'd be ... well, Poms if ya went back far enough I guess, but they've been here since Cook dropped anchor ... no congenital loonies, as far as we know.' Madden grinned. 'So you can go back to that shrink and tell her she's fulla shit.'

'I'm white, thought Roo heavily. That's if Maltese are white. What's a Maltese anyway? A wog, he reckons. I'm a Malteser – tell Leena that! He winced as he heard her say, sneering, yeah, that'd be right, brown outside and yella inside, ya weak prick.

'Have youse got any other kids?'

'Nuh.' The man stopped smiling. 'We tried, but Faith's ... we never had any luck. You're it.'

'Oh. Where is she anyway?'

'Angela? I dunno, haven't—'

'No, Faith,' Roo said.

'Oh, in Sydney. Her brother-in-law's dying of cancer. She's gone down to help her sister out. She's been there for about six weeks. She'll be back soon. She's just gotta stay for a bit longer, but there's no problem really,' Madden said, explaining too much. Roo tapped ash into his hand and fidgeted some more.

Madden passed him an ashtray. 'So have you seen Angela lately?'

'Nah, not for years. Not since it happened,' Graeme temporised.

'D'ya know where she lives?'

'Not round Brisbane I don't think. Dunno really. Guess I woulda heard if she was still around.'

Roo was silent again, desperate but afraid to ask: Why'd ya do it? Plenty of girls have teenage pregnancies, why'd ya let me go? And part of him wanted to abuse him, and part of him wanted to just sit and look at the man. Another part felt like running out the door – a *copper*, his father a *copper*, he'd be the laughing stock of his mates. If they even wanted to know him, that is. And another small voice said don't be too hasty. Maybe there's something in this, didn't he bail ya? Isn't he gonna help lower the charges? There's worse friends than boolimen when ya live on the edge of the law.

'So fill us in … who dragged you up?' Madden said finally, flicking the TV on with the sound down low. Roy and HG were still at it.

'No one. I was kicked in the guts and told to fucken get up.' Roo laughed and went on. 'Ah, I was in the orphanage for ages, then in the end they fostered me to Mum and Pop. They lived down the Gold Coast, they were first, and they were good, eh. Pop taught me to read and play footy and that, but then Mum got hurt in a car accident and had to go into this nursing place and they wouldn't let Pop keep me by himself. That was when I was eleven … no, twelve, no I was right, I was eleven. So then I just went to all these different places for years. Most of the ones that took me were a pack of arseholes. Some of 'em were okay.'

'These pair are funny bastards, aren't they?' Madden said, looking for some safe ground. 'You ever watch this show?'

'Yeah, sometimes.' Seeing that Graeme didn't care, Roo quickly buttoned down about the horror places he'd been put, houses that had bolts on the outside of all the bedroom doors. Places where they signed up for you for the welfare money and then forgot about you if you were lucky. Now he was grown, and he tried to forget about them in his turn. When he couldn't, there was always running – pounding the track round and round till all you could think of was your lungs and legs. It wasn't often that the memories came seeping through that harsh airless pain, but sometimes something'd happen and ya couldn't help it, eh, there'd be the flashbacks and shit. Coupla years back before he started running, it got real bad and he tried slashin up, didn't work, but. Ah well, life sux then ya die, what else is new?

Sitting in Madden's loungeroom, thinking about his life, Roo had a sudden premonition that everything was going to be as wrong as it ever had been. His fingers tingled and something marched across his chest. In an attempt to prevent the stress lines tearing him apart, he turned to the man. Look at it, willya, watching TV like it's just some ordinary night, the prick.

'So why'd ya do it?' Roo asked him bluntly. 'Why didn't youse keep me? Why didn't youse—' He couldn't say it. Want me. *Love* me. Am I that bad?

Madden flinched, looked away. He turned the sound down even lower on the TV.

'Oh, Jesus …' He paused for a long moment. 'Ya gotta understand, we were just kids ourselves. Her old man was this rich builder the size of a brick shithouse. He came round and talked with my parents and then they got together and said, right, she's adopting it out and that was it. Didn't want his daughter marrying a poor copper's son. I didn't have much say in any of it. Or Angela, I suppose. They kind of just shut us out of it,' he ended, almost believing himself.

Roo stared at the wall, *Reuben Glover, This Is Your Life!*

Guilt was an emotion that Madden was expert at avoiding, but to his surprise he found himself suddenly creaking under its weight. Would the kid have ended up a crim if he hadn't? He struggled for the words of reconciliation.

'Um, look, Reuben, I dunno what your life's been like ... '

'Yeah, well you got that right,' Roo answered harshly with no pretense at forgiveness. *Nineteen years of being kicked from pillar to fucken post, that's what, Dad.*

Madden frowned and went on, '... but in, what was it, 1978, I was just a dumb kid, too wet behind the ears to use a rubber. Okay, so probably we fucked up. I'm sorry, okay. But, ya know, that's the past. Ya gotta put it behind ya and move forward. Look, how about we get somethin for dinner – ya hungry?'

Roo grinned nastily at his father. *I don't think so.* 'That it, is it? You're sorry, let's eat.'

A heavy expression fell onto Madden's face. It was part of his uniform. 'Listen, sunshine, if you're trying to make me feel guilty, forget it, okay. And in case you've forgotten, I just got your arse outta the Holland Park lockup, so don't get smart with me, son. Now, do you want some dinner or not?'

Seeing that this was how it was, Roo wised up fast. Besides, he hadn't eaten since before training, and now he was mongrel starving, eh.

'Yeah, alright.'

'You want Chinese, or Thai? Or something else?'

'Thai, eh?'

His father nodded and went to phone the Thai Orchid on Logan Road.

'So whereabouts've you been lately?' Madden asked him as they were scraping the last traces of red beef curry off their plates, and he couldn't help it, the cop came sniffing back. 'When you're not a guest of Her Majesty I mean?' He forced a glum smile to take the edge off it.

Roo blew his nose unselfconsciously on the bottom of his Mad Dog T-shirt. Chilli.

'Oh, a few different places. I been staying with me girlfriend but she's—' and here Roo came to a screaming halt. He didn't want to go into all that. And wasn't particularly interested in saying she was a Murri, either. He could imagine Graeme's face when all that came up. He hadn't forgotten the way he'd looked at Todd in the car.

'Hmm? She's what?'

'We just split up, so I'm staying just up the road at me mate's.'

Roo evaded the question. 'Mount Gravatt. Till his dad gets home, anyway.' He'd met Todd's father once and once was enough – it'd been hate at first sight.

'Too bad about ya girlfriend. Were ya together long?'

'Nearly a year,' Roo replied. 'Met her last, um, Easter it was.' Down in Byron at the Blues Festival. It fucken went off, eh.

'Do ya reckon you'll get back together?' asked Madden with the first sign of real interest in Roo's life. 'What was the problem?'

'Nuh, I've had it with her. S'over. She shits me.'

'Uh-huh … yeah, I know that feeling alright. Ah, well, this is a big place and there's only me 'n Faith here. You could stay for a while if you wanted. Seeing as you're my responsibility now I've bailed you. Provided ya keep yer nose clean, mind you, none of this bloody pinching cars bullshit. I can't afford any more trouble at the moment, cos I'm under investigation already.' The desperate hope inside him didn't leak into his face, and when Roo looked around in disbelief at the flash surrounds, Madden knew the answer would be no. He quickly said, 'If ya don't want to that's okay. But—'

'You really want me to move in with ya? After the cars and doing time and that?' Roo was stunned.

'Well.' Madden looked suspiciously at him. 'If ya decided to do something constructive, like get a job, you could stay. Till ya front court, anyway – I can't see ya walking away from this one.'

Roo glanced at the expensive electronic equipment, the dozens of CDs that could easily be turned into grog down at the pawnshop or pub. The cleanness and newness of everything. The thick soft carpet. The *quiet*. Either Madden was a mug, or he was offering him something approximating trust. Then Roo thought about Todd's house, always chockablock full of blackfellas at every hour of the day and night, and about Todd's father. He thought about the TV that was never turned off or down, and the sticky brown vinyl lounge that was about an inch too short to sleep on comfortably. Fear of Graeme gnawed at his chest (a cop!) and yet so did hope, the hope that he always said was only for losers, and the trust that he knew very well to be a dead-end street. As he was deciding which way to jump, Roo saw that the sound system was a Pioneer, extra pricey. One of Jimmy's little sayings suddenly came into his head: *Do unto others as they do unto you, but do it first, and do it a fucken sight harder.*

'Yeah, okay, yer on. I'll come round tomorrow arvo,' he said flatly, unsure why he was agreeing. 'I'll hafta get my stuff and let people know.' He gave Graeme a wry smile. Inviting him home nineteen years too late, but it was something.

'Okay. Good. Great. I'll show you where your room is.'

Half an hour later, Graeme dropped Roo off at Todd's house, making no comment about the Aboriginal flag in the upstairs window. They could talk about his social circle later on. As he went to go, Roo leaned into the car, grinning wickedly. He'd saved the best for last. 'Oh, I forgot to tell ya, I've got a little baby girl lives in Newcastle. Eight months old. Her name's Hayley. Seeya tomorrow – Grandad.' He laughed out loud at the look on Madden 's face and went inside.

Lying on Todd's lounge half an hour later he remembered Madden's vague comment about being investigated, and wondered what he'd meant. Roo made a mental note to ask him about it, and then exhaustion won out over excitement. He fell asleep with his feet dangling irritatingly over the edge of the lounge.

The next morning Roo banged loudly on the Kings' metal security door. Having a father had given him new reserves of courage. New possibilities had opened up in his world. He imagined Graeme in at Roma Street Police HQ working at a desk, punching a computer keyboard, and Roo couldn't stop feeling the wonder, the amazement, the difference, of having someone that belonged to him, even if that someone was a hardhead and a copper. Even the words felt brand-new, ill-fitting. My father. It was weird. Half of him felt trapped, as though Madden was a ball and chain made flesh. The other half thought it'd wait and see what happened. He could always cut loose again, there was no law to say he had to live with him, eh? Even if he had fronted with the bungoo for bail. If Roo decided to fuck off, well, it'd be stiff shit, sucker, wouldn't it? Serve the cunt right for dumping him as a kid. If it didn't work out. Ya never know.

'Roo,' Darryl said curtly after opening the door, wondering what to do. He was glad Leena was over at her friends and Jimmy dead to the world inside sleeping off last night.

'I just come to get me stuff, man … okay?' Roo sussed him out.

Darryl hesitated, unhappy about the whole thing. There Roo stood looking fine as a whiteboy could in his Rip Curl singlet that showed off runner's muscles, borrowed blue jeans tight over hard thighs. It looked like he really was gonna skip out after all … go off and have his nice white life with his running career and his white mates, probably end up a doctor or lawyer or some fucken thing, while Darryl's sister stayed pregnant, and his brother stayed dead, d. e. a. d., gone, finished up.

There were dark circles under Darryl's eyes and his breath stank. He felt a million kinds of fool for having welcomed Roo into the family, and he knew what everyone was thinking about it, too. He pressed his lips tightly.

'Who's that?' Mum King called.

'Reuben,' Darryl answered.

She was there in a black flash, glaring. 'Whaddya want, ya little arsehole?'

'Me gear.'

Mum glanced at Darryl. 'Go get it for him Darryl. You can wait out there, ya cunt, you've worn ya welcome out round 'ere, eh? Gettin my daughter pregnant, and after all we done for ya too.'

'I wish I had your confidence that it was mine,' Roo said to her sarcastically, with his arms folded, 'but I reckon it might come out with a Cowboy's jersey and a flag tat on its little black arm, eh.'

Mum chose to deliberately misinterpret this reference to Max. 'Yeah, that'd be right, we're too black fer ya now, ain't we? S'orright when ya gettin ya bitta black velvet, but now ya got her pregnant it's a different story, innit?'

She looked at him in disgust, then decided not to waste her breath. Everyone knew Max'd been hanging around Shaleena before he got done for assault, but no one else would have had the bad manners to bring it up, not now. Not with Stanley dead and gone. If only Shaleena'd listened to her when she'd warned her about going with migs. Or Darryl. He'd picked a loser this time alright.

Roo shrugged and leaned against the carport pole. Fuck her then. He didn't give a rat's arse for any of em.

As he waited he could hear Mum and Darryl arguing about him. Then Darryl appeared with a green rubbish bag full of clothes. He threw them at Roo.

'You ain't exactly popular round here, mate,' he said dryly. 'Good time to fuck off, eh.'

'Yeah, I gathered.'

'Mum says to tell ya don't come round no more, right? And ...' Darryl paused, then said it anyway, 'I agree with her. Shaleena's got enough problems without being a single mum on top of it all, eh? Good timing, mate. So don't you fucken come round upsettin her.'

'Yeah, I know.' Roo got shame then, thinking again of Stanley. 'But I told ya already, Darryl, I'm not bringing up someone else's kid ...'

'Ya don't know that,' Darryl snapped. 'Ya can't know if it's his or yours, eh.' Roo stood before Darryl, hanging his head. He shrugged his shoulders, wondering if there was any way out of this dilemma.

'Jesus, Roo, ya picked ya fucken moment, din' ya?' Darryl lit a smoke behind a cupped hand as Roo sighed, knowing it was true.

'So is she gonna keep it then?' he asked, hoisting his stuff.

'Yeah, course.' Darryl looked less and less friendly, as it sunk in that Roo really was doing the dirty. 'We're gonna call it Stanley if it's a boy,' he added, rubbing it in.

Roo nodded – there was nothing to say in response to that. Darryl stood in the doorway and waited for him to leave. It was a pity, after all they'd been through, but there was no more to say. With Murries, you're either with em or against em, eh, and now Roo'd made his bed.

Jimmy was right after all, fuck it. Can't trust any of em.

'Fair enough. Well, I've gotta place at Mount Gravatt, so I'll see ya when I see ya,' Roo replied, hiding his sorrow. And for a while there he'd thought Darryl was a real mate, too. He was the one who'd stuck up for him being white in a black house, the one that showed him stuff. Educated him, so he didn't look silly in front of everyone. The one who'd said loudly to Jimmy, 'There's no colour bar in this family, he's with Shaleena so he's okay.' But it looked like Happy Families was over now, well'n truly over.

'Yeah. Make tracks,' Darryl said heavily, arms folded and breathing smoke out, as Mum yelled, 'Is that white cunt gorn yet?' Darryl warned him a final time. 'Don't go showin ya face, Roo ... and ya better look out for Jimmy. You think I'm being a prick, well he's real cut 'bout it ...'

Starting to jog away, Roo laughed his hurt away. A white cunt now, was he? Well fuck those black bastards then. Fuck the lot of em. 'Yeah, okay, I'll be leaving town tonight. Shittin meself – not.'

Darryl frowned, knowing Jimmy better than Roo did. Little smartarse. Then he had a sudden thought. He yelled out, 'What if it comes out white?'

But Roo either didn't hear or didn't want to hear. Darryl looked at his back for a moment, then gave it away. He went inside to the family and shut the door.

CHAPTER FIVE

On Friday morning Graeme had already started the Commodore when he heard the phone begin to ring inside the house. Deciding to leave it for the answering machine, or Reuben if the lazy little prick was awake yet, he kept backing down the drive. When he got to work *The Courier-Mail* was lying spread open on his desk at page four, weighted with his stapler and teacup. Ellen must have put it there, Graeme thought uneasily. *Second Report Throws Doubt on Black Head Injury*; the medium-size headline sat above a picture of suited men emerging from the coroner's office. A cold snake slowly began to stretch and uncoil itself in Graeme's guts. The original, favourable coroner's report was the main pillar in their argument that the death hadn't been caused in custody, but in the brawl beforehand. With a growing disbelief he read what the paper had to say. The facts of the case were stated (as if any bastard in Brisbane who could read didn't already know them). Amazing isn't it, Graeme sneered to himself, if it was a white that died no one'd give a flying fuck.

★

The youth in question, Stanley King, was arrested after what police described as a 'brief scuffle' in a Fortitude Valley park on the night of March 20, and charged with resisting arrest, assaulting a police officer and using obscene language. He was subsequently found dead in his cell at the City Watchhouse at 8.45 pm. King, who had a string of previous convictions, had been released from custody less than forty-eight hours prior to his death. On March 24 the arresting officer, Sergeant Madden, stated to the Police Internal Investigations Unit that King had appeared healthy though intoxicated when placed in his cell alone, a statement supported by other police officers who were on duty at the Watchhouse.

Yesterday's coronial inquiry, however, has cast further doubt upon the circumstances of King's death. Computerised analysis of King's medical tests has shown that, in addition to his head injury, his death may have been related to as yet unexplained internal bleeding inconsistent with a brief scuffle.

Further doubt, muttered Graeme to himself, whadda they bloody mean, *further* doubt?

Senior Sergeant Bruce O'Connor of the Internal Investigations Unit told the media yesterday that investigations into the matter were continuing. A representative of the Police Union said in a brief statement that she had every confidence the unit's original finding that King's death was the result of striking his head on a footpath during the 'scuffle' would be upheld.

Fear turns so quickly to anger. Enraged by what he read, Graeme threw the heavy wad of newspaper at his window. The sheets fell apart onto the floor, and Graeme scrunched them into small hard balls which he forced into the empty wastepaper basket beside his desk. Then he stood, hands braced against his desk.

Nothing in there, he told himself, about the bloody coon's criminal record, was there? Nothing about the sexual assault he'd been put into John Oxley for less than six months ago … nothing about him being pissed out of his tiny mind, and fighting every other black bastard in the park all that afternoon, was there? Nothing in the paper about the taunts that'd come out of its mouth when it saw Madden sitting in the patrol car on his way back from the Valley.

Nothing about King winding him up in that nasally boong voice that got on his nerves just to hear, let alone when it was saying: *Madman, ay madman, where's me taxi, madman? Ay, wanna root, madman, c 'mere and suck me black cock madman, eh madman …*

Graeme still had a perfectly clear memory of the thin body slumped on the floor of the cell. It'd been in basketball boots and jeans when they took it in, that and a 'Boonie our Brother' T-shirt, the ones that they all wore to make a martyr outta that other little black cunt that got what was coming to him. He shook his head, unsuccessfully trying to get things straight inside it. It didn't work. All Graeme could think of was the stink of the watchhouse that night, the ever-present stench of vomited beer and runny shit and the smell peculiar to old derros – overlaid with sweat and cheap sherry. And what had been the final fucken trigger: that the coon couldn't wait to get to the fucken cell to chuck his guts, no, he had to do it out in reception which meant yours fucken truly had to do the honours and clean it up. Servants of the public, that's what we are, mate, he'd told the Duty Officer, fucken glorified street-cleaners, picking society's shit outta the gutters so the nice people with their nice jobs and nice houses and rose-coloured fucken glasses don't ever have to see it. What a joke. The bird who was the Duty Officer just shrugged in agreement, but handed him the mop anyway when he lost the toss.

Graeme's two colleagues wandered over to his desk. 'You read it?' Ellen asked unnecessarily.

'Yeah, the fucken rag ...' Madden gestured uselessly at his bin.

'One day they'll print the truth and we'll all drop dead from shock,' she said.

'Yeah.' Madden began composing his own page-four article aloud: *'Well-known thief and rapist, the coon Stanley King got what was coming to him yesterday when he attempted to cross the thin blue line for the last time. After repeated verbal abuse of officers of the Queensland Police Service, King was taken into custody after a short scuffle, which he naturally lost, being pissed out of his tiny black brain ... this useless specimen, this drain on society was found dead in the lockup a couple of hours afterwards. No tears were shed except by a few other useless boongs. The arresting officer, Sergeant Graeme Madden, later said it was a tragedy, but these things happen when you break the law, don't they?'*

The phone rang, interrupting his recital, and Graeme turned to it, grateful for a distraction. But it was Bruce O'Connor, and a reminder that he had to front the inquiry again next week once they'd looked at more evidence.

Like he needed reminding. When he put the phone down, Graeme stirred sugar into his coffee, mindlessly watching the liquid swirl around against the inside of the cup. Fifteen years of hard work, fifteen years of service, and it could all be over cos of some little boong's smart mouth, and a dose of bad luck that'd cripple an elephant. He shook his head again. Who'd be a cop? *TJ.S. TJ. fucken S ...*

The sun crept up over the hibiscus in the front yard, and was well up the white trunks of the two gums by the time Roo stirred. A slice of yellow light was coming through a crack in the spare room's curtain and hitting him in the face. He rubbed at his eyes, and then pulled the floral material aside. It was a nice day out there. The cloudless sky real blue, that deep bright solid blue that he loved – an autumn morning sky. He gazed at it, remembering last year in John Oxley, and the way he'd looked out at that colour then, sick with longing for it to be the sky over a free fella's head.

He felt like he'd go fucken crazy before he got out, but he'd hung in, doing the little time he had to go cos what else can ya do, and dreaming of Sydney in the year 2000. Got through by running round the hard concrete compound risking stress fractures, pumping iron in the gym after work. And now he was out again. So sweet to be street legal, eh. And he had all day stretching in front of him before training at four o'clock. A whole day to do whatever he wanted. So why didn't he feel fantastic? So what, he told himself, if him and Shaleena split up – all they ever fucken did was fight anyway. Ah, forget about her, she's just another loser. A knocked-up loser with a jailbird's kid in her now. No way it was his, no fucken way, Jose. Roo pushed what he felt for Leena far down inside himself, too far to see or hear anything except this relentless chanting of her faults, real and imagined.

So, first things first. After a guilty cigarette that he told himself he'd stub out halfway through but didn't, Roo jumped out of bed and went for a long hot shower. This mig house felt a bit like a jail to him, but only in a good way. Like in the bathroom, there were no grubby clothes or towels on the floor, and everything was shiny and clean, like in prison. The toilet had a lid; there were no holes in the walls. There was plenty of soap, too, good hard soap, not that cheap stuff that disappears when you wet it, and heaps and heaps of hot water and three different sorts of shampoo and no one watching you and no one to watch out for. Roo revelled in the luxury. You're on easy street here, he told himself as the hot water battered him awake. When he stepped out steaming, the air surprised him with its sudden coolness. Winter was on the way. Athletics season in full swing shortly. He stood on the bathroom scales – seventy-two kay-gees, just right. Inspired, Roo decided that this week he'd definitely give up smoking for good. He could do it, he just needed a reason, eh, an incentive, that's all. He could do it, no worries.

Stuffing leftover pizza into his mouth for breakfast, he whacked on B105, turning it up loud, then thought he'd take the opportunity to have a good look around the house. May as well suss out his father properly. The first place he went was the tall cupboard in Graeme's room. Turned out to be full of clothes, no big surprise. Roo grabbed himself a dark-blue cop jumper. He pulled it on; it swung loosely below his bum, miles too big. He slipped it back on its hanger and tried a black Adidas top instead. That was better. Arms a bit long, but it looked sick, eh.

Roo admired himself in the full-length mirror. No doubt about it, the training was paying off. He'd bulked up in the shoulders and thighs since last winter, that's where them extra four kilos'd gone on. Getting in the habit of eating three meals a day in John Oxley hadn't hurt either. It was getting so it was hard to remember that they'd called him 'Stick' at school. His skin was clearing up, and if he'd cut his sideburns like Graeme wanted, he'd look like a real stiff, Roo thought. The black top with its vivid side stripes covered his forearm tats, and as for a couple of earrings, well, everyone wore earrings these days ... accountants, lawyers, poofs, everyone. Except pigs, of course, he grinned to himself.

But Graeme hadn't been on his case that much about stuff. Considering he was a cop and everything. In fact he'd hardly seen the bloke since he moved in, something to do with this Inquiry he was holding. The sucker got up at six-thirty every morning for work, unbelievable, and last night he didn't get home till after nine. Night before last Roo'd got sick of waiting up for him, turned the lights off and gone to bed. Lying there in the dark he couldn't stop thinking about Leena and Mum and that. Stressed himself right out – dickhead – and when he went to the kitchen for a drink it all kinda hit him at once. Started the flashbacks and everything, a full-on panic attack, but luckily he'd got to the front door in time and was out and running quick enough to kill the monster with speed and pain. Ran for ages, miles and miles, and then when he did get home there was a blast from Graeme about leaving the place unlocked and the security lights off. The man was obsessed by the dark; anyone'd think all the demons of the world lived in the bush there at the back of the house. That was about the sum of their communication so far, grunts about the news and a major reading of the Riot Act about home security.

They tiptoed around issues like Roo's history and his record and Roo not talking (not yet) about Murries getting bashed and murdered by the pigs, and where he'd been living and all that. Graeme'd said he'd take him to see the Broncos this weekend, get to spend some time together, do that bonding shit. Roo didn't tell him he'd rather watch NBL; he'd gotten the distinct impression that along with dole bludgers and crims and greenies and feminists, Graeme didn't like Yanks much either, or Yank sports. Left ya wondering if there was anyone he did like ... other cops, maybe? Although he was always whingeing about them, too.

Roo adjusted his look in the mirror, and went on rifling through his father's clothes. The jeans were too big, and you wouldn't wear ya old man's undies if ya didn't have to, eh. Some khaki Stubbies shorts, the zippered sort. Socks, a million pairs of thin black coppers' socks. Black shoes. One pair of black boots. Then Roo saw Graeme's cotton uniform shirts. Hanging loosely inside the other half of the cupboard, the pale blue shirts marked with the insignia of the Queensland Police jarred him up a bit. He made a face and superstitiously shut the door on them, trail of goosebumps ran up his back. Don't be stupid, he told himself, for Chrissake they're just bloody shirts. But all of a sudden the fun had gone out of his exploring. They made him think of poor bloody Stanley and that made him remember Shaleena again. And while Roo hated to admit it, he missed her. Missed her heaps. Darryl too. Even Mum – Roo had a sour, sick feeling when he thought about her words to Darryl. It still felt like she was saying it sorta by accident, just making a mistake. As if he could have said, *Hey! It's me – Roo*, and everything would have been okay. Only there was no accident, no mistake. He was wiped. Ah, fuck 'em, he said angrily, turning away from the mirror. Serves ya right for expecting anything better, ya dumb shit. Forget it. Who needs them?

Roo walked around the house for a while, close to tears. Then he went and put the TV on, but it was nothing good, just that midday shit. Five minutes of *Ray Martin* and he was on his feet, exploring again. In an ordinary house you could look under the sink for the bong, or check the bathroom cabinet for Seros and stuff. After knowing Graeme for three days, he didn't even bother looking. He was straight as, man. Roo sighed heavily. There were some beers in the fridge. And he wouldn't be home from work for how long? Ages … hours and hours. He'd said no ripping cars off, but he didn't say nothing about a few beers. Roo looked around the house some more. It was big and quiet alright – too quiet. When no one answered the phone at Todd's place,

Roo whacked both the cold sixpacks from the fridge in his sportsbag, stashed his house key and took off for the Gabba.

The pool hall was busy at lunchtime, because of it being Friday probably. Roo carefully hid his grog under the bench that ran along one side, and looked over to where a group of Murries were playing. Didn't he know that tall skinny fella from somewhere? He thought hard before he approached him, in case it was from a fight. Then he remembered. He was a mate of Shaleena's best friend's boyfriend. His name was Ross, or Randall, or something … Reggie? Something like that.

Russell remembered him, so he was soon in on the game playing doubles. No worries. He reckoned he might know where to score, too, he said, so Roo let him in on the beers quick smart. You scratch my back, pal.

The TV, which had been only a background hum of American talk shows, changed its tone as a newsbreak came on. Pauline Hanson's pinched bitterness appeared above them. Roo stood up from his shot. The woman's nasal drone drizzled its usual poison over the airwaves, and he felt a shiver of hate go through him. Russell noticed him listening to the TV.

'Fucken bitch,' he murmured to Roo in a gesture of solidarity.

'Give 'er some special treatment if I ever come across 'er.'

'Yer not wrong, bruz, yer not wrong at all,' Roo agreed, showing his middle finger to the screen. Even before the Kings took him in he'd had no time for racist shit. The whole crock sucked.

Then an unleashed comment floated towards him from the yobbos on the neighbouring table. '... be voting for her, before the fucken boongs and slopes take the place over ...'

He didn't need to turn to see the speaker. From the voice he knew it was the blond dickhead that talked that bit too loud; the one with the Marilyn Manson singlet and army daks. He'd given Roo the bullshit tough-guy look the minute he walked in, and didn't like being ignored in return.

'... packa lazy black cunts suckin piss on my taxes ...'

Russell was dark. Russell's nephew was dark. Russell's sister was dark. The whole room froze. Roo glanced over at Russell. His face was flushed under its colour but the Murri fella stood rock-steady. Rage shimmered off him like heat off an outback road.

'Ya white bruwa's a bit noisy, mate,' Russell said softly to him in sarcasm. A taunt. A challenge.

'Racist prick's no bruvver of mine,' Roo replied as he turned to face the dickhead. 'Yer voting for Pauline Hanson, I hear, eh?' The man smiled as Roo walked over to him, then lost the smile with, 'Ya look fucken stupid enough, cunt.' His usual plan: stir the possum, make him bite, then slam the fucker good, real good. The blond was big, but boofy, with a gut hanging over the camouflage pants and a second chin dangling just below where Roo planned to knock him out.

'Yeah, got a problem with it?' the man sneered, taking in Russell and the rest of them. A mocking aggression entered his remarks. 'Geez, I tell ya what, there's only one thing I hate worse'n coons and that's the kind of white trash that hangs round with em.'

Roo nodded at this, projecting an air of faint and detached amusement. 'This fuckwit thinks he can take me, Russ,' he noted. 'This poor, ugly, brain damaged, dogfucking dickhead actually thinks he can have me.'

Russell laughed.

'What's up, sunshine, didn't ya daughter suck ya cock for ya this mornin'?' Roo taunted. He waited only long enough for the bloke's face to be transformed by this remark before he threw his pool cue at him. It speared him in the midriff with a surprising force, forcing his breath from him and doubling him over at Roo's knee height.

Russell's crew whooped loudly at this new development. Girls screamed, and men protested. Roo didn't hear them. All he heard was Hanson, in his ear for weeks and months, shaming him in his whiteness, and making his and Leena's life harder than it already had to be.

'Want some special treatment, ya fuck?' he screamed in the ear of the blond. 'Try this,' and sank his right heel in the same spot the cue had hit. The whoof of breath this time was followed by spew and Roo spun sideways on the spot to avoid it.

'Dirty bastard!' he said in astonishment to the man who was now on all fours, retching.

'Get up 'im!' Russell's sister urged, 'Don't stop now, cuz!'

It occurred to Roo that it was a piece of good luck he'd worn a black T-shirt that day, and not the maroon and white Broncos shirt of Graeme's he'd been affecting lately. The thought was enough to make him pause, and in that moment his better sense spoke. Best lay off now, it advised, and at the same time Russell grabbed Roo's arm. Didn't want a murder charge on the young brother.

'The cunt's ratshit, ya proved ya point, so c'mon eh?'

Roo saw the sense of this, and allowed himself to be led away.

In the glass cage at the front of the building a small fat man stabbed furiously at the phone; he tried desperately not to hear what was happening on the wooden floor. When the police arrived several minutes later, the blond had been taken away by his group of stunned friends, and no one left behind had seen a thing. Least of all Roo who, mindful of his bail conditions, was hiding in the girls' toilet. The pool players pretended surprise when the cops pointed out the vomit on the floor, and wondered aloud how it'd got there.

'Went a bit over the top, didn't ya?' Russell asked when the pigs had left.

'I hate racists,' Roo said forcefully. 'Ya gotta stand up for what ya believe in.'

'You're fucken cracked,' said Russell, as they chalked up again. 'You'll be getting ya'self in some serious trouble one of these days, cuz.' There was neither praise nor condemnation in his voice.

'Yeah, yeah,' said Roo, tossing the chalk to him as if he'd never had the same thought, as if heading for jail was all a big laugh. 'Whatever.'

★

Training under the warm afternoon sun, Roo floated around the final bend, kicked it hard at a hundred out and roared past the guy struggling in front. The coach clocked him at 2.02.06 for the eight hundred. And it wasn't even his distance. Roo slowed gradually like you were supposed to, stopped, and bent over. He ran his fingers down the outside of his calves. He could feel their hardness under a film of sweat. The injury didn't seem to be coming back, or, if it was, four stubbies at Russell's place had killed the pain.

'Bit of regular training pays off, doesn't it?' the coach told him.

Roo grinned. 'Yeah, must do.'

'Reuben!' someone called from the sideline, and he turned around, still panting. To his shock, Madden stood there in jeans and a white polo shirt. Fucken hell, thought Roo, raising a hand in greeting, what's *he* doing here? He must have been home already and got changed. Roo frowned, hoping to Christ that Darryl wouldn't make his next surprise appearance at the track. He could just see them two at it. They'd get along like a house on fire. Not.

'More spectators?' the coach asked Roo, who didn't have a chance to answer. Graeme was there.

'Hi. I'm Graeme Madden. How's the kid doing?' Madden stuck his hand out. The coach grasped it, wondering who the hell he was.

'This is my, ah, father,' said Roo diffidently, and was rewarded by a proud smile from Graeme. Look out, he'll be putting his arm around ya next, like it's the fucken movies or something.

'Oh, pleased to meet cha. He's doing ... oh, not too bad. If he keeps training he'll have some sorta chance at the squad,' the coach said.

Graeme shot a curious look at his son, pleasure mingled with distaste. Roo had bragged about his place in the Queensland team to Graeme only last night. Roo decided it was a good time to do a couple more laps.

'Is it a strong squad?' Graeme asked, as he and the coach wandered off towards the centre of the field.

In the car, Graeme didn't look directly at Roo as he said, 'Well, you might not be in yet, but your coach reckons you've got a bit of talent. Thinks the sun shines out of your arse, actually.'

'What'd he say?' asked Roo, gut-starved for praise.

'Oh, most talented young bloke he'd seen for several years, blah blah blah. But he reckons you should train more. And lay off the fags. I can't believe you smoke when you're a runner.'

'Yeah, yeah, I know. I've just got a lotta stuff going on lately. You know, splitting up with Shaleena and that.'

Madden grunted, then asked, 'Did you take any beers outta the fridge today?'

'Yeah. That's okay, isn't it?' Roo bluffed it. Two sixpacks, twenty bucks worth of grog. Big deal.

'Yeah. But ask next time, alright? Doesn't grow on trees, you know. You didn't drink it all yourself, did ya?'

'Nah, I went round to a mate's place.' Roo relaxed, seeing Madden wasn't going to front him, not properly. Knowing the answer to his next question, Madden pursed his lips as he swung the car up the drive.

'So what's your mate do for a crust that he's home during the day?'

'He's … aw … he used to be an apprentice chef or something, but he's on the dole now. He's got that thing, that DDT thing. Attention deficit disorder.'

'Oh, right, so he works for me and every other stupid bastard that pays their taxes. Sitting around drinking piss all day isn't gonna help ya keep ya nose clean, son. 'Bout time you thought about doing something constructive with ya'self, isn't it?'

'Me?' Roo said, surprised. He'd only been outta jail five months. Why would he want to lock himself up again by taking on a job? If there was even any around, which there wasn't.

'Yeah, you,' Madden said, turning off Logan Road by the fire station. 'Or did you plan on being a career criminal?'

'But I'm training!' Roo said, to buy a bit of time. Bloody hell … here we go.

'When I was your age I used to work nine to five and then train four nights a week. Most blokes that play Club grade footy work all day. There's a bloke in at Roma Street represents Australia in water polo – he manages to drag himself in to the office every day.'

'Oh.' Roo had no response to this unwelcome idea. Work was the last thing he wanted to stumble across. Mugs game. Look at Graeme, he was hardly ever home.

'Have you ever had a job?' Graeme asked impatiently. Roo thought of all the hours he'd put in in jail, slaving over the weeds in the pine-bark garden beds.

'Yeah. I was a gardener in jail, eh, used to maintain

the lawns and that. And before I went in I used to wash windscreens sometimes. You know, at the lights? And the CES put me on this thing once, we fixed up the track at this national park out at Daisy Hill. There was a mob of us done it. That was alright. S'pose ...'

'Well, why not try and get a job gardening, then?' Madden asked. Roo grimaced. As if. Running was all the work he wanted or needed.

'Yeah, alright, I might go and have a look at the job place next week,' he said, to get him off his back.

'It's worth having a think about anyway. Can't stay on the dole forever, you know.' Then his tone of voice changed to a friendlier one. 'There's a work thing on tonight. Thought ya might be interested. I knocked off early to come and get you. Here, check this out.' He felt in his shirt pocket and drew out two squares of yellow cardboard. Roo read slowly and with difficulty:

Traffic Division invites you to celebrate the imminent marriage of Brian 'Jumbo' Jackson by joining us for a Female Revue Night – Videos, Live Strippers, Oil Wrestling, and a special variety show featuring 'The Thin "Blue" Line' at the Royal Hotel Function Room, 7.30 Friday. $25 per head.

'Wanna come?' Madden asked, grinning. 'Should be a good night. I'll pay for ya, don't worry about the twenty-five bucks.' Show the lad a good time, bit of father-son bonding. Take his mind off his girlfriend too.

'Yeah, sure.' This more than made up for the lack of porn Madden's video library. Roo had a stiff already, just thinking about it.

Graeme wore a stupid expectant grin for the rest of the afternoon, even when he warned Roo that it'd be better not to tell his copper mates about him having been locked up in the past. 'Not everyone in the Force is as broad-minded as me,' he said. Roo looked up quickly for his father's smile, but Graeme was serious.

The youngest and most attractive of the strippers was a darkie, Graeme observed, with jutting cheekbones and glistening cinnamon-brown legs. Indonesian or something. Whatever she is, she's a hot little spunk anyway, he thought, as he watched the groom-to-be running his hands up and down the girl's naked torso, squeezing her tits when she let him. She slid a leg across and straddled him, tongueing at the man's face, her bare brown breasts teasing the front of his shirt which she then began unbuttoning. Every man in the room had one thought: Lucky bastard. The girl's silver lamé g-string sparkled under the stage lights. She moved her head lower and the man began to groan.

Over the heavy, hypnotic thud of the music, catcalls came from the audience, suggestions on technique and lewd encouragement for Jumbo. But to his surprise and dismay, the girl didn't take her performance to its logical conclusion. She instead spun away from him to gyrate in front of one of the other men who in his turn developed a glazed look and troubled breathing. Shortly after, the music ended, the girl left and the video screen flickered to life. Jumbo sat in the dim light, frustrated and feeling bloody silly to boot.

When the dark girl beckoned to him from the wings a minute later he burst out of his seat, ignoring the enthusiastic noise from the mob. Seeing him go, Graeme half-jealously yelled, 'Ya not gonna, are ya, Jumbo?'

'Fucken watch me,' came the reply. 'It's my last chance!'

'Buggered if my last root before I got married'd be a boong,' someone behind him protested. Jeez, he was getting married tomorrow, or today it was now, to a gorgeous blonde ... couldn't he wait twelve hours?

'That's alright, I'm not racist!' Jumbo was dragging his shirt off over his head. A ripple of laughter ran round the room.

'Mate, she only looks about fucken thirteen,' muttered Graeme. It was one thing to look at little girls ... his lip curled with disdain.

'That's okay, I'm not superstitious either,' said Jumbo, disappearing quickly into the side room.

When Roo got back from the bar he got into a bit of a philosophical spiral, helped by the couple of Tequila slammers he'd had with one of the blokes who'd perched himself there for the evening. S'funny, he thought in a boozy haze, s'funny how these coppers are just like normal blokes, 'cept for being coppers and therefore arseholes, s'funny that. He sucked at the can of beer in his hand; finding to his disgust that it was empty, he threw it onto the table with the other empties. His head was spinning ever so slightly.

'Ay, Grae,' he called out to the blur of bodies in front of the big video screen. 'Graeme ...' Nothing happened. The blokes watching the last of the blue movies weren't moving for him or anyone else. Roo tried to focus on what was happening but his eyes wouldn't work properly. When the fog cleared a little he saw that his father wasn't around.

Wondering what had happened to Graeme, Roo staggered to the toilet and went julabai, then went outside in search of him. Near the entrance a group of the blokes was standing around a blue Magna sedan. Seeing Graeme amongst them, Roo went over. Inside the car a drunk had collapsed, snoring, on the back seat Most of the onlookers were indifferent, but the handful of cops closest to the car took a keener interest. Graeme's workmate Bill stood at the centre of the group; his right elbow rested on the car roof, his left hand on his hip. His chin jutted out in affront at what he was seeing.

'Look at this weak cunt, will you?' he was saying angrily to Graeme. 'He can never hold his piss, he's just a fucken weak prick. And he just about shit himself when that blonde piece sat in his lap. D'ya see him?' He looked to the rest of the group for support, miming the other man's reaction, flailing away from an imaginary stripper, palms held upwards in exaggerated horror. 'I'm married!' he parodied his workmate in a high falsetto, 'I'm married!' His eyes narrowed. 'Who fucken asked the prick along anyway?'

'Or so he reckons he's married,' Graeme interjected, tapping cigarette ash away from him onto the ground, 'but I've never seen her.' A faint trace of innuendo stayed in the air after he spoke.

Irritated, Bill banged his hand loudly on the car roof. It felt good. He did it again and everyone looked at him. He felt he had to say something to justify their attention. 'If there's one thing I can't stand it's weak bastards that can't hold their piss,' he announced. There were disgruntled nods and murmurs of agreement from some of the others.

Several sheets to the wind, Graeme suddenly had a brainwave. He unzipped his fly and took his prick in an unsteady hand. 'I'll show him how ta hold his piss.' He laughed hysterically, directing a stream of urine through the open window onto the sleeping body. The man in the car stirred but didn't wake. The others roared with approval. Three or four of them then did the honours as well, unbuttoning and hosing away till the man in the car groaned and suddenly sat up. He was half asleep, and dripping with piss. He put a bemused hand to his soaked hair. His persecutors found this hysterically funny. The look on the man's face when he realised what was going on sent Bill and Graeme into paroxysms of laughter, gasping for air.

Wiping himself down furiously, the man inside started to swear. One of the younger cops leaned into the car and spoke in the saccharine voice of an American receptionist. 'This is your morning wake-up call, sir.'

They exploded again. Graeme banged his fists together on the bonnet as tears ran down his face. Bill sagged at the knees and clutched his guts, sobbing for breath.

'Garn, have a slash, mate,' the young cop encouraged Roo.

Roo just looked at him, grinning weakly. He could sorta see why they thought it was funny, but even if he'd wanted to, the joke was surely over now. And the whole thing was pretty bloody off, eh?

'Nah, I can't mate, I just went for a leak inside,' he managed to say.

'Aaarrgh ...' The young cop dismissed Roo with a disappointed noise, and looked around.

The piss seeping from the car stank like a public bog. The men hovered, wondering what was next. The strip show was over, but they were too drunk and too excited to happily go home to their wives and girlfriends. Sensing their mood, Roo backed slowly away from the huddle of drunks – they were cops after all, and cops looking for amusement was something he'd experienced before from the sharp end. The victim climbed out of the car, still swearing to himself, and peeled his sodden clothes off down to his underwear. He stood there, shivering and ridiculous, but forced by group consensus to be a good sport, till someone took pity and threw him a dry jumper.

Feeling mildly sorry for the victim, Roo had no idea that his disorderly life was about to come crashing down. What he heard next slid a cold knife into his spine.

'Hey, Graeme,' said a tall redheaded bloke clutching a stubby and grinning, 'whaddya reckon we go and chase up a few coons?'

Before Roo could begin to know what to do or think, he saw Graeme stiffen and shake his head. Then he heard his father's reply.

'No fucken way, pal, the IIU's into me already over that other little black cunt. Last thing I need right now.'

Roo stared at his father. A thrill of horror began to stir in him.

'Yeah,' slurred the other man under the brilliant car park light. 'Yeah, well, listen. I know – we all know – they set ya up over it. So whassay we go teach his fucken boong mates a fucken good lesson … eh?' It was as close to a declaration of mateship as the tall man could make. He grinned lopsidedly at Graeme, a dog waiting for a bone.

The others waited in silence to see which way the night was going to go. The men's reaction to the idea ranged from silent disgust to mild enthusiasm; Graeme was still shaking his head. No way. No fucken way. Through the multiple layers of booze in his brain came an insistence that he watch his back. Because who knows? Maybe this bloke was part of some scheme to make sure they got him? What was his game, anyway? Bill reckoned he was alright, but …'

Roo finally recovered his voice. 'What black cunt?' he asked hoarsely. The conversation had drifted by then and no one took any notice of him. 'What are ya talkin about? What black cunt?' he shouted at Graeme, who looked at him through vacant drunken eyes. The noise died down again.

Something slowly stirred in Graeme's mind … there was something he had to be careful about here, with the kid. But what was it exactly? He'd had five or six too many beers to say exactly, and now two or three Reubens were staring accusingly at him. He tried to explain that it was a messy situation, he'd been set up, but nothing came out of his mouth. Roo was close to tears and choking on the incredible unfairness of his life. He managed to repeat his question. Bill overheard and came to Graeme's rescue.

'This Abo that died – it was in the paper – he kicked the bucket in the watchhouse a coupla weeks ago, and they're trying to pin it on Graeme.'

Graeme groaned in protest, wishing Bill would shut up about it. He remembered now. When he'd dropped Roo at his mate's place that first night, there was a boong flag in the window. He'd noticed it, but he wanted to get to know the kid a bit first, have some fun together before telling him about … about the situation. About him being deep in the shit. Or else Roo might not understand it, might get confused, eh. Might even blame him, in fact, before he knew the facts.

'It's nothing really—' Graeme began to say, but Roo's blurred faces stopped him.

Roo felt as if someone had carefully peeled the skin from his body. The air hurt. Breathing hurt. 'Stanley King,' he said quietly, not making it into a question.

Graeme nodded, but it was Bill who answered. 'Yeah, that's the one. No fucken great loss to society, let me tell ya. But don't worry, he's got a good case, they won't get him on anything. The inquiry's just to shut the papers up till it dies down. Hey, Al' – turning away – 'whaddya reckon we go to that place in the Valley, it'll be open for ages yet.'

Reuben didn't hear Al's reply. He was reeling out of the car park, getting as far and as fast away from the group of men as he could. He felt physically sick. *Unclean*, a voice shrieked from the back of his head, you've been drinking with him, eating with him. Talking to him. Sleeping in the same house, breathing the air he's breathed. And he's your father – you're tied to him, you belong to him.

You can't escape! Your blood's his blood. *Unclean!* Roo sobbed for air and space but neither came. There was nothing for him to do except run. Terrible fears lapped at his heels, speeding him on.

'Reuben! Roo ... whaddya doing?' Graeme called out in groggy confusion, seeing the lad take off. He started to chase after him, explain what Bill had really meant, make him see that whatever had happened that night wasn't his fault. But when he got just beyond the boundary of the car park lights he stopped. The vague outlines of the kid were already far away at the end of the street, and not slowing. He was a runner after all. Graeme didn't have a hope of catching him. The man stood impotent and fearful in the half-light.

'Reuben!' he shouted again into the blackness. No good. Even the sound of his feet was fading. Graeme stared in bewilderment out at the street, as the revellers began to drift away to their cars. Big engines started to rev; white smoke showed in clouds against the cool night air.

'Ah, shit!' Graeme spat the word out. '*Shit!*'

'Where's he going all of a sudden?' Bill asked in a hostile tone, draining his stubby.

'Fucked if I know,' said Graeme, too surprised to invent an excuse for Roo. Then embarrassment at the boy's behaviour made him terse. 'Ah, fuck him anyway, the little shit. He's big enough and ugly enough to look after himself.' He turned and walked back towards the car park. Bill had screwed it up for him nicely, but he couldn't say so.

'So you coming up the Red Garter with everyone?'

Bill asked, the empty stubby swinging loosely by the neck between his thumb and forefinger. Under his casual words lay the unmistakable and ever-present copper's question: are you still with us? Or is this mysteriously disappearing kid a sign of something bigger, some other betrayal lurking?

'Oh. Yeah, alright … whose car we taking?' Graeme frowned, his mind still on Roo.

'Scooby's only had a few stubbies he reckons.'

'Alright then, let's go.'

More or less satisfied, Bill moved back inside to see if they'd have to pay the bar tab. Graeme followed, but as he did, he turned and glared at the blackness of the night. His son was out there in the bloody dark somewhere, bailed and running, and he didn't have the first clue what to do about it.

PART TWO

HIS DEATH GROWS THROUGH OUR HEART

CHAPTER SIX

Roo slept little, woken every half an hour by the cold, or the lights of passing cars, or by screams coming from nearby streets and other parts of Musgrave Park. He put his hands over his ears and huddled further into the flimsy warmth of Madden's black jumper, trying not to hear, and trying uselessly to forget. Everything. Made miserable by the yoke of knowledge, he shrank between the industrial bin and the heavily graffitied wall of the public toilet, which were his shields from the outside world. Keep it tight lad, he reminded himself as he wriggled with cold, you can do it. You've been here before, just don't lose it now. Keep it buttoned down hard 'n you'll be right. He shivered the night away, his body whingeing, but the physical stuff was easy. It was what hadn't stopped roaring in his head since Graeme spoke that worried him. The best thing – the only thing – was to try not to think about it. Try and pretend it hadn't happened. Same as all the other shit that had gone down in his life, forget about it. The locks. The kicks. The boiling water, the cigarettes. The hands. Ignore it.

At first light the trucks started down Vulture Street and when Roo opened his tired eyes this time he could at least see the outlines of the big trees against the sky. He gave up on the idea of sleep then for good. His right hand went to his back pocket – lucky, he hadn't been rolled in the night. Then again, he'd hardly been asleep. He counted the money. Graeme had given him a fifty on Thursday and there was ten bucks sixty left. Heaps, he breathed in relief. Enough for a couple of days food if he stuck to cheap stuff like chips and that, and some for a bus fare and phone calls too. If he could just, like, work out where to go. Who to call.

Jesus, Roo, ya picked ya fucken moment didn't ya? We're gonna call it Stanley if it's a boy ...

If anyone had ever said to Roo that he'd one day go to a public bog for safety, he would have laughed and told them they were out of their tiny fucken minds. But snuggled between the wall and the bin he was in an animal-like nest of safety; he could see out and no one could see in, the way he liked it. Out of view of the parkies and the cops. Even a tap handy at the loo for drinking water. It was just the cold, eh. He was bloody freezing. The bite of early winter had arrived while he, lazybones, slackarse, was living in luxury in Madden's brick, carpeted house and now he was unprepared to go back to reality. Like in that song. He heard the woman singer's voice rising in his mind. *Gotta get black, black, black, to rea-a-lity ...*

Too right I do. 'Cept I'm white and on the outer, that's my reality. Get over it, he told himself. Cope. Plentya bastards live like this all year round, rain or shine, and not just when they've had a bitta bad luck. So stop fucken whingeing and get over it.

A hangover nagged behind Roo's temples while he ran through some options. He needed somewhere to crash, and second, some more bungoo, and third, a way of getting his training gear outta Madden's place, and fourth, a way to get to training and run every session like everything was normal. Really *really* normal, super-normal, cos do ya think they're gonna give ya a place in the Queensland squad if they think you live in a fucken park? If they find out your old man's a murderer? Roo remembered in a kind of daze that the first of the state trials was three weeks away. In only three weeks' time he had to run as fast as he ever had, or else kiss his squad possie goodbye. He swore under his breath about it, long complicated curses that rained down on the Kings and on Madden and on stupid dead Stanley and a few for himself too while he was at it. Then hearing noise outside, he lifted his head and looked through the protective screen of weeds.

On the far side of the park, on a small rise, a few crumpled people lay and sat around an open fire. Roo didn't know it but the park-dwellers were ignoring the young migloo stranger who was sleeping at Two Bob's place, poor thing. Bit of a laugh, eh. Hope Two Bob didn't come back last night and haunt him, like that last bloke who tried stoppin there steada headin back to Melrose Place. No wonder Two Bob come back sometimes, but. Horrible death, burning, horrible. White lady got him, and not the way he thought neither.

One of the parkies was arguing with a thin woman.

Roo couldn't hear what they were saying but the way they both flung their arms around in accusation didn't look promising. Sure enough, smack. He hit her in the face with an open hand. Roo flinched. He knew what that felt like. The woman half-fell, half-staggered away, and a watching child began to wail. Others raised their voices at it, then, and Roo shrank against the toilet wall. Seeing people fight usually made him wild, feel like lashing out – makem wake up to themselves, eh. Right now, but, he just felt sick. Knowing what his father was had hollowed him out, kinda sucked his guts away. Madden was scum, and he was the offspring of the lying dog. No wonder his life sucked. Goes to show ya, eh, that shrink was right after all. They could make a movie, starring him. *Son of Scum. Scum Two: The Inheritance.* Oh great.

The autumn air was turning everything outside Roo to pain. He felt abandoned in a cold, cold world of raised hands, voices, anger, death. Briefly, he thought of going home to Graeme's place. Trailing back there where a warm comfortable room waited and showing up like nothing had happened. Graeme wouldn't question him too hard; he had no idea what had made him bolt from the pub. He could say he got sick suddenly and was shame to spew in front of everyone, or … or thought he saw someone pinching a car (ha, that was a good one!), or, or … something.

Anything. It was so hard to be alone. Roo hung his head between his knees, not believing what was happening to him. He should have stayed with the Kings, worked something out with Shaleena, talked more to her about the baby. The fights didn't matter. Everyone had arguments with their chick, it wasn't no big deal. But how could he go back home now, knowing what he did?

This Abo that died, it was in the paper, he kicked the bucket in the watchhouse a coupla weeks ago, they're trying ta pin it on Graeme …

He shivered; the weak rays of sunshine that reached into his cubbyhole provided only light, not warmth. He saw himself jumping on the train over at South Brisbane, riding through to Salisbury, then hiking over the mountain to Madden's. He could do it while Graeme was at work. Wimpy knew him now, go there, grab some food, have a hot shower, and piss off before Graeme got home.

Even as he took the mental steps Roo knew they were pure fantasy. He was nauseated by the memory of last night, standing under those big bright car park lights, hearing Bill's words unzip his life. And as he ran up the street he could leave them fellas behind, but those first words Madden had ever spoken to him crashed in his head, wouldn't shut up, rang around his brain. Roo's cold aching body said *go to the station*, but he retched inside at what it would mean to go back.

He was bewildered at how it had all happened. After all that time in John Oxley telling himself every lonely night that it had to be the last time, that from now on, things were gonna be different. That his luck had to change soon. That he was gonna smarten up and stay outta trouble. How had he ended up sleeping friendless in a fucken park? He moved sideways to where the best shaft of sun was warming the grass a little, and wrapped himself around his knees. Maybe he was cursed. How else could you explain the way some people attracted all the bad luck? There was just no other explanation. He thought of Madden's big hard copper's hands, and marvelled at the way he'd been sucked into regarding the man – ah say it, ya father. Not as a cop, not as a murdering arsehole, but as a real person. There was no doubt, being careful just wasn't enough sometimes, you had to be *wise*, you had to be *lucky* and wise, and he'd fucked up yet again. Roo hung his head in shame, vowing that he wouldn't be taken in like that again.

Somehow when Graeme magically appeared that night, whisking him out of the pig car and ushering him into the world of the free, the fact of Stanley's murder had faded to the back of his mind. Or it had kinda slipped sideways, into another reality. Like, yeah, so he's dead, but it'd all happened a world away. Poor bastard, but shit happens, eh, ya gotta look out for ya'self, gotta expect trouble and not let it sneak up behind ya. Course the pigs'll bash ya, if ya give 'em the chance. Gotta not let 'em, eh, and anyway (Roo argued to himself, justifying his blindness) he wasn't me best mate or nothin, was he? They'd only met a few times, cos Stanley was always inside, and a few beers didn't make bosom buddies. Nearly come to blows one night, actually, Stanley being something like another Jimmy and Darryl jumpin in saying no colour bar, givit a rest, givit a rest. And even Shaleena'd said he was a loser, a goom drinker, always hanging with the drones when he wasn't locked up for stealing. If you wanted to be hard about it, if you wanted to be completely honest, you'd almost say the stupid little bastard had it coming, wouldn't ya? That's what Roo told himself when faced with Madden's blue uniform in the cupboard, Madden's old police newsletters on the kitchen table.

But now. Sitting on his twentieth birthday with his back to the cold orange brick of the toilet, surrounded by straggly weeds and old bits of dirty plastic, Roo felt the loss of the Kings tearing at him. His life had too many ragged edges. Roo began to realise that something had to be different if he was gonna keep going, something had to change. That something might even be him.

He realised he had been mourning the loss of his family – Stanley, Leena, Darryl. Even Mum King, the bloody old hard-case bitch. He stifled a sob – ah, ya weak bastard. But how could they do it to him? How? He didn't understand.

Has that white cunt gorn yet?

Roo tortured himself, let himself remember times at home, the way he'd laughed with Leena and Jimmy about TV shows. The fights he'd pretended with Darryl, both of em throwing punches and bottles designed to miss. Sweet times with Leena, going to the drive-in. That time they went and visited Auntie Mabel in hospital with pneumonia and flogged that wheelchair, Darryl sitting in it with a blanket over his legs and them all lying through their teeth saying, 'No, they said we could take it'. Coasting down the hill with all three of em hanging off it till it pranged and they left it, wheels spinning, by the side of Annerley Road. Ha-ha. Leena playing Zeppelin 3 so loud the windows shook and the neighbours chucked things on the roof. *Good times, bad times, you know I've had them all ...* And under all this remembering ran the poisoned stream of Madden's words: *Taking little smartarse cunts like you apart's my favourite occupation.* A strange man's grey eyes like rocks. A face that said it's a hard, hard world so just you try me, son, you'll do. I make the rules around here.

Taking little smartarse cunts like you apart's my favourite occupation.

Stanley'd never again sit back in the lounge at home. And he was on the outer too, looked like he'd never be there again neither. But if he thought about it, about stuff, he'd fall apart, eh. Roo bit his bottom lip and put a hand over his face. On ya birthday. Times like this ya wished ya had a gun. Fuck 'em, he thought through his tears. Fuck 'em all. Ignore it. Just get a grip, lad. Coming into the straight, tighten up. Sobbing for air. Whadda they call it? Home stretch. You can do it. Fuck 'em. Look for the line. Get over it. *Get over it.*

CHAPTER SEVEN

When Ellen picked up her handbag and left to get some more coffee and bickies, Graeme swung around to his desk and quickly made a call to a mate in Traffic.

'Chris. S'Graeme. Any luck?'

'Nah, sorry mate. Just a matter of time, but.' There were a million other things on Constable Breen's mind.

'Nothing at the Gabba eh?'

'Nah, not yet mate.' Impatient.

'Yeah … okay. Call us if you get anything, will ya?'

'No worries. Give it till tomorra if ya don't hear from us, eh?'

'Mmm. Righto, ta.'

Graeme rang off. No worries. No worries, except where the fuck is the kid? No worries, except I've put my arse on the line for him and now he's scooted. No worries, just a fucken boatload of trouble with a capital tee about to arrive courtesy of the I – I – fucken U. Graeme was beginning to understand how people literally tore their hair out. He grabbed his fags and went out onto the veranda. No one else up there for a change, too early for morning tea, bit late for the just-got-to-work-and-need-a-smoke-before- I-start brigade.

He lit a fag and looked out at the city landscape, clean and sharp in the autumn air. The weather was a bit Japanese these last couple of days, considering it was only April. Easter wouldn't be much good at the beach this year. Not that it worried him.

The view to Graeme's front was nearly blocked by the big cream-coloured block of the Transit Centre; the traffic of Roma Street blasted along its four lanes far below him. Other high buildings crowded around – the Courthouse, the old Post Office, the Sheraton, the tall white tower of the Hilton sticking up out of the mall. Others he didn't know by name. Graeme gripped the thick coolness of the metal railing and wondered if his son was somewhere out there in the CBD. Where would a nineteen-year-old – no twenty-year-old, it was his birthday yesterday – kid with no money and no job go? Pool halls? Pubs? Centrelink, God forbid? He's not locked up again yet, I know that much. S'pose that's something to be grateful for.

From what Reuben had said last week he had a handful of no-good mates round the place, but there'd been some sorta split in the ranks recently and he wasn't on speaking terms with a lot of em. That left, what? The bloke he'd been picked up in the hot car with was still on remand in SDL, so he was out. The ex-girlfriend – he'd never got her name, or anything about her, except that she lived somewhere near a fish 'n chip shop on Annerley Road, which could mean anywhere from Highgate Hill to bloody Salisbury. It didn't sound too likely he'd be with her, though. The kid said they'd been blueing for ages before they broke up on bad terms, and that he wasn't going back in a hurry.

Madden paced around angrily on the concrete deck, pushing himself off the end railings with extravagant force each time he reached them. Pace, pace, pace, *push*. Pace, pace, pace, *push*. How could the kid appear after nineteen years, move into home with him and then vanish again, all in the space of a week? It left the man stunned, pushed into a revolving door and spat out at random, not knowing where he was. Felt, in fact, as though he'd been bloody dreaming for a week, fantasising about having a kid to call him Dad, go to the footy with, take on camping trips (although Reuben had been less than enthusiastic when Graeme talked about going bush, the lazy little bastard). Now he was back to the crunch of reality again, with no son. No wife, either, if it came to that, but she'd left a message saying Peter was nearly gone so it wouldn't be long and she'd be home. Crying, blubbery message. And IIU still hanging over him like the Damoclean – was that it? – sword. His life held by a thread. Plunging through his body. O, crucify me.

Graeme ground his smoke out underfoot, dirtying the already grubby concrete, and then kicked the flattened butt over the edge. He peered down at the people on the street below. All the lucky bastards down there with their nice, straight, easy lives. Anger burned in him at his son's defection, and at the people who lived outside the cop world and could never understand. Work ya guts out, day in, day out, and then get kicked for it. Mongrels.

Graeme found some slight comfort from seeing the safety mesh that had been installed above the railings since that poor sod McEvoy went over last year. No one said anything of course, because of the insurance, but the next day the workmen arrived, and by the afternoon the temptation was gone. Graeme tried and failed to measure the immense drop. Just as well they fenced it, he thought. You could look down and get dizzy and then ... farewell, cruel world, you're cactus, cop á là tomato sauce. Maybe McEvoy was an accident after all.

He pulled himself away from the seductive edge, and went reluctantly back to the pretend work they'd given him. Here, keep yourself occupied with this garbage while the IIU's getting ready for your trial. You, the good guy. Yeah, you. Never mind the crims, it's you we want. Thought you wanted to make a contribution to society, eh, step this way, sucker, have we got news for you.

Three pm, Graeme's second-favourite watch said. There was just enough time before the anklebiters came for the Little A's. Roo jumped back as the cheap thin-shanked lock on the window snapped. You little ripper. He threw the Japanese screwdriver aside and wormed his way into the changeroom at the ANZ Stadium. The familiar smell of liniment and soap and smelly old shoes wrapped itself around him like a lover. To his amazement, he realised he actually had tears in his eyes. Get a grip, ya fucken wuss. He quickly dumped the few things he'd flogged off Graeme (shirts, a doona, a full bottle of some fancy scotch – probably cost a million bucks – a handful of easily saleable CDs) into a locker, then went outside carrying his training gear, and replaced the lock with another cheapie from the Ampol on the hill. No one would notice that it was a different one, one that he had the key to, cos no one ever opened that small, high, dusty window near the ceiling – why would they? He peered up at the wall. His flailing shoes had left streaks on the dust of the besser bricks. Roo collected a handful of fine sandy dirt and rubbed at the wall until there was no evidence of where he'd broken in.

With filthy hands and two days of sweat and park-dirt on him, he was dying for a shower, but when the wall was sorted Roo sat down outside with his training bag and waited for the coach to rock up and let him in. Discipline, he thought, that's what yer need to survive when yer on yer own. Discipline.

When yer cold in the park, and ya want to share someone's fire, ya stop. Ya remember what they do to kids in parks and ya stay where ya are, and never mind being cold. When the real hard screws hassle ya inside, and ya want to mouth off, ya shut up. Ya think about being dead and ya keep yer fucken trap shut. When ya want a shower and ya don't want anyone to know you've busted into the changeroom, ya wait. Ya do it the straight way. Then ya get to sleep somewhere warm that night.

If Stanley'd had a bit more discipline, a few more fucken brains, he'd be alive. For sure. What'd he expect anyway, doing crime all the time, sleeping in parks, drinking with the goomies? Ya gotta be sharp, gotta look out for number one, Roo thought in harsh self-satisfaction as he sat on the cold concrete, waiting.

★

The coach arrived at ten to four, pleased to see Roo there before anyone else. The boy stood up, rubbing his numb arse.

'You're early. First time for everything.'

'Yeah, I thought I'd grab a shower. Warm meself up, eh.' The coach nodded absently as he unlocked the building. It wasn'tcold in his airconditioned car, or in the swish office where he worked all day.

'How's the leg?'

'Oh, not bad. Needed to give them a few days off I reckon.'

Coach shot him a look. 'You still sucking on those coffin nails?'

'Hardly any, eh. Just one or two a day. I feel pretty good, pretty strong.' Roo bounced on his toes to make the point. As if. He woulda had four hours sleep, tops.

'Yeah, you look okay. But it might be those one or two a day that'll make the difference, Roo. Mark Grogan doesn't smoke, you know.' Talented kid, crying shame to see it go to waste.

'Yeah, I know. I'll cut 'em right out soon, altogether,' he promised. And yandy. And speed. And grog. And trips. And stealing. And getting in fights. And getting girls pregnant. No worries.

The coach looked his protégé up and down. Unshaven. Slightly untidy, the way kids look when they need to say *Fuck you, world*. Still that light in his eyes, though, still ready to take on anything, anyone. Bigger in the arms and chest than the other runners, bulked up from years of kickboxing he says. Just unsteady in himself. No other runner in the squad smokes. The lad's a bit ... wild. But if he settles, if the father helps, if the family's there ... where'd he say he lived?

'Your dad coming to watch you today?'

Roo turned his head away from the question. 'Nah, don't think so.'

'He must be pretty pleased with you, though,' the coach prodded. If you were my son ... Fast. Got guts. A bit wild, but anyway ... good kid. Come from behind. Push the limits.

'Mmmm. S'pose so.' Voice strained, pretending to undress. A bruise on the chest where he ran against something in the dark that night, what was it? Corner of an industrial bin. Shoulda slept in the tucker, it woulda been warmer. Too dangerous, but. What if they come and collected it? Keep it light, Roo. Let the man see ya got ordinary problems. Nothing serious, not really. Not like yer only friends in the world, practically, gave ya the arse. Not like ya slept in a fucken freezin park, and ya been living on chips and stolen lollies.

'Gonna have a bash today?' the coach encouraged him.

Roo turned around smiling. The Art of Facade, one of the guys in John Oxley's called it *putting on a front*. 'Yeah, sure. What's today?'

'David Wiseman might be coming later,' Coach says.

Roo's eyes widen. The Australian coach. In town for the Queensland titles and the trials. 'Yeah?'

'Just for a look. Mostly at the sprinters, but you never know. I mentioned you to him.'

Roo's stomach flips. Today. The big man.

He runs a bad fifteen hundred, stiff, unbalanced. The

rhythm not there, concentration gone. Third in a mock race of six runners he shoulda creamed. Grogan won, the weak bastard coming over to shake his hand like it's the fucken Olympics or something. Breath harsh and ragged. Lousy time. Roo waited till Wiseman left, then kicked into the side-panelling of the track.

Shit. It reverberated with his anger.

'What went wrong?' the coach asks later. Second-sensing something going on – this is a kid thrives on pressure. Loves it, always rises to the occasion.

Roo shrugs. 'Just screwed up, I guess.'

'Everything's alright at home?'

Roo smiles sarcastically, laughs. He doesn't care anymore. 'Yeah.' No.

'Really?'

'I split up with my girlfriend,' he said in a low voice.

'Oh, right. That's no good. But try not to let it wreck your training. Girlfriends come and go, son, state squads come but once a year. When she sees you on TV waving that Australian trophy around she'll be begging you to take her back.'

Roo grinned. Bit more complicated than that, mate. Still, he had a point. Plenty of fish, eh. He went inside. The coach watched him disappear into the changeroom. Twenty-six athletes to look after, and you could beat 'em all, if only you'd train. If only you'd settle. Bugger the girlfriend, Roo. Just run, lad. Just run.

Graeme looked sulkily into his grog cabinet at the hole where his Laphroaig should have been. The little bastard.

Couldn't have flogged the bloody Grouse, or the Bundy, nah it had to be the friggen good stuff. Little bastard. That'd be where my watch went ... and those jumpers. Blanket off the spare bed, of course. Typical. Blind Freddy coulda seen it coming. Once a crim, always a fucken crim. Bloke shoulda fucken known he'd just use him for what he could get, eh. Wait'll I catch up with him, the pimply arsed little ...

Madden's big blunt copper's hand grabbed the Bundy. He sat and poured a heavy dose. Thieving little bastard. An hour and a half later, a deep resentment said: *No shon uv mine.*

A cup or two of rum angers the man's belly. He sloshes to the phone. As for that fuggen bitch. Stab. Stab. Ringringringring.

'Graeme. Chrissake Graeme, it's one o'clock here!' Her tired voice almost hysterical.

He sways slightly as he composes himself. Bloody run off on me. Musht think I'm shtupid or shomethin. 'Thing ish, thing ish Faithy, when 'ah comin home, eh? THASH THE THING INNIT, EH?'

She hangs up. Fuggen bitch runnin round on him. Stumble, clutching the edge of the table, the phone. Wild stabbing. Ringring.

'Doan ya fuggen, DOAN ya ever fuggen hang up on me ya fuggen bitch okay jus FUGGEN DOAN HANG UP!'

Silence.

'WELL? I jus wanna know when ya fuggen gonna come back home, Fai, jus can ya tell a bloke that? Eh? How's he, eh, how's Pete?'

Ingratiating. Get on good shide.

Faith bit each of her words off. 'He's very sick, Graeme. He's dying of cancer. Have you been—'

She is crying.

'Oh fuggen shmartarsh now? I KNOW he's dyin a fuggen cansher, doan I?' He pauses, gathering his wits. Poor dead Petie, poor cunt. Thass right. 'But anyway, wha I wanna know's whenna ya comin home?'

'I ... I ... don't know whether I'm ... I dunno,' his wife says hopelessly.

He looks at the handpiece, a piece of slapstick out of the movies.

'YOU WHA?' A terrible truth is dawning beneath the rum.

She snaps. 'Ah, Christ, if you keep this drunken bloody bullshit up ... I dunno what I'm bloody doing, Graeme. Now look it's late, it's the middle of the—'

'Ya dunno wha? AH FOR THE LUVVA GOD FAITHY ... if ya leave me I'll fuggen kill ya, you know that, eh? I'll blow ya fuggen brains ... No, I won't.' Graeme suddenly turns into McEvoy, sailing over the side of Roma Street waving ta-tas as he plunges four floors. 'I'll knock meself, I'll do it, I fuggen promise ya. That make ya happy, eh? No worries, then, eh. Collec the fuggen shuper?? Eh? Shave ya the fuggen trouble!'

Silence again.

'Graeme ...' Weary, weary woman. Wanting to say, well don't talk about it all the fucking time, if ya gonna do it, do it. Sick of hearing it.

'I tell ya, Faithy, ya gotta come home. Ya gotta, I can't make it wishout ya. They wanna get me, ya know they're

after me. If I didn't have … ah, wass tha point … I …
(more threatening now) I'm warning ya. I'll top meshelf,
doan say I'm not warning ya. And I'll fuggen take ya
wish me, I can't live wishout ya Faithy.' He changes tack,
wheedles. 'When'yre comin home, luv?'

'Ah, Jesus …'

'Come on, Faithy, just tell ush when?'

'Next week.' Sobbing. 'I'll be on the plane next week.
Okay? Next week. Don't do anything stupid, alright?
And for Christ's sake try not to drink too much—'

'Wha day? Eh?' Sneaky, grog-cunning.

'Wednesday,' she quickly improvises. 'Two o'clock
Wednesday. Now I'm going back to bed. Okay?'

'Uh, yeah.' Only half-believing.

'Alright then.'

Graeme replaces the receiver. Wenshday. Back on
Wenshday. Bloody bewdy. 'Bout fuggen time. Fuggen
bitch.

Chapter Eight

Mum King poured boiling water out of the still-switched-on kettle over her two teabags; not a coffee drinker, she wanted it nice and strong, cos of not sleeping. She plonked the scarred plastic kettle down and flicked the power off at the wall. The kettle subsided with a last aggrieved, breathy whistle. Black like me, Mum thought, as she stirred the bags with a fork, then pressed the last drop from them, making the tea darken, black like me. Me and me boys. Funny the way they all come out. Me dark, and Joe and Frank both fair, Lord bless em, ya'd think it'd be the girl's what'd be dark, but it was me boys what all come out black. Lose us in a dark room, ya could, we shut our eyes. Ah, no matter 'bout colours. Only I lost my beautiful dark boys, see. Sadness suddenly welled up in her. She tried to stop counting the loss of Stanley over and over, tried to consign him to that place where John and Trev already were. Lost ones. Too hard. Tears pricked at her eyes.

Mum found the sugar packet and stirred in a heaped spoonful. She hesitated, then added a second, grabbed

Leena's smokes packet and lighter and carried her kit outside to the steps overlooking the street. A little possie to watch the street from. Her cup rasped as it met the concrete stair tread, and left a wet semicircle underneath. Mum lit a cigarette and looked out at the world of Park Road. Nigga's busy feet had worn a dusty path in the grass around the house, and as she watched he came trotting along it to say hello.

'You're a big Doris you are,' she told him, wiping her eyes.

'Poor old Nigga ...' The dog stood foursquare at the base of the stairs, panting with love and drool. Dogs now. Jimmy was the one for dogs. Stanley never did like 'em much, always too scared, him. Same with Roo, eh? (the little shit). Even with Nigga, he never really clicked, never trusted him not to turn and go him. Jimmy slept with the dog, talked to him, did everything with him, short of that, a course. But not Roo, and never Stanley.

'Why zat, Nigga?' Mum growled at the animal. 'Eh? You too uptown for 'em, uh? Cos ya white. You'n the parkies' dog, both whitefellas you are, sha-ame.'

Brindle and white, Nigga stood and panted, impervious to her teasing.

'Which way now? Jimmy gorn out an left ya, has he?'

Nigga cocked his eyes in her direction, understanding everything. Mum sighed, wishing Uncle Eddie was around, but he'd gone bush again. The city was no place for a Lawman, he'd say, and disappear, for a week, or a month. There hadn't been hide nor hair of Uncle to be seen since the funeral.

'C'mere Nig, c'mon,' Mum urged, suddenly wanting

him close. The dog climbed the stairs heavily, then tossed his head up under Mum's hand for a sook. 'There, that's a boy.' She rubbed his neck with the side of her hand.

Hoping for a crust or crumb, Nigga sniffed at her and finding none turned away in disgust. Down the stairs, back to the dust.

Mum snorted. 'Ah, garn. Woss the matter with ya? I'll flog you,' she threatened as he wallowed in dirt. 'Don't think I won't. Ya turn ya big black nose up't me, ya cunt.' Good go, knucklin up to the dog. They'll be lockin me up soon. Mum smiled a tiny sad smile, forgetting to grieve for just an instant. The first moment of forgetting that would stretch, soon, to minutes, then the minutes to hours and the hours to days, until one morning she'd wake and her first heavy thought wouldn't be of Stanley at all, but something, someone, else.

'Nigga,' she called as he searched for fleas along his spine. 'Nigga!' He turned a lazy eye in her direction, then sprang quickly to his feet, whining and cringing. 'Ah, what now?' Mum asked, exasperated.

Nigga flattened himself onto the grass, looking up to the open door. Mum turned where she sat. When she looked behind her, her fingers forgot themselves and she dropped her cup, strong black tea and all. It shattered on the tread, tea splashing and running along the concrete grooves, dribbling into the dust. The broken pieces lay where they fell. In the doorway stood Stanley in his Broncos shirt. Behind him, Mum could see the stereo system and TV, and Leena asleep on the lounge. Facing Mum, Stanley beckoned her inside. His face bore the same energetic persuasion it had when he was alive, as if he was saying, *look la! Come see in ere* … Ashen, Mum shook her head. Stanley frowned and pointed to his shirt. Stains began spreading across it, a crimson blossoming that soon covered the white folds. As it spread, Stanley pressed his hands against his chest, as though trying to stop the flow. A strange, gurgled lingo rose from his throat.

'Stop it!' Mum ordered him in a stem whisper. 'Stop it, Stanley! You got no call!'

On the lounge Leena shifted her weight and moaned a little.

'You stop it now, boy.' Mum said fiercely. 'We ain't done nothin to you, now you go – you hear me? You go back! There's nothin for ya here now!'

Stanley turned and pointed at Leena. Mum's heart stood still.

No, no. God, no, not another one, please. No! Not another one, no oh no. Dear God.

A rage started within her, a deep, menacing rage of protection for her daughter. 'Whatchoo mean? Leena belongs here, with me! With us. You bugger off where you belong, steada trying to frighten an old woman, shame! Gorn – fuck off!'

He began to laugh at that and to move down the stairs. Mum took a step backward and then another. She glanced behind her. Nigga had disappeared. Typical, fucken useless thing like its owner. Leave her in the lurch. The black woman stood on the front lawn, alone and barefooted, standing in the cup's broken shards and facing the ghost of her baby son. Shaking, she mustered the courage to address Stanley once more.

'Tell me whatcha want then,' she pleaded. 'I din't mean to call yer name, St … son, I just … gets so lonely at night, thassall. Thassall, I din't mean ta call fer ya to come, not really. I'm sorry if I disturbed ya, boy …'

He stopped on the middle step, shook his head and pointed once more in the direction of his sister. This time Mum finally understood, and the terror left her. Her tone turned to a mother's counsel. 'Ah … okay, okay. I know. I know whatcha mean. I'll make sure. Garn, then. Go back, boy … this no place fer you. We love ya, son, but it's no place …'

Stanley turned and went up the stairs into the house. Mum held her breath, waiting for Leena's shriek, but there was no sound.

'Leena?' she called. Then a bit louder. 'Leena?'

A bloodcurdling scream and Mum bounded upstairs.

'Wha …' she cried, but Leena was standing in the middle of the lounge and Stanley was gone. 'What is it?' Mum demanded, her eyes fixed closely upon her daughter.

'I dreamed, I dreamed …' Leena was shivering. 'I had this nightmare, that Stanley …'

'Now, girl, don't you be saying that name to me. There's been too much talk. No more. No more saying it. That name's not to be mentioned in this house.'

Leena gulped, her eyes still frightened. 'I dreamed he come back. And he said Roo hadda come back too, and we all hadda live here, with him, with his ghost, here in this house. That we couldn't ever leave, none of us. Never.'

'Ah, now, s'just a bad dream, you gotta expect them

when yer this way, eh. Nothin unusual there, just being pregnant, thassall, doan worry 'bout it.' Mum soothed her.

Leena felt like having a go at Mum, but a sudden brightness about her mother held her back. There was something of the old Mum King in the woman facing her. Despair had fallen from Mum's face, and even her newly grey hair couldn't take away the strength in her stance. The girl contented herself with a muttered, 'Well ya coulda bloody told me' and a fast hard stomp to the loo.

Chapter Nine

Roo waited outside the Annerley dole office for his turn in the machine. Kicked at the pavers and checked the time twice a minute. He successfully bludged a smoke off a lady he didn't know. That wasted five minutes. Then back to waiting again. Wait to be born, wait to go to school, wait for school to kick ya out, wait for your dole cheque, wait for the right girl. Wait for the memories to go away. Wait to catch up with the pricks from Community Services and slit their throats one dark night. Wait to die.

Roo tried to find some inspiration in the concrete and pine-bark of the courtyard but failed. It was dreary, dreary, dreary, this life of Social. A dreary little scabby garden. Dreary noisy buses thundering past. More interesting, the pub over the road was open to the lucky bastards that just got counter cheques; not open to him, with no ID and no bungoo. Could ask someone to go to the bottleshop and hope they didn't fuck off with his grog ... get paid first, he reminded himself. Can't spend it till it's in ya hand, not at pubs. No mercy there.

He looked back inside the Social at the digital readout, red numbers. Thirty-nine. Two more to go. Smoke-lady went in, she was thirty-nine. Roo wondered what really being thirty-nine would be like, as in thirty-nine years old. Fuck, it was beyond imagining. He'd never get old anyway. Him! Fat chance. Probly die of thirst first, ha, ha.

That big bloke standing over there – who's he? Face looks familiar. About thirty, beer gut, grizzled black hair. Roo puzzles this for a while then it drops. Bouncer in town at the other pool place where he doesn't go cos of the skins. Nice enough guy. He's about to go and say g'day when – blackfellas crossing the road – Leena! Darryl! His heart sped up. Bang, bang, bang. Ah, ya weak idiot, don't pretend it isn't why ya came outside, hoping for her to walk past. Roo made a sour face at himself. They wiped ya, whaddya want to be friends with them cunts for? No choice, they're coming to the Social too. They both spot him at the same time. Darryl stops, saying something to Leena, then swings inside, ignoring him. Leena stops too, but she stays stopped, looks at him. They don't know what to say. Roo starts it off.

'Hi.' Ah, give us a smile, it won't kill ya.

'Hi.'

'How are ya?'

Leena shifts awkwardly. Her back hurts standing and walking around on concrete. Three and something months. Keeps on this way she'll be crawling by the end, Mum reckons. S'if it was twins. 'Ah … You know, alright. Same's usual … Jimmy's in lockup again, but.'

Roo shoves his hands in his pockets. Mr Cool. 'True? Whaffor?'

'Oh, he musta decided he's a black yuppie or somethin, credit card fraud this time.'

'Credit cards! Jimmy!' Roo cracks up at the idea, and most of the tension between them dissolves. 'I didn't even know he could fucken read.'

'He can't, not properly. Oh, the dickhead, he's been going on lately about never having any bungoo, ever since, since Stanley. I think it's cos he thinks, like, if Stanley'd had any money it wouldna happened, somethin like ... like having bungoo'd protect him or somethin. So, anyway, he ripped these coupla tourists off and then tried to use *her* cards, the dumb fuck. Cops picked him up in the Myer Centre.' Shaleena is blank-faced, dismissive about it, but Roo is falling about laughing. Straggly black Jimmy in his Gunners T-shirt, flashin a Mastercard. The fucken idiot.

'He gotta trial date?' Roo wheezes.

'Not yet. He's bin in the watchhouse for five days now, still ain't shifted him out.'

Roo recovers a bit. He knows the watchhouse is no joke, specially not for Jimmy. Plenty of ghosts in there for a blackfella. Still, credit card fraud, what was he thinking? Tats over both arms, slashed-up face, yeah right.

'Christ he's a fucken card, isn't he?'

Leena's mouth was set in sharp disapproval. 'It's not funny, Roo. Mum's goin spare over him, eh. Her hair's goin all grey, and she just—' The girl stops. Mum's been crying, sleepless at night, cranky in the day, and terrified the whole time that Jimmy was going to be the next phone call from the cops or the P.A. 'Mum's stressing out bigtime, and he just keeps doin crime and stupid shit. He needs ... I dunno what he needs. Needs ta smarten up before he gets himself into some real trouble one day soon. But he won't listen, he never listens, he don't care.'

Roo's grin fades away. He changes the subject. 'Yeah ... hey, you, ah, doing okay and that?' She's a bit thicker round the middle, but not so you'd really notice 'less ya looked. Lotta Murries like that, eh, don't show all that much.

'Yeah. I went for a check-up yesterday at the medical centre. They reckon it's okay.'

'Mum knitting booties and shit is she?' Roo asked, crinkly-eye smiling like he isn't dying inside.

'Yeah. Oh well, no ... but St Vinnies give her a bit of stuff. And Jimmy brung the cot over from Nicole's the other week, eh. We're putting it in the boys' room, and I'm swapping with Daz once it's 'ere.'

'All set then, eh?' Roo tries to prolong the conversation.

'Yeah, just gotta wait another five and a bit months. Waddle around till Christmas.' The girl finally cracks a smile.

'Oh, well, good luck with it, eh.' He half-turns away, and then back to her, courage building. 'Ya know I miss yez, eh.' Meaning it, but it's the wrong thing to say. Her face tightens. He's not forgiven, not like that. Arsehole, running out on her.

'Me 'n someone else's kid?'

He says nothing, shrugs.

Leena sniffs. 'Yeah, well, shit happens, eh?' Then her tone softens into practicality. 'Ah, Roo, look, it probably is bloody Max's, anyway—'

Some wild animal is chewing on his bones, sucking the blood out of his heart.

Shaleena keeps talking, slicing away. '—so we might's well just forget about it. The boys are still pretty cut. Mum's got over it, she's sweet, ya know she always liked ya.'

'Are you over it?' he asks bitterly, pain in his chest soaring.

Leena looks away, changes the subject. 'Where ya stayin?'

Roo laughs silently at her tactic, brushes his scalp with two splayed hands, and sticks a finger in his ear. 'Oh, well, now that's a bit of a long story …'

'Why?' Her interest is pricked.

'I found me old man.'

Her eyes goggle. 'Ah-weee!' Standing in her Hong Kong shoes beside the road roaring with traffic, she gives him a sound that is older than dust itself.

'No, I did, truegod. He's a …' Roo snorts in self-deprecation, 'a cop'.

Leena laughs in disbelief.

Roo grins and flexes his arms jokingly. Superman. 'Yeah. He fucken loves me, eh?' Like – not.

'Are you staying with him?' Incredulous. 'Does he live in Brisbane?'

Roo stared at the concrete. God, if she knew. Lucky he can bluff like an expert. 'Yeah, but I ain't livin with no pig … I'm stayin out at Mount Gravatt mosta the time, jus cruisin.' Let her think he's at Todd's.

Leena is amused about the booliman. Smiling, she rubs her arms briskly and Roo notices her goosepimples in the cold shadow of the waiting area. 'You cold?'

126

'No. Aw, yeah, a bit. None of me clothes fit properly no more, eh.'

'Here.' He takes off Madden's black top and gives it to her. 'Ya can have it, I don't want it.'

She looks at it sceptically. A hundred dollar fleecy-lined job, nice. Warm. 'You sure? Did ya steal it?'

Someone sticks a head out the door. 'FORTY-ONE?'

Roo jumps. 'Nah, it's sweet. That's me.' He goes to leave.

'Here.' Leena suddenly has an idea. She opens her shoulder bag and pulls out her outgrown red nylon jumper. She thrusts it at him. 'Take this then.'

'Oh, okay, ta. See ya, eh.' Smiling.

'Yeah. See ya.' She doesn't quite smile back.

Inside the office Darryl looked sourly at his sister's jumper on Roo, but the two males didn't speak. Roo followed the clerk into the cubicle and talking them into the counter cheque took so long that by the time he came out Leena and Darryl had done their business and shot through. The pub was still there, but.

The Commodore's big V8 motor rumbled magnificently as Graeme pulled up at the Herschel Street lights. He touched the accelerator with his right toe, and the car's low sexy roar bounced off the crash barrier beside the vehicle. Geez, if a car could root, he thought, this baby'd be the biggest rootrat in town. Then he felt a bit silly, thinking about shit like that. Cars rooting, what sort of nut thinks like that? He checked himself in the mirror for incipient signs of insanity.

He still looked pretty normal considering he was going, or should say being driven, round the bend. Getting old though. He had flat tanned cheeks. Deep furrows ran between his nose and mouth, lines that looked deeper than they had before all this IIU bullshit started, he was sure. Crow's-feet radiated out from his eyes; three horizontal creases decorated his forehead. You old bastard, he told himself, fucken not even forty yet and you're old before your time. He gave a melancholic grimace at his reflection and ran a hand over his hair. That was on the way out, too. Couple of years since he'd started wearing it ultra-short to hide the grey, but ultra-short or not, there was less for the girl to run the clippers over each time. He gave a deep sigh, and resolved to go to the gym more often at lunch instead of to the club. It was too easy to get on the piss with the boys once you were in the door.

The lights changed. Caught daydreaming, Graeme put his foot down a little too quickly, stalling the car. He swore as he started her up again; the cars in the queue behind him blared their horns. That was the only problem not being in uniform – no respect. He eventually throbbed through the intersection as the light changed to orange. Three cars followed him through the red and he thought about pulling them up, then decided, ah fuck it. QPS wants to have my arse on a silver platter, let em do their own dirty work. He pulled in sharply underneath the Roma Street HQ and did the whirly-go-round in the car park until he reached the fifth floor below.

Monday morning, and here he was feelin okay about it. If that wasn't a sad bloody reflection of the state of his life, what was? Every other bastard sitting around moaning, the Moaning Minnies, and him happy because now he'd see another human being after forty-eight friggin hours. Graeme didn't know whether to laugh or cry. To avoid the whole question, he made coffee for everyone, filled the pot with a brew you could stand a spoon up in.

Ellen was in already. She was usually first in. She reckoned it was because girls had to do twice the work for half the recognition, but Graeme knew it was really because she went to a morning gym class in town and came straight in after. Bill arrived twenty minutes later, claiming to be seriously hungover. The Fat Controller rocked up in another five, nodded grimly to their good-mornings and went straight to his office up the corridor. His door banged after him.

'Snaky!' Ellen made a face. 'What's his problem?'

'He's fifty years old, forty kilos overweight, and thirty light years away from promotion,' said Bill as he took his coffee from her.

'Wish you lazy buggers'd put the top down on the milk,' complained Graeme from the fridge. 'It goes off in about ten minutes if you don't. Ah god, smell that!' He gestured towards them with the offending carton, provoking loud disgusted noises. He raised his voice, comically camp. 'It's not *difficult*, people.'

The boss's door opened again. The Fat Controller looked thunderous. 'Sergeant?'

Graeme quickly put the carton down. 'Sorry, just—'

'I need to see you.' The Fat Controller was terse; Graeme hesitated. Then with a worried look at Bill, he went in. The door closed behind him, and Bill and Ellen raised eyebrows at each other. It was only a couple of minutes later that Graeme came out, dark-faced with anger. He came straight over to Bill.

'Cover me for a half an hour, will ya?'

'Yeah, mate, course. What'd he want?'

Graeme snorted, and shook his head in disbelief. 'Tell ya later.'

Graeme went outside the building and gazed at the traffic, not knowing what to do. The Fat Controller had been kind, by his standards. No sarcasm, no interrogation, no drawing it out. Just: 'There's a restraining order out on you from interstate, and I've been asked to get your QPS pistol off you. Do you have a problem with that?'

'No, sir.'

'Fine. I want it by knock-off time. Is there anything you want to tell me?'

'No, sir.'

'If you've got any other firearms they'll want them too. Just for the time being.'

'There's only the one.'

'Okay then.'

And that was it. All of society's trash out there, useless scumbags that'd be better off dead, murderers, rapists, armed robbers, child molesters, and all the Service was worried about was disarming *him*. What a laugh, eh? What-a-fucken-joke.

Graeme ran his hand over his hair once again, feeling a bit dizzy with anger and grief. What the fuck was Faith up to? Jesus, they'd been through all this years ago, when she'd nagged him into going along to that AA crap a few times.

He stormed out of the building and went to the cafe across the road where he bought himself an orange juice, lashed out on one of the fresh-squeezed type. He tried ringing her, but it was engaged both times. Off the hook no doubt. He hung up and stood wondering what to do next.

Afraid of looking stupid, he went over to the counter and absentmindedly bought a packet of smokes. The place was full of cops, blokes just finished night duty, or trying to look like they weren't having affairs or just skiving off work for half an hour like he was. A couple of them said g'day, and he muttered back at them, preoccupied. A headache that had troubled him on Saturday was threatening to come back. City workers streamed past on their way to work, and a tribe of Abos waltzed past as they came out of the Transit Centre. Must be on their way to do a bit of shoplifting or something. Well, that's work for them, isn't it? And if one of em decides to do an armed rob while they're at it, what am I sposed to do? Point me finger at em, drop it or I'll … I'll point me finger at you.

Sourfaced, Graeme finished his drink and got ready to go. As he tossed the bottle in the rubbish from where he sat, Graeme noticed one of the gins had on an Adidas jacket like the one of his that Reuben took. Must be all the rage with the criminal set, he sneered to himself. Little prick. Then he had a sudden brainwave. He'd go and see the kid's coach. Of course, he'd know where the kid was staying. Bloody brilliant. Why didn't he think of it before? Graeme started to cheer up as he left, and it was a whole half a minute before he remembered about the restraining order and got depressed again.

Chapter Ten

Maybe wearing his suit hadn't been such a good idea after all, Graeme reflected. The coon Legal Service bloke had a suit on, and so did all the other legal eagles. The Police Union rep wore uniform, and he looked better for it, more impressive. I'll wear uniform too next time, Graeme promised himself, bugger what they say. If there has to be a next time, that is. Might get all this bullshit cleared up today with any luck.

Bruce O'Connor, the heavy-set head of the IIU shuffled some papers and cleared his throat. 'Right. Let's get started. Sergeant Madden, step up here please.' He sat Graeme down at the desk in front of the committee, just like the Fat Controller had explained they would. Graeme hoped his nerves weren't showing. 'You understand, Sergeant, that this is not a Court of Law, and that the findings of this investigation are not binding in any Court of Law?'

'Yes, sir.'

'Okay. You've heard what the defend ... I mean what the family representatives have had to say earlier. I'd like to hear your account of the events in question.'

Graeme took a deep breath. Here goes nothing. A reporter started scribbling in a notebook – Graeme could hear the pen scratching away.

'On the night of March 20, at approximately five-fifty pm, I was returning in a police vehicle to the City Watchhouse from the Valley Police Station. Constable McGregor was driving me because he had a duty to undertake in the CBD.'

'You were on Watchhouse Duty in the City at the time?' O'Connor asked.

'No, sir. I was at that point in time stationed at the Valley on a temporary assignment.'

O'Connor looked confused. 'Then how did you – never mind. Keep going.'

'We had come to a halt at an intersection at the corner of Ann and Gotha Streets, next to the Centenary Park, when we noticed an altercation between two Indigenous males in the park. Both of these individuals were very well known to police: Stanley George King and Anthony John Chandler. We observed them in this altercation and after a short time I decided it was appropriate to intervene.'

'How long is a short time, Sergeant?'

'About two or three minutes, sir.' Hilarious it was, at the time, these two coons swinging away at each other and missing, and the prick with the beer bottle smashed it, only it cut his arm and the other one got in with a good kick to the guts. Him and Macca pissed themselves sitting in the truck. Shame to have to break it up, really. Best laugh he'd had for ages.

'And then?'

'And then Constable McGregor and myself approached the assembled group, whereupon we were verbally abused by a majority of the individuals in the vicinity, particularly King—'

'What did King say?'

'He suggested I perform indecent acts upon him, sir. And he asked whether his "taxi" had arrived. Referring to the police vehicle.'

'Go on.'

'I decided at that point in time to take him into custody as he was obviously heavily intoxicated, and Constable McGregor stated to me that his patrol had been called to the park earlier that afternoon to break up a previous brawl in which King had been involved. When I instructed King to get in the back of the vehicle, he refused and stated that he would prefer to—' Graeme looked at his papers in embarrassment. 'He made an obscene suggestion to me.'

O'Connor looked up. 'Can you be a little more explicit, Sergeant?'

Graeme's jaw tightened. It was rapidly becoming obvious that this whole, whole … charade was meant to publicly humiliate him.

'I instructed him to get in, and he stated that he would rather—' Graeme read in a flat voice without looking up '—shove his black cock right up my white crack before he got in there, so we'd know who was fucking who right from the start.'

A couple of people snorted their laughs down, and the scratching of the reporter's pen stopped for a moment. No way they'd print that.

Graeme went on, with a glare at the ALS lawyer. 'As you may be aware, sir, King had a history of violent sex offences.'

There was an angry murmur from the family who were seated well away from the action. An elderly woman cried out repeatedly, 'Who's on trial here?' till O'Connor was finally able to quieten the room. Nobody was on trial, he explained, it was merely a departmental inquiry to determine what had transpired on the night in question. Dissatisfied, the audience shifted and muttered among themselves. 'If it was a whitefella dead and a blackfella in the hotseat there'd be a trial, wouldn't there?' insisted the same woman angrily. O'Connor threatened to evict her, and she sat, silenced.

'Are you saying King resisted arrest?' O'Connor asked Graeme when they resumed.

'That's correct, sir. There was a brief scuffle between himself and myself, during which altercation his head hit the concrete gutter edging outside the public convenience. Then Constable McGregor and myself put him into the van, and cuffed him.'

'How was he handcuffed?'

'In view of his aggression, and being intoxicated to the point of ...' Graeme paused. 'He was cuffed behind the back.'

O'Connor merely grunted, and Graeme took that to mean he should continue.

'We arrived at Herschel Street at six-twelve pm and took him inside. He appeared alive and well, although, as I already said, he was heavily intoxicated and I judged that he may have been smoking marijuana as well. Then, a call came through that as a result of the wet roads there was a pile-up on the freeway at Greenslopes with seven vehicles involved and at least one fatality. Constable McGregor left to attend the scene while I booked King into the watchhouse. However, there was a change of shift at Herschel Street while I was there, which meant I waited for about an hour altogether.'

'That sounds like a long time for a change of shift,' O'Connor interrupted sharply.

'There was a power failure, sir, from the storm that had caused the pile-up, and the computers were down for forty minutes. Also,' Graeme's distaste showed on his face, 'King, he, ah, well, he vomited and, ah, excreted himself in the courtyard. I spent about ten or fifteen minutes disposing of the mess.'

'Why didn't the watchhouse staff do it?'

'It was during the changeover, sir, and because it was in the courtyard ... in the event we ended up tossing a coin. I lost.'

O'Connor grunted. He'd been there before, hadn't they all.

'So King was conscious when he was put in his cell?'

'Yes, sir.'

'He'd stopped vomiting?'

'Yes, sir.'

'Did you have any further contact with him that night?'

'While I was waiting for the generators to come on, King called out for assistance. He was making a lot of noise. A lot. I went and checked him through the peephole and asked him what he wanted. He said he was frightened and he wanted to be put in a cell with another

Aboriginal prisoner. He was breathing heavily but otherwise seemed normal. I put the respiration difficulty down to stress. I told him he was the only inmate of any persuasion at that point, and that the lights would come back on as soon as the generator cut in. He settled down and so I went back to the front office.'

'Was he the only inmate?'

'Yes, sir. It was still quite early, before seven.' Graeme was finally beginning to feel less agitated.

'When did you see him next?'

'The change of shift arrived and after we completed the paperwork I, we, that is, went in to check him once more before I left. We were surprised to see him lying on the floor of the cell, unconscious. We couldn't detect a pulse, and we attempted heart massage. After a short time we detected a pulse but he wasn't breathing. We had rung an ambulance by that stage.'

'It was quite conscientious of you to check him before you left.' O'Connor's tone was dry.

'Because of his heavy breathing, sir. I wanted to …' Graeme trailed off.

'To cover yourself.' O'Connor finished his sentence. 'Who rang the ambulance?'

'Constable Corcoran, while we were engaged in the CPR.'

'You say "we" – who was there besides yourself?'

'Sergeant Jones, sir.'

'Did you attempt to resuscitate him before the ambulance arrived?'

'We judged there to be a significant risk of infection, sir, and there was no one-way mask available.'

'So you didn't attempt mouth-to-mouth?'

'No, sir. He was bleeding from the mouth and nose. And anus.'

'I see. Had you arrested King before that night?' O'Connor asked.

Graeme hesitated. He couldn't remember what the Fat Controller had said to say. 'I'm not sure, but I think so, yes. I'd certainly had contact with him, because he was a regular in the park with an extensive history, and I think I arrested him about six months previously, but I couldn't say for certain. He had only been out of protective custody for less than seventy-two hours at the time of death, sir.'

'Never mind, the record will show whether you did or not. Very well, Sergeant, you may step down for the time being. Mr … Phillips? Can Mr Phillips come forward please.'

Graeme left the room and went to the Mens. As he sat on the toilet, he noticed that his knees were shaking. What a nightmare. O'Connor was a cop, but he was a bosses' cop, and he wouldn't trust the prick further than he could throw him.

CHAPTER ELEVEN

'Hello' said the voice on the other end of Graeme's phone. I was wondering if I could speak to Roo Glover's father please?'

Roo. That means Reuben ... contact!

'Speaking,' he said cautiously.

'This is Bob Abbotsford, here, Roo's coach.' A wave of relief swept over Madden. The coach.

He was effusive. 'Oh, g'day! Yeah, how's he doing? Showing up for training, is he?'

'Well, that's why I'm ringing. He's showing up alright, but I just get the feeling that there's something not quite right with him. He seems kind of, um, I dunno, if he wasn't always cracking jokes I'd say he was sort of depressed, or something. Look, I don't want to go sticking my nose in your business or anything, but—'

'No, that's okay.' Madden reassured him. Fucken busybody cunt.

'I was just wondering if everything was okay at home, you know, or, you know, if you could speak to him? It's just these trials are coming up and he's got a pretty good chance at the state squad if he runs at his best. Could you have a word with him? Or maybe if there's anything I can do?'

'Nah, you're right. Thanks for taking the trouble but, eh. He just split up with his girlfriend, you know. I think that knocked him pretty hard—'

'Yeah,' he said.

'But I'll double-check anyway. I know he thinks a lot of you, he'll take notice of you more than me. Thanks for taking the trouble, Coach.'

Madden rang off. Depressed, eh? And the coach doesn't know where he's living either. I'll give him depressed, I'll go to the track and I'll tan his thieving little hide, that's what I'll bloody do. Depressed! What's he got to be depressed about?

That afternoon Graeme waited impatiently in his car just inside the high metal gates of the ANZ stadium. A mediocre bronze statue of a galloping horse, a 'bronco' – as if any Australian ever called a brumby that; broncos were cars, Fords – stood between him and the main part of the complex. There was a fair chance Reuben would head out this way afterwards, in a car or on foot. He'd see him either way, he hoped, and front him where there wasn't anyone else around to see. Graeme sat smoking and listening to the radio until at five-thirty, just as the sun was approaching the distant hills and the light beginning to fade, his effort was rewarded. Roo walked out from beneath the stands in athletic shorts and a cheap red nylon jumper. He had his sports bag over his shoulder. The close-cropped hair over his ears was black with sweat, and his face looked

141

freshly scrubbed from the many laps of the track he'd just done.

Roo saw his father sitting behind the steering wheel of the Commodore. As he recoiled, his heart skipped a beat in anger and fear. *Run, Rabbit.* He swivelled on his heel away from the bus stop, and headed down the hill, putting the stadium's high wire-mesh fence between him and the man. Walk away, walk away, away from death and lies and having to say it all out loud.

Surprised by Roo's sudden evasion, Graeme got out of the car and went up to the fence. Silly little prick, running away all the time. Why didn't he stop and face him like a man – what was his problem? Probably it was the stuff he'd flogged. Graeme called out to him.

'Reuben, I don't care about the scotch! Just stop!'

'Fuck off! Leave me alone!' his son called over his shoulder.

'Reuben!' Graeme insisted.

Roo stopped and snarled at him. 'Leave me alone, willya, ya murderin cunt!'

Graeme slowed with a jerk when Roo's words reached him, momentarily thrown by this new charge. What was the kid saying? Then the two separate pieces of his life, the running figure that was his son and the saga of dead Stanley King, hurtled into each other. It felt like something burst inside his brain. He stared through the wire mesh at Roo, who had paused thirty metres away.

A rage rose up in him and he wanted to lay hands on his son and sit him down hard. Force him to see reason. Make him see that he, the cop, was the good guy in all this and that what had happened to King was ... well, was simple bad luck, really. And anyway, the useless piece of shit had it coming. It wouldn't take much, if he could just have a chance to explain properly. If anyone'd listen. Why was it always this way? The truth was easily available, if people just looked at things the right way, instead of deliberately misunderstanding him. Graeme began to breathe in painful gulps.

'Reuben! Stop, willya, you stupid litde prick! They set me up!' Graeme felt ridiculous. A grown man, arguing like this beside a busy suburban road. He said it again, as if someone in the back of his head was analysing his behaviour, and finding it wanting. You don't do this, the voice said, it's weak. Let him come to you. Anyway, fuck him and what he thinks. Graeme yelled anyway. 'Reuben – THEY SET ME UP! I didn't do anything … JUST STOP WILLYA!'

It was no use. Madden stood leaning on the fence, chest heaving and perspiration breaking out on his brow. He threw a disgusted hand in his son's direction and looked around as if for someone to agree with him, be on his side for once. Ah Jesus, a bloke tries his best … ungrateful little turd. Ungrateful thieving little turd. Typical.

'Ah, well, fuck ya then,' he shouted at Roo's back which was now disappearing down the hill.

He watched in frustration as the lad veered into the bush beside the stadium and disappeared. Then he made fists of his hands and bent over in angry despair. *Ya murdering cunt.* The words echoed in his ears. Ironic, eh? His criminal son, rejecting him for the worst crime of all. What now? Madden thought, first the inquiry, then

Faith and her restraining order bullshit, now this. For Christ's fucking sake, what else could go wrong?

Roo ran a kay or so, dodging through the trees, then listened intently. There was nothing close, just the distant, muted thunder of traffic from Kessels Road. He'd lost him. Feeling suddenly weak, Roo sat shakily against a big smooth-barked gum and put a thin twig in his mouth. He liked the acrid taste of gum tree tannin. As he chewed the twig into a brown pulp, he got his breath back and wondered about Madden's shouted claim. Set up, he reckoned. He put the idea in front of him and looked at it from several angles. Who would set his father up as a murderer – who'd want to, who'd be able to and why? Well, a cop would have plenty of enemies, for sure. He didn't buy it, though. Nah. Words, that's all it was – words. And they wouldn't bring Stanley back, eh? Or Leena, or his old life, before the funeral. What was a copper's word worth anyway? Not a pinch of shit, in his estimation.

From where he sat Roo noticed the many living things in this scrap of bush. Black ants there, sniffing around an empty soft drink tin. Something small and mobile rustled in the grass behind him. A magpie regarded him amiably from above; Roo narrowed his eyes at it. He was too much of the city boy to know its black beak wasn't danger except when the bird had nestlings. He prised a lump of chalky rock out of the earth and hurled it. The magpie flustered into the air, and departed for the next tree along. Roo was beginning to feel a little calmer now he'd made his escape; the drying sweat was making his forehead and back feel cold. And the sun was almost gone, too; the shadows of the big trees surrounding him were long, thin fingers and the hazy air looked full of dust even though it wasn't.

Don't sit here too long, he thought, or you'll end up stumbling around lost in the dark, stepping on snakes and shit. Still, may as well have a think while you're here. The image of John Oxley came to him, and that bloody big sign that greeted you when you walked in the gates: *Think Before You Act*. Said it all really, eh? He remembered what Darryl had taught him too: Don't move unless you have to. Nine times outta ten, do nothing, and you'll be better off in the end. And – confronted with Roo's wild hypotheses about the state of the world – facts, lad. Deal with the facts.

Okay, then, facts. Stanley was dead, and dead while the pigs had him. So, obviously, the pigs killed him. Unless he had a heart attack or something, but he was only, what, seventeen – how likely is it that you'd have a heart attack when you're seventeen? Nah, fuck that – someone knocked him off for sure. So, fact two – Sergeant Madden was a prime suspect for the aforesaid crime. Roo'd seen it in *The Courier-Mail* that someone left lying around in the pie shop near the park and there it was, fair and square. Couldn't argue with that. It said so in black and white, eh. Senior Sergeant Graeme Madden (funny, I always thought it was spelt Graham) was under investigation by the Internal Investigations Unit.

Okay, Roo thought, using his fingers and thumb, that's two down. One, Stanley's dead and, two, Madden's in the frame. Fact three: Madden claimed to be innocent, but (and for some reason Roo sensed that this was important), he didn't claim that no one at all had killed Stanley. He just said it wasn't him, that he was set up. Which meant … which meant … but Roo couldn't keep adequate track of his thoughts. He hit his head with the heels of his palms. Think. *Think!* It was hard to keep things straight in his mind; all he was doing was feeling – feeling confused. Feeling ripped off again, more even than when he didn't have a father. How's that for luck, eh? Born a fucken orphan and when ya do find the cunt, he doesn't know where ya mother is *and* he's a murderer! He dropped his head, hearing Darryl. *Do nothing. Do nothing and it'll be alright.* But overriding everything else in Roo's head was the terrible fear that he didn't know what to do because there simply wasn't anything to be done. That maybe this was as good as it got.

He stared at the ants tracking over his shoes. In lockup, you knew the story, because you didn't bother trusting anyone, not unless you had a real close mate in with you at the same time, and even then … fuck the screws, fuck the other crims, fuck the police and look out for your own back. Simple. So, what was going on here, what was he worried about? His head was full of mud. Jesus, he could use a smoke. *Set up* – how many times had he heard that chant, or used it himself. Anyway, probably Madden just wanted him to come back because of the bail business, eh. Just bullshitting to save his own mangy hide. Because, let's face it, if he wanted a son, all he had to do was come looking, eh? Years ago, he could have found him, if he'd really wanted to. He wasn't hiding …

Years ago, when Roo really could have used a dad, when he was little and helpless. Before all this shit went down.

And yet.

And yet.

Roo's heart started thudding hard again as he imagined the other possibility.

If he *wasn't* lying, if he was set up, it'd mean … things would be different. Way, way different. There'd be a kind of belonging. Another chance at a family. Sort of. *If* he was telling the truth. Big if, Roo told himself. Don't be a sucker for that kinda crap. And deep down, way down, sat the idea that if Graeme wasn't lying, if he really wanted to be believed, he'd have chased Roo further, not stopped, not given up on the other side of the fence. If he cared enough, he'd have kept going, he would have climbed it, run his guts out, he wouldn't have given up on me. Roo bared his teeth at his own thoughts. There was a lost and lonely boychild to be found at the bottom of that one, and he wasn't about to listen to him. Not now, he wasn't. It'd be his undoing.

He got to his feet. Enough bloody philosophising. He brushed damp remnants of brown rotted gumleaf off the back of his bare legs. Then he straightened himself and walked back up the hill. As he'd expected, the Commodore had gone. He crossed the busy road and bought himself a Coke at the Ampol. It was a waste of precious dough because he could break into the machine at the track tonight and get it free. But he was thirsty now, eh, and patience wasn't his primary virtue. He took it across to the window and sat down. The sharp sweetness of the sugar soothed his razored nerves.

Set up.

Jesus Roo, ya picked ya fucken moment, didn't ya?

Set up.

Is that white cunt gorn yet?

Set up.

Nine times outta ten do nothing and you'll be better off, you'll be alright in the end. The change from the drink rattled in his pocket, and the public phone was right there. A blue one, one of these new friendly looking ones, not like the orange ones that glared at ya, holding all kinds of grief inside. Roo looked around rapidly, feeling like everyone in the world was staring at him. If only he had some real bungoo, some speed, some mull. That scotch wasn't gonna last past tonight, and booze was one thing. When you were strung out, it was yandy ya wanted, yandy, trips, speed, not grog. And strung out was putting it mildly. Jesus, getting chased into the bush by a copper and he hadn't even done nothing for once! His gaze drifted over to the cash register and the young woman operating it. Have to be, how much in there? Hundreds. His mouth watered. The girl saw him staring, and he quickly looked away, guilty. At least one hundred, maybe three or four. Even more. Could be off his face for a week on that. A month. Easy street. He wasn't into smack because of the running, but he could be, if he wanted, with all that money. Graeme's desperate face came into his mind, chasing him down the road.

Set up.

If it was true, it would mean he could go back. It'd mean dough for living and dough for partying.

Set up.

148

If he believed it, or pretended to, it'd mean somewhere to live until the state titles. It'd mean food in his guts instead of slobbering over the discarded wrappers of burgers he couldn't buy.

Set up.

It was easy salvation in two little words. Of course, Madden was lying – and yet.

Set up. The thing was, see, the thing was ... that even if it was a lie (and it was for sure, probably) then Madden had at least taken the trouble to find him, and he'd bothered to lie to him. That was something, eh. His father had come looking for him. It wasn't all that much, but it was definitely something, it meant something. He didn't know what, but, like, something. Twitching with nervous tension, Roo made the call. Got the answering machine, thank Christ.

'I'll, ah, I'll meet ya at the Ampol on the hill near the track tomorrow arvo. Same time.' He hung up, and then waited out of sight till dark, when it was safe to break into his home.

Chapter Twelve

Roo leaned his back against the cubicle door and took the last big swig of scotch he'd – miraculously – saved until now. Man, it burned alright, fumes in his throat, but it worked. He could feel the tension draining out of his arms and neck. His tongue loosened in his head, a flap of soft silly meat. Madden's watch told him it was well past five. Go on, then, the Roo inside him taunted. Go and front him then. Recklessly, he opened the door and barged out to the restaurant area. Slid to a halt on the large white tiles.

His father was looking out the glass windows at the pumps. It was a cool afternoon, and cold in the shadow of the overhanging roof. There was a low hum of conversation and rock music, noise from the till, car engines stopping and starting. Roo called out in a low voice.

Madden swung around to face him. 'Oh, it's you. G'day.'

Roo slid onto one of the orange plastic seats and his father took the one opposite. Madden offered him a smoke and they both puffed away awkwardly, arms folded in a mirror image of each other. Roo gave close attention to his bootlaces, dirty white strings fuzzy from wear.

'You go to training?' the man asked stiffly.

'Yeah, I go all the time,' Roo said. It was the truth. What else did he have?

'Going okay?'

'Yeah.'

'Do you want anything?' Madden waved at the counter. 'A burger or anything?'

Yes, Roo's stomach screamed, for the love of god – yes yes yes!

'Yeah, a steakburger. With the lot. And a Coke.'

Graeme went over and ordered, then sat down again. 'It's on its way.'

'Ta.' Roo smoked and stared; he wasn't gonna bust a gut trying to make polite conversation. The whiskey was enough company for him, for the moment.

Madden leaned back, crossed a leg over an ankle and spoke heavily. 'Ya coach rang me the other day.' Tapping of ash.

'You? What'd he ring you for?' Roo was startled by this unexpected adult collusion.

'Said he thought something was bothering you,' Madden said. 'I guess he was right. Was he?'

His son was silent. Madden gave an irritable sigh. 'You think I'm responsible for what happened to Stanley King, is that it?' His tone was hostile without being over the top. 'That's why you took off the other night, is it?'

'I dunno who was responsible for it. I wasn't there, you were.' Roo was shrugging, looking out the window.

This was stupid – how could you look your father in the face and agree you thought he was a murderer? Come on ... anyway, what did he think he thought? That Stanley died from a mozzie bite or something? Obviously someone knocked him, and if it wasn't him it was one of his pig mates, which pretty much amounted to the same thing.

'Well, d'ya wanna know the truth, or d'ya wanna believe what the fucken bullshit newspaper tells ya?' Graeme was trying to sound hurt, but it came out as pissed off.

Roo shrugged again. As if he gave a fuck for his lies. Suddenly, he thought he'd explain exactly where he stood. 'I knew Stanley King,' he said icily to the laminex tabletop. 'I went to his funeral.'

Inside, Madden wavered. This was even worse than he thought. Externally he stayed cool, calm and collected, the ideal cop. He ignored what Roo said. 'Yeah, so d'ya wanna hear my side of it or am I wasting my breath?'

'If ya want. I don't read the newspapers, but,' Roo added.

'Well that's something ... Look, I picked him up out of Centenary Park that night, okay? We were just passing, there was another bloke, a policeman with me. We took him into the watchhouse. He spewed up everywhere, and shit his pants, he was pissed out of his tiny brain. He'd been drinking sherry all day, drinking and fighting, they said. Blood alcohol of .21 – and that's enough to paralyse most people. We celled him, and half an hour later he was unconscious. He died on the way to hospital. It was from a head injury he got fighting in the park. Cerebral contusion. No one bashed him. No one "murdered" him, alright, specially not me. He died in the ambulance from punching on in the park.'

'No he didn't,' Roo said flatly. 'He died in the lockup.'

'Whaddya fucken mean, he didn't? I'm tellin ya he died in the fucken ambulance. They got a pulse before they put him in.'

Madden's eyes were ugly. Roo stared out at the gums that lined the Stadium fence over the road. More lies. Graeme wasn't gonna change. Something had to change, he himself had to change, but this was going nowhere.

'Yeah, whatever,' he said.

'What does that mean, "whatever"?' Madden asked angrily. 'Hey?'

Drunk with the power of rejection, Roo lifted a careless shoulder. Then the girl came over with a big plate of steaming food. Madden gestured to put it in front of Roo, who began to eat. Madden watched him tuck the burger away. Neither of them spoke for a minute. Then Roo wiped tomato sauce off his chin and said, 'It means ... I'll never really know, will I?' And started eating again.

His father shook his head. This wasn't how it was supposed to go. He was supposed to tell Roo his side of the story, what really happened, and Roo would accept it and apologise and then they'd go on from there. Not ... his jaw twitched. Try again.

'You'll know if ya listen to what I'm telling ya ... he died in the ambulance, and if the Coroner did his job properly that'd be the end of it. But no, the bloody bleedin hearts are at it again, and someone's head's gotta roll, and I'm it, apparently. It's a set-up job, son, ever heard of them?' Madden was sarcastic now.

'Yeah, sure did.' Roo stared him down with contempt. 'Every crim I was ever inside with was set up, every single one, there must be that many crims running around free, eh, cos no fucker in jail never did nothin. Look, look, he … Stanley was just a kid, alright? A bloody dumb, harmless kid. So what if he was drinking all day? Hey? So fucking what? Blood alcohol! Who gives a fuck what his blood alcohol was … he was alive and now he's dead. I seen his mother bawling her eyes out for days, I seen em put the fucken box in the ground.'

'He was a convicted rapist,' Madden interrupted. 'That's how harmless he was. And—'

'That was bullshit, it was a set-up!' Roo blurted, then stopped abruptly, desperate to take the words back.

Madden just lifted his eyebrows and said nothing.

'Anyway, that's not the point!' Roo said defensively. 'He's dead, and for what? For nothin. You was there that night, you could have stopped em, even if you didn't do it! Why'd he have to die?'

'Stopped *what*? He collapsed in his cell and died in the ambulance. For your information, I was one of the ones giving the little cunt heart massage,' Madden said. 'Yknow, I'm the good guy here. I don't appreciate—'

'Yeah, right,' Roo stood up, his cheeks flushed. This was getting nowhere. Packa lies. 'I'm going.'

'Where?'

'Whadda ya fucken care? All you care about is ya bail money.'

'What? How'd we get onto *that* all of a sudden?'

Madden was perplexed. It was like fighting with friggin Faith, all over the place like a madwoman's shit. Roo was looking at him like he was dirt. What'd he have to be shitty about anyway? Christ, anyone'd think the kid was the one that was hard done by.

Roo was trembling as he spoke. He felt like dropping the big cunt where he sat.

"Yez just think you can do whatever ya want and we've just gotta take it and take it and take it. Don't lie to me,' shaking his head, 'just don't lie to me, alright?'

'If I'm lying then this bloody investigation'll find out about it, won't it?' Madden replied, raising his voice. 'I'll lose my job, and my super, eh? Willya be happy then? Will justice have been done when I'm on the dole with me reputation in tatters? Would that make ya—'

'Oh, what? Cops investigating cops – as if they're gonna say ya did anything! That's so-o fucken likely, isn't it?' Roo curled his lip, and Madden steamed some more. His breathing grew heavier.

'It's not just cops investigating cops! Why don't ya come along and watch it, you might learn something, ya little smartarse,' Madden cried. 'Why d'ya think I'm worried about it, if it's all bullshit?'

'What have ya got to worry about?' Roo shot back. 'The truth?'

'How many times do I have to tell ya, I'm being set up 'cos they don't want it to just ... it's all garbage, it's a set-up,' Madden ended limply. 'I've got ... enemies.'

'Yeah, and I'm the fucken Queen Mother,' Roo said. 'Thanks for the burger. I'll see ya when I see ya.' He went to pick up his training bag and leave.

'How did ya know him anyway?' Graeme asked Roo. His voice was hopeless, a last question to satisfy his curiosity.

'He was my girlfriend's brother,' Roo said nastily. 'His brother was my best friend – before he died anyway. But you lot've cruelled that for me. Now he doesn't even wanna know me.' Ha! That'll show him, he thought, as he waited to see what Madden said to that.

His father had no immediate reply; when he did eventually speak it was with resignation: 'Well, obviously, it doesn't matter what I say, cos you've made ya mind up before ya got here.' Graeme suddenly put his head in his hands. It was no use. Nothing was any use. Nothing mattered anymore.

Roo stood and heaved with emotion. This was bullshit. It was like when he fought with Leena, and she said, 'Well, why don't ya fucken leave insteada talkin 'bout it?' A turning point, but he hesitated to turn, just like he didn't leave her so many times. Fight or flight. He spoke more slowly. 'I haven't made anything up, I just hate being lied to, ya know, cos I've been lied to all me life. Not that you'd know about that.'

Graeme heard the indecision under his son's bitter words. A bird of hope lifted in him. He looked at Roo. 'Well, maybe someone isn't lying for once. Come to the Inquiry – I mean it. Come and see for yourself, instead of letting other people decide for you.' His voice was hard and insistent, unforgiving, and it forced a concession out of Roo. The slight, faint, insane possibility that he could be telling the truth after all. Roo was still for a long moment.

'Mmm. Alright. Maybe.'

'Right then.'

Madden was the one to shrug then, and he got up. He paid for the food and they went outside.

'Where ya going now?' he asked his son. They both shivered as they came out of the air-conditioned restaurant. Another cold night coming.

'Nowhere.'

'Ya coach said something about state trials coming up.'

'Yeah.'

'When are they?'

'Coupla weeks. Saturday week.'

'What if I come and watch you run?' his father asked, conciliatory.

'Suit yerself.' Nothing to do with me, buddy, what you do. Freeze him out.

'Alright. Just remember what I said, won't ya? Come and see the inquiry in town if want to know the truth. There's still something called the burden of proof in this country. Means you're innocent till you're proven guilty.' Madden fitted his wallet into his back pocket and got his car keys out.

'Pity Stanley never had the benefit of it,' Roo said stonily. 'Death sentence for being pissed, that's a bit rough, eh.' It was a line he'd got off the ALS blokes at the funeral.

Madden stared at Roo's gold-flecked eyes for the count of three, then he threw his hands in the air. Fuck it. 'Yeah, okay, well, if that's your attitude, fine. You know where to find me.' He turned his back on the boy, got in the car and drove away.

PART THREE

FORGIVE US

CHAPTER THIRTEEN

Still half-asleep, Roo rolled over yawning on the thick vinyl-covered high jump mat. Too soft – was that Mother Bear's bed, or Father Bear's? Tough, eh, be whingeing about being too well fed. His mood darkened as the memories came flooding back. They sat sourly in his empty stomach. He saw his father's reptilian eyes and thought, *Set up, yeah, I just bet*. The liar. Then he forced himself to think about something else. Leena came immediately to mind, but that was another no-go area. Anyway, no way was that baby his. It vaguely occurred to Roo that he should ring Newcastle and see how Hayley was doing. She'd be turning one pretty shortly. Should try and get her a present or something, eh. Or could he find a way to go see her? Scrape up a bus fare outta thin air, and just lob there. He sighed. Most of his bungoo had been in the zipper pocket of the Adidas jacket, and while he didn't regret his decision to pass it to Leena, givin all ya money away when yer on the dole cuts ya options considerably.

Goosepimpling as a cold breeze whipped under the double wooden doors, Roo considered his domestic situation. The spartan locker-room with its concrete floor was too big for his meagre body heat to warm it throughout the night. Besides, the toilets down the end had them windows with the built-in mesh part, to let fresh air in, so it was a waste of time hoping that he'd ever get properly warm living here. If only he hadn't left the doona behind. It woulda been five-star luxury-living for his white arse if he still had it here, but it went west long ago. With Leena's jumper on, though, and huddled under the old towels he'd found in the cupboard, it was way better than the bloody park had been.

Slatted wooden benches ran along the long sides of the besser-block room; he'd tried sleeping on them but they were just that little bit narrow. After the first night he'd decided the risk of putting the big mat out in the middle of the floor was worth it, just to have some sleep. He needed rest to run properly, rest and decent food, though the food was less important for the time being. It was all about trade-offs, living like this. Like when ya slept in the park, hiding was important, but it wasn't that much of an issue, because you could always run from trouble in the open. Here he had to stay undetected, had to be absolutely fucken cunning about it, or else the coach'd find out, and then … well, who knows what'd happen? Back to the lockup, more than likely. It had been six days. So far so good. He'd even begun to feel proprietorial about the place, with a crazy resentment at the others in the team using it morning and night, wetting *his* towels, throwing things on *his* floor.

Roo's new accommodation was grubby and in need of paint, but brightened by some outdated posters of

Carl Lewis, Allan Wells and Daley Thompson. A large permanent banner dominated the big wall. It said in the coach's red, hand-painted letters (betraying his bias towards the track, to the annoyance of the throwers and jumpers): 'To run is to live – everything else is just waiting.'

It was some quote or something. It was true but, eh. Roo repeated the commandment to himself frequently, heard Coach telling them to be able to run and race was a privilege they should never take for granted. Think of the buggers born without legs, he'd lecture their deaf ears, think of the millions and billions of people in the world born with legs and no talent. You can't put in what god left out. But you can squander what meagre ability you've got – can't you, Roo Glover? And Roo'd look at his shoes, shame at not working hard enough, at playing the fool, at missing training cos he could get away with it, sometimes. At being bad here, as well as everywhere else. Born that way, maybe.

To run is to live. Roo knew it was true. Running meant a chance at freedom, it meant everything. When you came around the bend as one of a sweating, gasping group and you still had something left to kick with, when you surged to the front, when you lined up in a starting line and knew beyond any sort of doubt that you could win, when you floated past the rest of them, hit the empty space in front and all the pain fell away to glory … it felt like nothing on earth. Way better than anything else, better than sex, better than drugs. That's why it was worth it, to put up with the coach's homilies and strange ways, to live in a fucker of a freezing shed, to push your body till it screamed every day for mercy. To train so hard you could only hobble the next morning and had to walk downstairs one painful step at a time, bringing your feet together on each one cos your quads and hammies were full of knives. Roo looked at the red-lettered banner each day and clung to its promise, which was a conjuring trick showing him everything and nothing at the same time.

The young athlete sat up on the edge of the spongy mat, dived in his bag for the watch and found to his horror that it was already five forty-five. He'd slept in! Tuesday training started early and they'd be here any minute. Panicking, he quickly jumped up and dragged the heavy mat over to where it belonged, leaned up against the wall next to the shower cubicle. He grabbed the towels and crammed them in the cupboard – no time to fold them – then scanned the room for remaining evidence. His drink bottle! He thrust it into his bag. He roughly dragged his shoes on without untying the laces and wondered whether to risk breaking out. Five-fifty. Training started at six, but you never knew if some try-hard had insomnia and had decided to turn up early. Reluctantly, he retreated to one of the toilet cubicles, shutting the door but not locking it. Ever so quietly he opened his last packet of Maggi two-minute noodles and began to eat. At six-o-three, sitting with his feet drawn up invisibly onto the white plastic toilet seat, he heard the coach unlocking the wooden doors. The rusted tongue of the bolt scraped back and half a dozen blokes came in.

Jesse was saying: '... was gonna buy them new, but then I thought, you might pick up some just as good second-hand, hey? So I waited till Thursday ...'

Someone else chipped in: '... I'm hanging out for my birthday. I've told Dianne I want those new Nikes, Monsters ... I dunno if she'll come at them though, they're a hundred and eighty ...'

And then Coach cutting in with friendly sarcasm: 'Oh, I know how important it is to you lot to look good, but it's training that wins medals ... Abibe Bakila didn't need two-hundred-dollar shoes, cos the bastard could run. Now c'mon, let's get cracking, you lot'd be late for your own funerals ...'

In a few minutes the room was clear and Roo emerged. He threw his bag onto the bench, stripped his jumper off and jogged out to the cluster of runners in the middle of the oval. He didn't really want to train this morning, but in the circumstances there wasn't much choice. It was either that or squat on the bog for another hour and a half.

Waiting again, always bloody waiting. That banner in the locker-room was closer than the coach ever knew. It was Thursday night and Roo felt conspicuous lurking around the basketball hall by himself after training. In an attempt to look meaningfully occupied, he bought an expensive and unsatisfying bucket of chips at the tuckshop (and pocketed some little packets of tomato sauce and sugar while the girl wasn't looking). He looked morosely at the tepid yellow straws in the bucket. Chips for dinner. Again. A bloke could get sick of chips. He went outside to a distant alcove and leaned against the wall, smoking and trying not to look as impatient as he felt. It was six-twenty.

He'd had no idea, when he used to bugger-off back to Kings on the quarter-past-five bus, that the coach and the field athletes hung around this late. Actually, this whole deal, sleeping in the locker-room, which had seemed so ideal to begin with, was starting to like, suck. It was warmer than the park, and probably safer, but it meant a constant minor level of hassle all the time, staying out of sight and always having to worry about getting sprung. *And* it was fucken boring. It'd been ages since he'd had anyone to talk to, drink with, or have a pool game with. He sighed. No friends, no Nintendo, no TV, no videos. No music. You could almost say he was getting lonely, eh. Then he grinned at himself. One thing there was plenty of – training. Morning and bloody night. Just had to hack it for another ten days, that's all he had to do. Ten long days that seemed like a year stretching out in front of him, but after the state titles he'd be free and clear. Something else'd turn up then, he knew it. Ten days. He felt like a kid waiting for Christmas.

Six twenty-seven. Roo dragged the last traces of nicotine out of his smoke and threw the butt down a drain outlet. It hissed as it hit the black water. Have to cut down on them, too. He couldn't be bothered with rollies, and at seven bucks a pack it was nothing but a mug's game. Maybe tomorrow he'd stop. Waiting. Six thirty-one. *Mark Grogan doesn't smoke, you know.* With relief, Roo finally saw the coach and the last of the shot-putters trail across the oval to the car park, still yakking. Bingo, dingo, you're on your way.

Ten minutes later he was safely inside his room, which

was dimly lit by the hot glare of the basketball lights from the other side of the track. Roo unzipped his bag and spread his belongings out on the high jump mat. Time to take stock. One maroon Adidas training bag, stolen. Two T-shirts, dirty. Two pairs of running shorts, pretty dirty. One pair of jeans, filthy from sleeping in the park. Two disposable razors, blunt. Running shoes. One pair of socks, dirty. Three pairs of undies, not too bad (he'd washed them in the shower some days and dried them at night). And the jeans and jumper he had on, dirty but wearable. One drink bottle. One pair of street Nikes. One wallet (slim). Exactly three dollars to last him – what – one, two, three, four, five days till the rest of his pay came through. One pair of stolen Ray-Ban wrap-around sunnies. One towel. Two *Penthouse* magazines he'd found in the park, old and torn and getting boring. The bit of the *White Pages* with Madden's and some other phone numbers written on it. TallyHo papers. A big roll of Leukoplast from the chemist, for blisters. Half a packet of smokes and a lighter (a bloke really should chuck em out, eh, seeing as how he was giving up tomorrow.) The six CDs he'd cash in when it was time to pay registration fees for next weekend's meet. That was it. He'd sorrowfully left Madden's doona stuffed away in the hidey hole at the park and when he went back it was gone.

Roo ran his tongue around his teeth, imagining that he could feel the green fuzz growing on them. Should have thought to grab a toothbrush from Graeme's, but he hadn't. Wouldn't think you'd need a toothbrush when you only ate chips and that, eh. Thinking about chips made Roo feel a bit off. He was stuffed to the gills with bloody chips, but he was still always hungry, hungry, hungry. Sometimes as he pounded the track he dreamed about pizzas, about roast chicken and great big dripping hamburgers with egg and pineapple and that. He imagined that waiting for him at the finish line were chocolate milkshakes, spareribs slathered with sauce. He'd wake up in the mornings starving, knowing that just over the hill at the Ampol people were having whole platefuls of bacon and eggs with great mounds of toast, washing it down with coffee and tea and orange juice. Once or twice he'd gone in there in the morning and bought coffee, just so – oh shamejob, eh – just so he could eat other people's scraps when no one was looking. Leena had his bungoo, and that was a good thing, but the result was that he now thought more about food than about drugs or fucking. His fantasy was a huge t-bone with mushroom sauce and vegies and garlic bread, followed by an endless chocolate sundae. Roo's guts gnawed at him, but there was nothing to appease them with, except a cigarette. Better than nothing.

He winced as his probing tongue found a huge new hole in one of his molars. Holey or not, these teeth were definitely slimy. Roo had a vague idea that blackfellas used to use sticks as toothbrushes, and made a mental note to get a hold of some gum twigs tomorrow. Then he finished his smoke, stuffed his worldly goods back into the training bag, covered himself with half a dozen towels and tried not to think about food. He slowly drifted off out of an immense hungry boredom into fitful nightmarish sleep.

★

Something woke him in the deep night. He lay frozen with night panic. There it was again, something scratching and banging at the double doors. The half-nonsensical paranoia of 2 am gripped him. He was gonna get sprung! It was the night watchman, prowling around, they were onto him! No, it was Graeme, after him again! He'd realised where he was, and had come to settle the score for stealing his stuff, for running away, for not believing him! Roo lay rigid in bed, too frightened to hide, waiting desperately for the lock to creak open. After all his hiding, all his running. It was no use. When you were a crim like him you had it coming. He tried not to breathe.

After five minutes he was sane enough to sit up despite the noise. And in another couple, he realised that if it was a person they'd either be in or gone by now, which meant it had to be an animal. Probably a mongrel dog sniffing round for rubbish. Ah, bloody hell, he swore softly, pulling himself up to look out the window. A hump-backed animal was creeping around on the grass, sniffing at bits of rubbish that had blown over from the canteen. Not a dog, a great big possum. Look at the bastard poking around there, scaring the shit out of people. Big fat cunt of a thing. Big, fat ... Roo suddenly had an idea.

He looked around and found the bit of broken chair frame that had worried him that time with Darryl. Yep, it was solid, heavy too. Perfect. He carefully wormed his way out of the high window and ultra-slowly placed himself in the best position on the ground, his legs spreadeagled, club held above his head. Then he launched himself. The possum, cornered between locker-room and the external toilet wall, screeched in terror. Roo lunged with the chair leg and missed. He crashed heavily against the besser bricks. With nowhere else to go, and an instinct for climbing, the possum rocketed up Roo's legs and body. It clung to his scalp with its sharp claws. Roo howled in horror as he danced. Oh-oh. This wasn't the idea at all. He shook his head frantically and pawed at it, but it was no use. He began to yelp with pain and fright.

The possum clung tighter still, raking great channels in his short hair. Blood sprayed from his head as he desperately tried to pull the animal off. And then the possum bit his hand. Snarling with pain, Roo gathered his wits and clubbed at the clinging beast with the chair leg, but it was the wrong moment. At that instant the possum chose to leap free in favour of the higher wall close by, and Roo struck himself a mighty blow on his head. Dazed from the hit, he staggered after the capering animal. He wasn't about to give up on the prick now. Not only was it nearly a week since Graeme bought him that steak burger, now it was *personal*.

Chapter Fourteen

By day Roo walked. He walked and walked and walked, risking blisters, so he wouldn't crumple under the boredom and loneliness. Nowhere to go but the shops, no bed, no friendly house to welcome him, and so, you walk. If the stadium had been closer to the railway, he might have jumped trains and run from the ticket people, but the station was forty minutes away by Shanks' pony and he needed to keep some energy in reserve for training. He walked instead to the big shopping centres, Garden City and the slope ones at Sunnybank. Chinese faces surrounded him, and Chinese women in alien clothes dripped gold in his face, inviting assault. Snatch it and bolt, he thought, but never did. Gutteral Cantonese told him nothing new about the world. He didn't mind the slopes, didn't care one way or the other. They were loaded yeah, but they still copped it, same as Murries.

There were brown faces in the shops, too, Arabs, Islanders, Murries, Malays. Honeyed girls tossed their hair, and it was Leena all over again. His heart broke a hundred times a day, seeing them. Girls of all descriptions noticed his muscles. The noticing made their faces soft, their eyes bright. He opened himself to their scrutiny, but then the tattoos frightened them. Poverty screamed its name, and the girls slid away. If he followed, it just made things worse. The security guards began to know him, and they stood up a fraction straighter when he walked past. Roo looked at the floor and disappeared for them.

One morning, he stood after training in the vast car park at the stadium and ached towards the Gabba and his lost life. Walking the opposite way than usual, towards and not away from town, he found himself outside the Mount Gravatt cemetery. Roo had absorbed the Murri dislike for things of the dead, and he paused. The concrete slabs on top of the graves were broken in places. Grass spiked its way heavenward. Yuck. The boneyard. He thought of horror movies, zombies, the living dead. Stanley. He was about to turn back to the shops when dew on a bunch of plastic flowers winked at him. He made a face at himself, then spoke apologetically to the grave before snatching the flowers away. The white girl at the Ampol knew him, too.

'White coffee, three sugars?' she asked, knowing he'd say yes.

Roo flashed her a brilliant smile and used her name as he leaned closer. A spray can jangled illicitly in his bag when he sought the coins to pay. The girl would have liked conversation, but Roo had business to conduct. He gulped and went. She watched him until he was out of sight.

In the midst of the sheltering bush Roo pulled the top off the paint and aimed it at the flowers. He gently waved them in the sun and breeze, spraying and drying in turn for ages until they were a uniform glossy black. Leena was crazy for anything black. He lay on the grass and admired his handiwork. How could she refuse such an offering?

The sound of the final lap bell faded in his ears. Onetwo went his legs, onetwo, onetwo, onetwo. His lungs were being pumped full of acid. This was what dying would be like, pain and pain and pain again. Pain doubled, agony tripled and don't think about it, don't give it anything at all. Just run. Roo's mouth opened for air on the final turn and he found he didn't have the strength to close it. He ran the last one hundred without legs, almost without eyes. The world was turning red in front of him, but he was winning. Winning! *To run is to live*, no, the banner was wrong, to run was shit, to run was to hurt, to be flayed alive. Running was pain and pain was death. Roo dipped and breasted the line well in front. The banner was wrong. To run was nothing. To win was to live. He looked to the coach from where he lay on the grass, heaving for breath as he pulled on his jumper over his sweat-soaked tee-shirt. The man slowly nodded in approval and Roo's heart grew large.

'John,' said the coach to the guy who came second, 'you're still holding your arms up like I told you, okay? Liam, your stride's not as rough as it was, but you need to lose three more kilos before you're gonna get anywhere, okay? You want to cut out those bloody Mars Bars you've always got in your face. Look at Roo, he's not carrying any extra weight, is he?'

Pimple-faced Liam blushed.

Then the man turned to the winner. 'Run like that this time next week, will you?' he said. 'Please.'

'I quit. Never again.' Roo smiled in a pale exhausted face.

To cover his emotion the coach wrote their times in his notebook with grim satisfaction. Roo's was good, less than a second outside Olympic Qualifying Time, but that was a detail. It was the instinct that mattered, the pure driving obsession that had made the kid push through pain when the pack was three metres away. Any other runner in the club would have been content with first, would have eased up once it was obvious he'd win. Roo had ignored the others and had run like a man without a body.

It was what would make Roo a champion, the coach reflected. At training – when he got to training that is – he was a slackarse, lazy, preferring to rely on god-given talent than on putting in the hard yards. But he'd been doing well this week, turned up for every session, and it showed – he'd fined down and lost the tiny bit of excess fat he'd had. Now the lad was a study in athletic physique, tall and lean, with a whipcord body of hardened muscle.

Before, he'd been fit enough and fast too, but the heavier muscle in his upper body had made him look unbalanced, more like a decathlete or even a lightly built thrower. Now he looked like the runner he was. He was ready to race, and when he raced, Roo was a man possessed. Nothing was more important in an athlete. The lad was going to do well.

High in the stand, Madden had used his binoculars

to spy on his son. He saw Roo run with a steady fluid motion, staying in the pack of five till the last two hundred metres when he drew away without apparent effort, accelerating until there was a big gap between him and the rolling, stumbling others. When Roo crossed the line first, Madden lowered his glasses. He stared down at the athletes who had all collapsed onto the turf. Now he understood what the coach had meant about his son. Watching Roo's long striding steps take him over the line, Graeme was shocked to find that he had a lump in his throat. Little sod's not completely useless after all.

Suddenly enthused, he walked halfway down the grandstand to the exit tunnel and stood waving his right arm. Another runner said something to Roo, who was flat on the grass, and he looked up, shielding his eyes against the afternoon sun. Graeme! He rapidly sat up. The man didn't approach any closer though and Roo hesitated for ages, then lifted a low tentative hand, bandaged white with Leukoplast where the possum had bitten him, before turning away to say something to Peter. Graeme's arm dropped and he quickly disappeared down the stairwell leading to the car park. Roo was left to warm down alone, disconcerted and puzzled. What was he hanging around for? What did he want?

'Something stinks,' complained John as he came out of the shower on Monday afternoon, provoking an avalanche of comments about his personal hygiene. He grinned, but insisted, 'I'm serious, can't youse smell it?' Their noses led the team outside the locker-room and into the nearby bush. With the bloody gouges in his scalp visible (he'd blamed them on a horse-riding accident, now there's a flight of fantasy for ya), Roo shrank back as the coach looked curiously at the fireplace. It consisted of a ring of blackened stones just inside the bushy fringe of gums which surrounded the oval. In the ashes, mixed with half-burnt pages from *Penthouse*, was something greasy and hairy that looked a bit like a mangled cat.

'Ah, noooooo!' Jesse pretended to stagger and vomit.

'What in Christ's name is it?' asked John.

Coach squinted at it in puzzlement and turned it over with his toe. It was the scant remains of a possum, seething with maggots. His nose wrinkled and he stepped back from the smell. Bloody weird – who'd kill a possum and then eat it? He would have said a dog, maybe, yeah, but there was no clue, no empty beer bottles to denote a party, no rubbish, nothing. You'd have to be pretty damn hungry to catch and eat a possum, the coach thought, mystified. Unless it was some sick cult thing. But no …

'Any of you lot know anything about this?' he asked, and of course no one did. Roo's plastered hand caught the man's eye, and an almost forgotten idea glimmered in the back of his mind. 'I knew times were tough but this is ridiculous!' he quipped and told everyone to forget it. Later he pulled Roo to one side. The man contorted his face and pulled awkwardly at his permanently sunburnt ear, wondering how to say what he wanted to. Ten years of managing athletes had taught him a lot about human nature, and you didn't need a university degree to realise Roo was a bolter. Get this wrong now and he could easily bugger-up the boy's chances at the state titles. He couldn't just let it slide though. The lad needed help – careful help, arms-length help.

Mentioning the locker-room might be the right way in. He hoped so.

'Um, yeah, Roo. The night watchman told me he thought someone might be hanging around here at night. Said they might even be sleeping in one of the buildings.'

Roo felt sick as he stretched his hamstring against the railing of the track. His stomach fell to the ground, a great yawning drop.

'What do you reckon?' the man asked him, a question within a question. 'Have you seen anything unusual around lately?'

Roo simply shook his head, dumbfounded. And he'd been so careful.

'No strangers running around with sleeping bags?' Coach smiled.

'Ah, geez, how desperate would ya have to be to hang around here for fun?' Roo replied lightly.

'That's just what I don't know.' Christ lad, the way you can run, why do you live so wild, from moment to moment? Can't you see it's wrong, that you'll waste it ... wake up one morning and it'll be gone? 'Look, don't get me wrong, I'm not gonna call the cops or anything, it's just ...'

Roo thought hard for a moment. Then he knew what he had to do. He kicked at the bottom of the wall as he spoke, his arms folded. 'Ah, probably if anyone was, um, like, "staying here", they'd probably only stay a few days, hey? Probably they'd bugger off after about a week. Not as if it's the Hilton, eh.'

'I guess they might,' said the coach slowly, testing this new ground, 'I guess that would be the best thing for them to do. Seeing as it's trespassing on Council property.'

'Yeah … Not that I'd know,' Roo added quickly.

'Of course not,' the coach agreed. 'But I think you're right. Probably they'd be careful to look around the place, too. Have a look in all the lockers in case they'd missed anything. Or, ah, even ask someone for some help, maybe. But like you say, who'd want to stay here?' The man shot a sudden piercing look at the kid and then went off to other affairs with the team, hoping that would do the trick. Touchy business. Touchy lad. Funny life he must have.

Roo pounced joyfully on the twenty dollar note lying crumpled in the dark corner of locker twelve. Ah, too, too deadly! Thanks, man. He held the treasure in his hand, torn between using it as bus fare to go and pawn the CDs, or spending it immediately on food at the Ampol. It wasn't a hard decision. He was desperate for protein. He slipped the note into his pocket; with what was left of the money he'd borrowed off Jesse he had exactly twenty-two bucks. He felt like he'd won Lotto.

Half an hour later Roo pushed the plate away from him, sure that he couldn't fit in another molecule. When the waitress came and took the plate she raised her eyebrows as its cleanness. Not a trace of egg or sauce left, no toast corners, no fat or rinds. It was like a bone. She threw the plate on top of the others on her tray, gave Roo an absent smile and went on her way.

Full of food and hollow optimism, Roo braved himself to ring Mum King. Time to get his living arrangements sorted, now he'd got the shove-along from Coach. He'd ask if she'd vouch for him at the Hostel, not lie about him being a Murri or nothin, but just sorta put in a word for him, see if he could get a room for a coupla weeks or something. Even for one week, till the finals were over. There was whitefellas stayed there sometimes, Daz reckoned, parkies and that. Would she talk to him? Leena said she was sweet, but sweet several days ago and sweet now were two different things. He steeled himself. It had to be worth a go, and anyway, no pain, no gain.

Ring-ring. Ring-ring. Roo checked his watch. One-thirty on a Saturday, someone should be there, unless they all went to see Jimmy play. Ring-ring.

'Hello?' It was Darryl. Roo tried disguising his voice.

'Can I speak to Mrs King please?'

'Who is it?' Suspicious. Sounded like he was charged. Couldn't be – Darryl didn't drink, hardly ever. Roo sighed, sensing already that this attempt was doomed.

'Roo.'

'Who?'

'ROO.'

'Roo who?'

Giving him the very slim benefit of the doubt, Roo replied wearily, 'Roo, Reuben Glover, remember me? I used to live there.' Mate.

Darryl made a loud and sarcastic announcement to the household. 'Ah, there's a Reuben Glover on the phone here, do we know a Reuben Glover? Anyone? Nah?' He waited for one beat, then, 'Sorry, pal, must be a wrong number.' Clunk.

You arsehole. Roo hung up too and leaned his forehead against the phone. You fucken racist arsehole. Wiped. If only Shaleena'd picked it up instead. Or Mum. Now what? He gazed hopelessly out at the greyness of the sky. He knew one thing, with the wind whipping the tops of those trees around like that, it was only gonna get colder, and he wasn't going back to freeze his nuts in the bloody park, that was for sure.

CHAPTER FIFTEEN

Roo stood on the track tugging at his satin athletics shorts, and dying for a cigarette, ha not likely. It can wait, brother. He put his palms flat on the ground, then grabbed the back of his knees, stretching his hammies for the millionth time that morning. He tried not to look over at the apparently nerveless Mark Grogan who was chatting with a pretty reporter from the *Southern Star*.

Grogan wore a flash Nike spray-jacket which protected him from the light spits of rain. Unwilling to shame himself in Leena's cheap jumper, Roo stood and shivered in his racing singlet. He'd given up shaving on Thursday, and now a dark stubble, beaded with rain, covered his lower face. After some deliberation that morning he'd left his earrings in, and, as always, the racing singlet exposed the crudely hand-inked Harley Badge on his left shoulder, a red heart with 'Leena' and 'Roo' intertwined on his right, and the Chinese symbols for war and victory on his forearms. Some race days he felt sorry for his criminal appearance; today he was glad of it. Grogan (the dickhead) had stared gormlessly the first time Roo had come onto a track to race him. Roo had leaned into his face with a *Whatthefuck'syourproblem?* – half-shitty, half-bunging it on, and Grogan, the flustered Grammar boy, hadn't recovered enough poise to win. Blew the fucker away. Ha.

The coach came over to Roo as he was enjoying the memory. The man felt his neck and shoulder muscles with probing fingers. He was the only bloke Roo'd let near him, and that'd taken a few months. Now the man had his trust – he was fair dinkum – and Roo accepted the physical intimacy that their relationship sometimes required.

'Loose enough. Good. There ya go.'

Roo touched each of his ears to his shoulders in turn, and blew rain out of his nose.

'Ready to win?' Coach growled, revving him up.

'Ready as I'll ever be.' Roo shrugged. He wondered if Graeme had come to watch him. Or Leena even. He scanned the crowd, but the only black faces belonged to Jesse's mob, that island breed.

'See that skinny prick over there?' The athlete turned to where his coach's finger pointed.

'Danny McQueen?' Nice guy, but slow as a wet weekend.

'Mmm.' The coach's voice was low and clear. 'Run like you did last Saturday and Grogan's got as much chance of winning as he has. Sweet FA. Now get out there and show David Wiseman what you can do. Sydney, Roo, just think Sydney.' The coach clapped Roo on the back, and then left as the stewards marshalled the runners.

The row of athletes came together then, all focusing

on the track, trying not to notice each other. They settled onto the line. Run in the tunnel, thought Roo, forget Grogan, forget who's watching or not watching, run in the tunnel. Weight even on your toes, relax …

Set. The gun fired and Roo began to live.

The rain was buggering Graeme's binoculars. He swore as the pack ran the first lap in an indistinguishable blur. Roo was in blue and white – he thought he could see him running four or five men back but couldn't be sure.

Onetwo onetwo easy does it yeah that's right you can fuck right off pal stick an elbow slightly further out to avoid getting boxed in yeah and don't try it again ya prick goddit? Where's Grogan? Just up there, okay, onetwo onetwo onetwo this feels too easy its nice and slow – we don't want that we want a record, so pick it up pushing pushing that's it but don't go to the front...

Another lap and another. They were still bunched tight and now beginning to breathe hard. The rain got heavier. Umbrellas went up all around him and Graeme grew impatient. He used his bulk to push his way down the stadium and through the crowd. Eventually he was close enough to the finish line to see clearly. The pack sped past as the last-lap bell sounded. As if it were one pounding gasping organism, the pace of the group picked up once again. There he was! A fair way back, come on son, you can do better than that. The leader was a nondescript man in his twenties, hollow-cheeked with a blonde crewcut. Behind him, the announcer was bellowing; Mark Grogan was poised to make his move.

Ah Grogan you mug, you think I've haddit don't ya sucker? Cos it's getting late and you're ready to kick. Stay there you onetwo onetwo breathe breathe stay relaxed as I go past you mister McQueen that's it son ah now he's seen me gotcha worried ya should be ya prick onetwo onetwo starting to hurt now ah me lungs onetwo relax relax breathe onetwo ah Jesus the pain hello Grogan how's tricks sunshine? Ah forget the legs the burning legs rain trickling down my face and arms breathe breathe whaddayareckon we go for it? NO Wait for him to go, wait, wait … this is it, state titles Roo how long you bin waiting boy ? How long? Ah Jesus me lungs relax onetwo onetwo Is that it, Grogan, is that what you call a kick? But still, wait, wait —

Madden couldn't tear his eyes off his son, moving up relentlessly, overtaking one, then two, then three runners. The crewcut was wobbling, he'd gone out too soon and couldn't hold it. Smooth but hurting, Grogan took over the lead thankyouverymuch and flew towards the finish. Roo was in second place. Madden started to yell. He'd left it too late, the stupid little bastard.

Readyreadywait — to run is to live — ready NOW!

Burning, Roo could feel every individual fibre of his calves and quads. He was soaring, the others were standing still. Grogan was wearing number sixteen and the sweat and rain were prickling through the cotton. His face was sweating, the rain still coming down in great silvery slashes, spikes tearing into the track. The coach was running beside him, hair plastered flat screaming something, something GO GO. Passing Grogan like he's not even there. I'm loose, I'm free, I'm a runner, I'm a runner. Ah Jesus, the crowd, hear em, hear em, keep going, keep going, ah God the pain, hello sweet line Shaleeeeeenarrrrgh …

The animal roar of the crowd when the Olympic qualifying time was announced. A glimpse of his father, pretending not to cry. He *did* come, he *did*! Grabbed ecstatically by the coach, by John, by Jesse, by Pete.

And then the pain.

Half an hour later, walking on legs made of wet string, Roo limped over to the locker-room. Then he stopped. Something made him slowly turn back towards the stands. Today was no ordinary day. His eyes sought Graeme's close-clipped head in the crowd. He'd just say g'day to the bloke quicksmart, then tuck off to the barbecue and pig out on about ten steak sandwiches. He was mongrel starving, eh.

'Looking for someone?' Graeme asked. He loomed unexpectedly beside Roo in jeans and a plain navy-blue cop jacket. Roo was shocked to find him there; whenever he wasn't with him he forgot how tall and bulky Madden was. Every time he saw him again he was surprised by his size. Now Roo was jittery, extremely conscious of the strain in his right leg. Take off now and he'll catch ya.

'You came, eh.' The young man's neck was stiff as he spoke, and his eyes cold with judgement.

'Yeah, and I'm tellin ya I'm glad I made the effort. Bloody good race, mate. Ya had me worried for a bit there. Congratulations.'

Madden was smiling as he stuck his hand out. Roo looked at it. He didn't shake hands much. Reluctantly he grabbed his father's hand for a quick hard moment. Madden beamed.

'OQ, eh. Not bad son,' he went on blithely. 'Must take after your old man. I was a pretty fast winger in my younger days.'

Roo winced, and stared at him. Either the man was a monumental bloody egomaniac, or else he was innocent of murdering Stanley. How else could he say stuff like that? Look so happy and carefree?

'Thanks,' he muttered.

'You'll be in the squad for sure now, eh?' It was a question.

'Probably.'

'Good one. So, ya gonna come along to the Inquiry next week?' Madden asked suddenly.

Roo shrugged a mild shoulder. What did he think this fucken was? *Oprah*? 'Maybe.'

Encouraged, Madden threw caution to the winds. 'Well, listen, I know you reckon your old man's a bit on the nose, but whaddya reckon I shout you a beer anyway. To celebrate?'

Roo's dismissal was instant and blunt. 'Nah, no way, I've gotta run the eight hundred this arvo and I'll probably lose even without getting pissed. But I reckon I'll be picked for the fifteen. For the squad.'

'Oh. Right.' Madden's smile faded. 'Okay. Well—'

Before he could rephrase his offer, Roo ended the conversation abruptly with another lie. 'I've gotta bolt, the coach wants to see us all inside. I'll, ah, catchya later.'

Graeme watched the young man favouring his right leg as he jogged over to the changeroom. He was insulted by Roo's quick refusal and by his sudden disappearance. Seemed like every time he had anything to do with the kid, he had to rub it in that his father didn't own him. Cheeky little prick. Same old problem, no respect. The old man would have tanned my hide for that.

Madden watched Roo disappear into the throng of athletes around the locker-room. His son, state champion and criminal. Runaway, thief and athlete. He shook his head. How had he come to have anything to do with this young bloke? Life was never simple.

Several days later, Roo looked out the bus window at the city stiffs crossing Adelaide Street in their six-thousand-dollar clothes and fancy briefcases. His forehead creased in disgust at the idea of working in an office. Some of them weren't much older than he was. How did they stand it? It didn't make sense, he didn't understand why they had to, who it was that made them do it. He gazed at the crowd and knew he would never understand such people, never ever.

The doors hissed open and he hit the street, heading across King George Square. It was busy with people putting up notices about some march or something. He read one on his way past – Palm Sunday, it reckoned. What? There was a chick handing out leaflets, and he took one off her when she proffered it.

'What is it?' he asked.

'Palm Sunday – we're having a peace rally to protest the build-up of troops in the Gulf. And war generally.'

'Palm Sunday ...' Roo laughed out loud and the poster girl gave him a funny look. She didn't get it, eh. It was always Palm Sunday in the square, with the Murries drinking there and the derros. Still laughing, he went on his way, and foolishly wandered close to the metal sculptures where the parkies sat quietly on the grass.

The city people walking through took no notice of this group, just as the city people had no faces to the parkies, either. They were just walking wallets, most of them shut nice and tight. Likely to stay that way, too, especially since the pigs started foot patrols. Roo wondered why the coppers let the drones stay there at all. Very tolerant of the bastards, eh. He hesitated a little too long and one of the younger black men in the group got up and came towards him. Roo swore under his breath.

'Hey, man, you got twodollar? We's hungry, shout us a feed, go on …'

Roo surveyed the flat black hand, its creamy-tan palm creased with dirt, sticking out of the sensationally ugly sleeve of a St Vinnies suit jacket. Wild mop of hair over a dark face, teeth missing and a red triangle of flesh exposed over one eye. He sighed heavily. 'Youse doan wanna feed, yuflajus wanna go for a charge, eh?'

'Nah, we bin chargin las' night, man, we's hungry now. Wanna go for kai over …' The man gestured with his chin towards the Transit Centre.

'Ah gammon, don't fucken bullshit me, bloody kai. Salvo's feed you mob.'

The man just grinned, not bothering to argue.

Roo scratched at the itchy scabs on his scalp, irritated. He was supposed to go and see this inquiry thing, not start sinking piss with blackfellas. Shit. The thing was, he didn't know if he had the right change. If he had a two-dollar coin, he could escape, but if he only had the ten and the five … Who was this cunt anyway? 'What's ya name?' he asked, as he pulled his wallet out in despair.

'Paul.' The man's attention was on Roo's hands. 'You Murri, bro?'

'Nuh, migloo. What's ya last name?'

'Ah Sung.'

When Roo looked more closely he could see a bit of Chinaman in the fella's eyes and face. The name meant nothing to him, but.

'You know, Robbie Ah Sung and them at New Farm?' Seeing Roo's intentions, the man offered extra information. 'Jamie and them?'

'Oh yeah. Look, take this.' Defeated, Roo gave the man all the coins in his wallet, about three bucks worth. He pushed the wallet back in his jeans pocket, giving it an extra hard shove as if that'd make it easier to say 'No' next time.

'Thanks, bud.'

'Yeah, no worries.'

Money in hand, the man buggered off quickly, holding his right hand high to show the others his success. He had already forgotten Roo's existence.

Ten minutes later Roo stood outside Police HQ. He didn't even know where this inquiry was supposed to be, and the idea of walking into the building made him quake. It was pig-land, a total blue-out. He breathed heavily, remembering his bail conditions for the first time in weeks, and was about to give up on the idea when he saw a middle-aged Murri woman in a business suit get out of a taxi. She was carrying a briefcase, and looked as though she was in a hurry as she headed through the heavy glass doors into the building. Without thinking, Roo followed her into the air-conditioning. Warmth hugged his body and he realised how cold he'd been outside.

Inside, a long counter stretched away to his left and a high staircase with silver railings rose on the other side. The black woman flashed an ID badge at the uniformed copper standing at the foot of the stairs, and briskly started climbing. Roo slowed down as he neared the pig. Lucky he had Leena's jumper on, he thought. He looked half respectable when his tats didn't show. His heart was pounding as he fronted the pig.

'Yes?' said the constable suspiciously.

'Ah, can you tell me where the inquiry is?' Roo blurted.

'Which inquiry would that be?' said the cop unhelpfully. 'There's about a million inquiries going on right now.'

'Into Stanley King's death.'

The cop looked coldly at him. More boong-lovers. They were all coming out of the woodwork. 'Third floor.'

'Ta.' Roo was about to bolt past when the cop spoke again.

'You need a security pass to go up there. Have you got one?'

Graeme never said nothin about a pass. Anger spiked in Roo. Looked like Graeme didn't want him to come after all, it was all gammon and he knew they were gonna stop him at the door.

'I lost it.'

'Well, you can't go upstairs without it.' The cop folded his arms. He got about two of these a day, trying to wangle their way in.

'But I lost it!' Roo repeated in distress. You fucken blue-suited prick, standing there like a fucken statue. All of a sudden, his indecision evaporated. He had to see what was happening with Graeme.

'If you haven't got it, I can't let you up there,' the cop repeated automatically.

'Ah, Christ, I can't help it if my wallet got stolen, can I?' Roo blustered.

'If you haven't got a pass, perhaps you should leave the building and come back when you've got another one.'

Roo bit his tongue from asking where to go for one. 'So you're not gonna let me in?', he argued. 'He was my best friend and you're not gonna let me hear what they say about it.'

'It's only for legal representatives and immediate family,' the cop told him smugly. 'So if you ever did have a pass, you shouldn't have been given it in the first place.'

'Jesus Christ,' Roo flared, torn between rage at his powerlessness and a sickening fear of all police. 'Who are you to tell me that I shouldn't be let in anywhere? Anyone'd think it was the fucken Crown Jewels ya had in here instead of a bunch of bloody pigs sucking each other's poxy dicks.'

At which the cop rapidly unfolded his arms, grabbed Roo and propelled him, swearing, out onto the street. 'I wouldn't bother trying again, sunshine,' he told him. 'Not unless you feel like spending a few hours in the cells.'

'Yeah, well, fuck you too, Constable Faggot.' Roo spat the words as the doors shut behind him. He hitched his bag over his shoulder and headed back to town thinking that he was never gonna be able to find out the truth about Graeme. Ah, today sucked. In the circumstances, a bloke felt like a drink and Roo knew just the place to get one.

Graeme stood in line in the police cafeteria, waiting to be served. The inquiry seemed to be going alright for a change, he mused. The Union guy thought it might even be swinging in his favour at long last, but Roo still hadn't showed up. Typical. The uniformed blokes in front of him were talking loudly as they sipped from styrofoam coffee cups. 'Little bastard about eighteen. Sixty million earrings and a crewcut, eh, and he reckons, oh, I lost my security pass. I was like, yeah, right. Outskey.' The man laughed and made a sideways tossing gesture.

Graeme's ears pricked up. He spoke to the man. 'Excuse me mate, I couldn't help hearing what you just said. What was this kid up to? Just that he sounds like a case I'm working on. Skipped bail for an illegal use.'

The man looked at Graeme indifferently. 'Ah, doubt it, mate, it was this young bloke this morning. He wanted to get into the King inquiry. Reckoned he'd lost his pass, but he was just a walk-in. Isn't this the wrong place for a bail-jumper to be hanging around, mate?'

'Yeah, I know mate. Was he solid-built, but? Hazel eyes, short brown hair, about five eleven?'

The other cop nodded slowly. 'Yeah, that's him.

Heaps of earrings. *Shit.*' He got cranky at himself for missing the opportunity to arrest a bail-jumper.

'Ah, well, don't stress too much mate, he's harmless,' Graeme assured the young cop as he paid for his meal and left. So he *did* come after all. Screwed it up, like the fuckup that he was, but his son had tried to come and see him defend himself. Graeme suddenly felt good. He was gonna get off this bullshit charge, and Faith had dropped her restraining order on Friday ('bout time the silly bitch woke up to herself) and if only Roo'd come back and apologise for running out on him, things might maybe, maybe, just work out for once in his fucken life.

Chapter Sixteen

Roo moaned softly. His guts hurt. Worse, someone was sitting on his head, someone large with sharp edges. No, they were holding his head between their hands and squeezing it till his eyes were watering with the pain. Ah, Christ, stop it! Now they were trying to pull his eyelids off. Unwillingly, he opened his eyes. Harsh sunlight flared at him through an unfamiliar, non-institutional window. What? If he wasn't locked up, where was he?

Outside he could hear the traffic rushing past; a city sound. The room itself gave few clues. The door opened onto an unremarkable hall; the window showed him the side of a brick building. There was the grubby single bed he was on, a brown dresser with an ashtray and a couple of newspapers on it, and an old wardrobe. The floor was made of dusty bare wooden boards, some of which were stained dark by anonymous substances. Some sort of doss-house or squat maybe. Bit clean and neat for a squat, but. Could be a hostel. But then why the single room all to himself, hostels usually crammed you in.

He lay on the strange bed trying to make sense of things. He couldn't remember much, just going back to see Paul Ah Sung and him saying he knew where to score some – vomit rose unexpectedly in Roo's throat and he lurched rapidly over to the open window. The effort of throwing up exhausted him, and he hung limp across the window frame, half inside and half out in the cool morning air. Oh boy, here we go again. His veins ran with bile. After a while, he gathered the strength to fall back on the bed. The boy shut his eyes and in three seconds was back asleep.

When he woke again it was late afternoon. Cold air flooded into the room from the open window, and the pain in his head was almost gone. Roo sat on the edge of the bed, puzzled as to how he'd got to this place. Paul said, '*Yeah yandy's choice but speedballs're a fucken blast, man, at twenty bucks apop,*' and he knew a bloke who knew a bloke. And so they'd walked with a couple of others down to the valley, stopping in for a quick drink at the Mall, and then … nothing. It was all dark and blank. Mentally Roo threw his hands in the air. Fuck it. So he blacked out. So what. Wasn't the first time. Maybe he'd OD'd or something and they fucked off and left him. Probably thought he was dead and didn't want the drama, eh. He looked his arms and legs over for injection marks and found what might have been a bruise on the inside of his left elbow. Ah well, shit happens.

He checked his wallet. Empty. Of course. Roo suddenly realised he was starving and had a raging thirst for Coke. He wandered out to the front of the house, warily in case he'd broken in or something. It was barely furnished and apparently deserted. To his relief, Roo saw his Adidas bag sitting on one of the orange kitchen chairs. A fucken miracle. The others must've bolted when they thought he'd bought it. Roo grabbed the bag and fled outside to the street. Ah, so he was in New Farm, eh.

A Night Owl was open conveniently close to the mystery house and Roo limped over to its inviting lights and food. All that walking yesterday seemed to have buggered his leg up again. He noted that the shopkeeper standing behind a rack of chocolate Easter eggs was a small harmless-looking Asian woman. Roo barely gave it a thought beyond whether or not he could get away with it. It wasn't like stealin off your mates or nothin. Roo waited a half a minute for the pair of poofters buying groceries to leave, and then there was no one else in the shop besides him and the woman.

'S'cuse me ...' he said to her. She was wary of him, saying nothing. Well, spose I do look a bit of a crim. 'Some of those biscuits have fallen under the rack over there,' Roo said, mock helpful. The woman rose to where he was pointing. She came out from behind the counter and crouched to see what he was talking about.

One can, two cans, while her back's turned, that'll do. Fast and smooth, he slipped them in his bag along with a packet of Winfield, oh yes! Dry-mouthed and nauseated, Roo went to hurry outside, but the woman made an angry sound.

'You show bag!' she said repeatedly. Roo laughed in her face. Her tone grew more threatening and he walked out fast before he lost his temper and smacked her one. He cracked open the first can, ah sweet. He heard angry slopetalk in the background and grinned again. The coke began to glug down, reviving him. Ah, that's better.

He stopped grinning when two men with sticks came out. The first strike cracked against his skull with a sound like gunshot, and then their heavy sticks descended on his head and arm and ribs with sickening thuds that felt like his body was catching fire where they made contact. The men weren't so much angry as methodical. They didn't speak. They just did their job and didn't blink when Roo began to cry. They hit him six, eight, ten times, and only laid off when the poofters came back and started arguing with them. There was an angry exchange between the four men which allowed Roo to creep, red-spitting, out of the puddle of spilt coke and blood that he was lying in. Heart hammering, half-crying with pain, he propped himself against the glass window of the shop, and found that standing up was definitely out of the question. He shut his eyes and wished for other things.

When the car arrived, the pigs slowly got out adjusting their hats and belts. They were quite relaxed as they stood over him, where he lay shuddering in shock on the footpath, talking to the slopes about junkies and capital punishment. It seemed his blood-spattered, busted face was invisible. When they finally got around to asking him who he was, they discovered that – for the second time that day – Roo didn't know where he was or what he was doing there. They discussed what to do with him, and before he passed out Roo heard them tell the arse bandits that if the kid was only shoplifting they might possibly have let it go at that, but not the aggravated assault on the two blokes, be reasonable.

★

Graeme hung the phone up carefully. Right. Time to play superheroes again, was it? Well, this time he wasn't gonna be taken for a ride. This time they'd do it his way, or they could throw the book at the little shit. He was tired of being taken for the mug in all of this.

Concrete. Ah Jesus me arm, me head. Metal cold on me skin. Heavy material on the walls, quilted beige canvas. More concrete. I'm cold, cold, cold. Another anonymous room to wake up in but not such a happy story this time.

Stainless steel shelf for sleeping on. Headache, a real fucker of a headache. A grey blanket. Everything dimly lit and a padded wall between him and the world. Just his luck to be on the end of the row of six with no view of the waiting room, no view of nothin. Heavy floor-to-ceiling bars at the front of the room. Not room. Cell. *Fuck*.

Roo sat up gingerly, mourning his lost freedom of a few hours ago, and wondering what in God's name he'd done to be put in a padded cell. Wetting a fingertip, he rubbed at his face. Grains of dry blood came away from beneath his nose and ears. He wiped until it felt like it was mostly gone. There was a lump on his head the size of a golf ball, no wonder it fucken hurt. He lay back down and depression lay down with him. What happened this time? Something about the Valley, and a Coke can. Ah, yeah, them Asians with the sticks. That's right. The fucken arseholes.

Lockup. Again. Herschel Street. He hadn't been in here for ages but the grottiness of the old watchhouse was unmistakable. He lay and wondered why bad luck followed him around when it just passed other people by. His thoughts drifted to home – Leena, Mum, and everyone else. He didn't even know what day it was. No idea what them mob'd be doing. Then as he stared at the ceiling Roo had a sudden realisation about where he lay. A kind of gaping horror entered him. He sat up and peered at the graffiti on the walls, hoping and praying he didn't find Stanley's name, dated six weeks ago. He squinted to read in the dim light.

All pigs are fucking lying counts.

A five-pronged marijuana leaf drawn with loving accuracy on the back of the door.

DM.4 BD 4 EVA.

A three-dimensional swastika.

Jacko '89.

West End Niggers Dont go to Heaven or Hell wen they die there dirty Spirits hang around the Boundry Hotel.

ACDC with the lightning slash in the middle.

More swastikas.

F.T.W. (a popular one).

And then, low on the wall near the toilet cistern: *S.K. Broncos Rool.*

Panic oozed up Roo's arms and legs; he stood transfixed in the middle of the cell. Then he began pacing the floor. It coulda bin any old time. It coulda bin from earlier this year. Don't think about it. One two three four turn. How'd he die? One two three four turn. Don't fucken think about it! It was no good. You couldn't control what was in your head. Stanley's face came to him, and enraged, Roo threw his steel bucket against the railings set into the door of his cell. He howled and picked it up and threw it again. The metal clanged dramatically on metal and the noise echoed through the corridor. The duty officer yelled out to him to shut the fuck up or there'd be trouble. Roo didn't give a shit – he threw the bucket again. Even though it hurt his head, it felt good. BANG. BANG. He didn't give a fuck anyway. Why should he? What was to care about?

Then the prisoner next door yelled out, telling him to settle down, that he'd be alright. When he heard him, Roo nearly fell over on the concrete floor.

'Jimmy! That you Jimmy?'

'Yeah,' wary in case of being set up. 'Who's that?'

'Roo.' He couldn't believe it. Although, then again, the amount of time Jimmy spent inside …

'Roo.' It was a flat sound. Roo was too surprised to hear trouble, too pleased at hearing a familiar voice.

'Yeah. How long ya been in for? What they pick ya up on?'

'Trifecta.'

'True, yeah, me too probly. I got knocked out, I dunno. Plus stealin, I reckon. But listen, these Asians, they owned this shop, eh, and they bashed the fucken shit outta me, eh, two of em, big guys, and when booliman come—'

Roo spilt his story out. When he finished there was an unfriendly silence. Then Jimmy said, 'So?'

Roo shrivelled. 'Whaddya mean, so? So that's what happened.' His headache suddenly got worse.

When Jimmy spoke, his voice shook with anger. 'You fucken knock my cousin up, ya white dog, and take off on her, and then you expect me to give a fuck what happens? I hope they string ya up. It shoulda bin you what died, not Stanley.'

Roo swallowed, his eyes pricked by sudden ridiculous tears. There was nothing to say to this.

Jimmy continued in much the same vein for five or six minutes. Much of what he said centred on Stanley and the fact of his death at the hands of whitefellas like Roo. Then there was a silent spell lasting almost twice as long. Roo lay on the bed, numbed, in the foetal position; mostly while Jimmy was talking he held his arms over his ears. Shaleena, Graeme and Stanley took turns visiting his cell. He paced the cell and his head hurt. He lay down and his head stopped hurting, but then the faces came back. Up and down, up and down. Faces. Angry, accusing faces in the walls, the ceiling. Leave me *alone*!

'But, ah, ya lucky, Roo!' called Jimmy sarcastically from next door, starting up again, recycling his lifetime of hate. 'You've got the penthouse suite there, man, that's the Death Cell, eh. That's where they done it. Took that goonah paper and wet it and plaited it up nice and tight while Stanley watched em – ya migloo mates I mean. He seen em alright. He was yellin out while they put it round his neck, see, that's the story I got told, and they got stuck right into him then. Put the boot in good and proper and then slung it round the toilet tap under there. He managed to hang himself six inches off the ground, eh. And they reckon blackfellas are stupid! Can ya just imagine his eyes sticken out, there, just there, eh, near ya toilet there, just think what he woulda bin thinkin while they was—'

'Ah what a loada bullshit, the autopsy never said nothin about hangin,' replied Roo, horrified. 'And he was in ere, by himself, too, so how the fuck'd you know what happened? Eh? No one knows.' Except Graeme and one other bloke, he didn't add. It's bullshit, more of Jimmy's lies. Don't listen. He's lying.

'The autopsy never said nothin about hangin,' Jimmy mocked him in a little kid's voice. 'Never said nothin 'bout murder neither, you dumb white fuck—'

'Ah just fucken shut up willya Jimmy.' Roo couldn't take this much longer.

'Eyes stickin out and them kickin 'im and kickin 'im ...'

'Fucken shuttup! Just fucken shuttup or I'll fucken smash ya mouth in.' The faces spiralled around Roo. Leena, Graeme, Darryl and Stanley. Lying there, two feet from where he sat. He turned and faced the other wall. Lying there ... my father. Sins of the father shall be visited. Roo started crying silently into his hands.

'And that pig that done it, Madden or whatever his name is, yeah, they reckon he was jumpin up and down on his chest while he was hangin off there, eh—'

'I'm not listenin to ya, I'm not listenin!' Roo screamed. He started throwing his bucket against the bars again, this time to drown out the sound of Jimmy's voice. Tears streaked down his bloodied face as he clanged it over and over. After a couple of minutes he was exhausted and fell onto the bed, close to passing out. He hadn't eaten for twenty-four hours. Traces of speed still swam in his bloodstream.

'Dunno what you're worried about,' sang out

Jimmy merrily. 'He was just a coon, just a boong, just a blackfella. Nothin to you mob. Youse can knock us off like fucken – hahahahaha – like roos!' Jimmy found this witticism very funny.

'You don't shut the fuck up I'm gonna come in there and wrap those fucken footy socks round ya neck, ya black bastard.' But it wasn't Roo speaking. It was the duty officer who'd wandered down to check out what all the noise was about.

'Ya wanna fucken try, mate,' Jimmy taunted him. 'I'll be back to hauntya. Wooo-ooo-oooo!' Past caring what happened to him, he waved his arms, goggled his eyes and made ghost noises.

'Just keep the noise down, ya black cunt, if you want any breakfast,' said the officer, walking away. He flashed his torch quickly into Roo's cell and saw him crying, but to Roo's relief said nothing about it.

Roo lay still, praying that Jimmy would take notice of the screw. Not that he probably would. He resolved to ignore him, not react to his provocations. Just lie there and forget everything and start to do the time. Same old fucken story. Waiting.

Jimmy had stopped tormenting him, intentionally anyway. He sang instead, country and western off the radio.

And the biggest disappointment in the family was me,
The only twisted branch upon that good old family tree,
I just couldn't be the person they expected me to be-e-e,
And the biggest disappointment in the world was me ...

Desperately tired underneath the last traces of speed, Roo finally managed to force himself into sleep. It felt like it was about an hour later that he woke to the sounds in the waiting room. He stared dully at the ceiling. In the cage again. You *loser.*

'Thass MurriWatch there come ta get me,' Jimmy suddenly boasted, 'So your white mates can't fucken string me up too.'

'More's the pity,' Roo muttered, wishing that the screws would go in and bash Jimmy into silence. He'd do it himself, given half a chance. Now that he'd slept his head wasn't killing him as much. But he was way hungrier and now there was less pain to cloud his immense self-loathing. You stupid fuck, he castigated himself. You had it all, ya had a family and a woman and a place to live and ya threw it away for nothin. Darryl woulda done anything for ya, Leena too, and look what you've gone and done. No wonder Mum kicked ya out. He bit his lip, feeling with sudden horror that he was going to start sobbing.

Then it happened again. Graeme did his magical appearing trick, towing the duty officer beside him. He had a talent for it alright, popping up outta nowhere. Roo leaned back against the far wall of the cell, stirred to terror by Jimmy's stories.

'You must like being locked up, do ya?' Graeme asked sourly through the bars of the door. He told himself his sarcasm was for the benefit of the duty officer.

Roo gulped; he couldn't say anything. Darryl whispered in his ear: *He's going to kill you. He hates you, man. He's going to come in this cell and put them big hands around your skinny neck and …*

'Well?' Graeme said.

From the next cell Jimmy requested a stretch limo to take him to the casino. He was universally ignored.

The duty officer shone his torch straight in Roo's face – blackened eyes; rivers of dry blood, smeared where he thought he'd cleaned himself up; hair matted with blood. Roo trembled in the beam of bright light.

'Jesus,' said Graeme, 'What happened to you?'

'I got flogged up.' There was no self-pity in his voice. Fear made Roo defiant. *Think I'm gonna crawl to you, think again, mate.*

'Well, I'm sure you no doubt deserved it.' Graeme said harshly, assuming the cops had done it. He shifted his weight and folded his arms to ask the next question. 'So are you still too high and fucken mighty to talk to me, or are you seeing the world in a different light all of a sudden?'

The massive metal door that stood between them – between Roo and the whole rest of the world – was the thickness of a man's spread hand.

We're gonna call it Stanley if it's a boy.

Set up.

Is that white cunt gorn yet?

Set up.

It shoulda been you that died, not Stanley.

Set up.

It took him four heartbeats to decide. 'I'll talk to ya,' Roo said. 'I talked to ya the other day,' he added, attempting to salvage a crumb of pride.

'Just get him out,' Graeme said to the constable.

★

205

Roo stumbled out into the corridor behind the two cops. He turned and put both his hands on the floor-to-ceiling bars of Jimmy's cell. He was careful to hide his rage from Graeme. The power Roo would happily have put into killing Jimmy went into his words instead. He leaned close to the bars. There was no emotion in his voice.

'I'm gonna fuck you up, Jimmy,' he said very gently. 'You hear me, you lying cunt? I'm gonna fuck you right up.' Jimmy's eyes narrowed, but before he had time to respond, Roo let go of the bars and walked up the corridor to the brightly lit waiting room.

'Paperwork's done, is it?' Graeme asked the nervous young Duty Officer.

'Yea-ah, but …' The constable wasn't too sure about releasing Roo into Graeme's custody.

Graeme took pity on the greenhorn. 'Consider it an order, son.'

The constable sighed with relief and tucked his papers back into the folder on the desk.

'Okay, let's go,' Graeme said to Roo as he threw him his sports bag. The flying weight of the bag nearly toppled him. He stumbled backwards against the wall, his face ashen under the dirt and blood.

'What's wrong with you?' Graeme asked. 'Apart from terminal stupidity, I mean?'

'I got the shit bashed outta me,' Roo answered. 'And I'm starving.'

The man's eyebrows rose. The kid did look pretty rooted. 'Well, the car's over at the Railway, it's only five minutes' walk. You can have a bath and a feed at home, before we discuss your … lifestyle.'

I need something to eat, Roo thought. I gotta eat or I'll faint. *Don't faint.* He couldn't in front of Graeme. He was stricken with shame at being locked up again; how could he ask for more than his freedom? But I gotta eat, I gotta.

One painful limping step at a time, he followed his father out of the watchhouse yard. It was dark and cold outside. The sun had long set behind the high pillars of the skyscrapers, and the moon was a thin yellow sliver behind thick cloud. Follow him, keep up. *Don't faint.* Gotta eat.

All of a sudden, not far beyond the wire mesh fence of the watchhouse yard, Graeme stopped. 'Wait here.'

What, thought Roo, in sharp irritation, leaving me here to fucken starve to death on George Street? The big man walked briskly back towards the watchhouse, his breath condensing against the night air, and re-emerged holding a police torch. 'Let's go.'

Graeme waited impatiently at the traffic lights across from the Transit Centre. Something was bugging him, Roo realised through a fog of pain and hunger. The big man fidgeted, running his car keys through his fingers. Probably shit off cos he had to come and get me. Shit off his son's a crim. Shit off he's missing something good on that big flash TV of his.

'C'mon, hurry up, will'ya?'

Roo was lagging behind. He tabulated his woes. Strained tendon. Busted nose. Arm wrenched and bruised. Head feeling like a horse kicked it. And hunger you wouldn't believe. Roo found himself looking at the street for scraps of food. An apple core. An unfinished lollypop stick. Anything.

'C'mon, it's on, *walk!*' Graeme said. 'Let's go!'

Roo made an enormous effort and managed to speed up a little. His head throbbed like an amplifier. As they crossed the road and entered the small park next to the Transit Centre, Graeme flicked the torch button but no beam of light broke the dark shadows around them. I gotta eat, thought Roo. *Don't faint.*

'Ah, fuck it!' Graeme shook the torch, banged it against his thigh. It was still no good.

'The batteries must have had it,' Roo suggested weakly.

Graeme unscrewed the end of the torch and swore some more. 'Nah, it's been broken for weeks. I told them to fix it that many times, the lazy bastards, but they just bring their own to work instead.' Graeme shook his head as he began to put the torch back together. Lazy cops, they shit him to tears. 'That could've been important, you know,' he commented angrily, tilting the tube at Roo. 'A torch left like that, that little bit of effort it woulda taken—'

'We don't need it really,' Roo said in a thin voice. The shadowy street was dim but hardly the kind of pitch black that left you at risk of falling over stuff and breaking a leg. Graeme had some sort of paranoia about the dark. He wouldn't even go and put the garbage bins out if the sun was down. That's why he kept the house lit up like a birthday cake. Roo wasn't surprised. Even if Graeme hadn't killed Stanley there'd be plentya other things on his conscience to make demons out of. There'd be other ghosts on his mind.

'That's not the point.' Graeme snapped. 'They're a

packalazy—' He stopped abruptly. Ya didn't slag off cops to crims. To anyone, 'cept other cops.

Roo made a face – don't be such a fucken uptight white – but Graeme was hurrying him to the end of the railway yard. The car was in the far corner, standing at an angle to the white painted lines that marked the car spaces. He musta been in a hurry when he parked. Roo felt a bit strange about that – he was hurrying to get me outta lockup. Like he cared where I was, what I was doing. That's … nice.

'Why din'ya park at the cop station?' he asked. 'Or the watchhouse?'

'Forgot me access card,' Graeme said tersely. 'This was the only space I could find for miles. This …' gesturing to the empty car park, 'was all chocka block half an hour ago. I'll give ya the drum, pal, it took a fair talk to get ya out this time.' He unlocked the car.

Roo fell in and lay breathing heavily across the back seat. The silent drive to the house at Mount Gravatt took fifteen minutes. Roo scarcely noted as they turned into the street that someone had taken out the signpost on the comer.

Tell-tale skid marks veered up onto the grass footpath. The steel bar of the signpost was bent close to the ground; Circle Street had lost its 'l' and now read Circ-e.

'Look at that.' Graeme grunted, unimpressed. 'Woman driver, I bet. And it'll take em six months to put up a new one.' Just as well a bloke's not trying to sell his house, eh?

At the house, Roo got out and put an unsteady hand on Wimpy's smooth bony head. It took Graeme five minutes to disarm the security system. *Don't faint.*

Eons later, Graeme unlocked the front door. Roo wobbled to the fridge. He ate where he stood, more than he knew it was possible for a human to eat – cold baked beans out of the tin, chocolate, hunks of cheese, an old lamb chop, milk out of the container, meatballs, an old bit of apricot pie with drying yellowed cream on top. He crammed it in like he was a refugee; not chewing, not tasting, just biting the food into swallowable pieces as if it were medicine, and then moving on to the next thing.

Graeme stood watching, swigging from a Fourex can. He watched his battered starving son, and mingled with his anger was an inexplicable sense of obscure nagging shame.

CHAPTER SEVENTEEN

'You're bloody filthy.' Graeme said when Roo finally stopped gorging. 'You better have a shower. Do ya want some clean clothes?'

'Yeah.'

'I wanna see ya before ya go to bed.' Graeme added heavily. Before anything else goes wrong. See if we can put the brakes on whatever is happening here. Jesus. What did I do to deserve this crap?

Roo went to shower while Graeme threw some clean things onto the spare bed, then went back and opened another beer. The red light was flashing on his answering machine; it was Faith. Crying as usual, only this time cos Pete had snuffed it at last.

'Pete died an hour ago. He was ... unconscious, so it wasn't... he wasn't in too much pain (sob). Margie's in shock though, I think. I've gotta go and see her now. Give us a call in the morning if you want. Bye.'

Graeme frowned. He didn't like the sound of that much. No mention of when she was coming back. Bloody Marg better not take over from Pete as the excuse, now he was dead. So he'd gone at last, the poor bastard. Graeme upended his stubby. Made you think, eh? Dead at forty-two. This time last year he was playing B-grade baseball, and now. Just goes to show, if your time's up, your time's up, and there's nothing you can do about it. Ah, well, crying about it wasn't gonna bring him back, was it?

Graeme had that empty feeling inside that you got when people died, that feeling that life had slipped sideways on you, but he pushed it down and it didn't take very long to fade away to nothingness. Deep down he was shocked that he felt anything. Dead bodies had been all in a day's work for him; after a few months, like everyone else, you got to the point where it was only hard if it was a little kid. That, and telling the families, and he was the family in this case, so ...

He shrugged mentally. Ah, fuck it. No point worrying about Pete. Wasn't gonna bring him back, was it?

Shortly afterwards, Roo limped into the lounge, clean and dressed in his father's loose clothes. His face wasn't too bad now that the blood was gone.

'You look a bit more presentable than you did an hour ago,' said Graeme.

'I feel a bit better,' said Roo truthfully, as he sat down. Headache was the worst thing, the remnants of the fucker that felt like it'd split his head inside.

'What're ya limping for?'

'Buggered an old injury up,' said Roo. 'Tendonitis in my knee. I probably need a reconstruction or something.' He sat with his legs drawn up in the mock leather armchair, smoking, wondering how he was going to find out the truth he needed from this hard man. He had a sudden sense of deja vu. A few weeks ago he was sitting in this very seat, bailed from Holland Park. Only this time he had a better idea who he was dealing with. This time the element of surprise wasn't waiting to snare him and leave him gasping with horror. He knew – sort of – what his father was. He hoped.

Graeme pursed his lips and exhaled heavily at the sight of his son. Roo had a cut lip that would heal quickly, and a black eye that wouldn't. Sitting there smoking calm as you please, looking like it was him that wanted a few answers, like it was Graeme in the wrong. What was there to do with a kid like that? A champion runner and yet a total fuck-up off the track. Like Mike Tyson, and a thousand footy players you could name, and that weightlifting guy, too, the one that sold dope after he'd won Commonwealth gold.

'Well, mate, you wouldn't have to be a university graduate to figure out I'm not very impressed.' He began reading the Riot Act. 'I don't want to have to fucken come and bail ya out every couple of weeks, you know? Apart from anything else this is becoming an expensive bloody habit, and—'

He broke off suddenly as Roo stood up and looked out the window at the streaming traffic.

'Are you listening to me?' Graeme demanded, fists bunching.

Roo folded his arms and turned around to face his father where he sat. Somewhere in that padded cell, looking at the initials Stanley had scratched onto the canvas before he died, he had discovered what it was he

213

really wanted. No more bullshit. No more lies. He stared at Graeme, deaf to the lecturing, oblivious to his body screaming for painkillers and sleep.

'I want to know what happened. That night in the watchhouse, with Stanley. What really happened?'

'Am I just wasting my …' Graeme spluttered.

Roo ignored this tangent, this … irrelevance. His strength was inexplicably growing. Knowing the truth would free him, either way. Saints and sinners. 'Tell me what happened to Stanley King.'

'I've told you.' Graeme was exasperated. 'He hit his head in the park, and when we locked him up he … he passed out, and then he died in the ambulance. How many times do I have to say it?'

'Did you bash him? Or anyone else?' *Did you force a noose of plaited toilet paper around his neck and jump on his chest while he strangled to death?*

'No, I didn't bash him.' Graeme put the word 'bash' in inverted commas, then halted. When he spoke again there was a different, lower note in his voice. 'I gave him a good clout around the ear cos the little cunt deserved it.'

'At the park.' It was a question. Roo was darkly silhouetted against the freeway.

'No, after that … Look, will you fucken siddown? What is this?'

'Just tell me what happened.' Roo remained on his feet. There was too much at stake here.

Graeme swore in frustration as he lit a cigarette. He was shitty enough not to offer Roo one. 'We picked him up at the park because he was hassling the people driving past, chucking bottles at cars and stuff. Then when we went in to pinch him, he hit the back of his head on the gutter, resisting arrest. When we got to the watchhouse, he mouthed off at me again for about the millionth time, after he spewed up and shit himself, and I just snapped, alright? I'd just had to clean his shit up, and I'd had enough of the little bastard. I thought, right, you ...' Graeme drew on his cigarette. It sounded bad. It sounded *wrong*. 'It wasn't ...' he stopped.

'So you did bash him?' Roo pressed the point. Even though he felt sick as he looked at the size of his father and remembered Stanley's bone-thin arms and legs, his chicken-neck, it was almost a relief to hear it. The truth. Graeme rolled his tongue in his cheek, staring for a long moment into the middle distance.

'I didn't 'bash' him,' he finally said. 'I smacked him across the face a coupla times, I got him in the chest once, I was aiming for his face. I belted him then, and I'd belt him now. He was a useless smart-mouthed little boong cunt and if you think otherwise ya fucken dreamin.' Graeme's face was ugly with the memory. 'But I didn't kill him. He wasn't bashed any worse than he woulda been a thousand times before. No worse than you are now. Alright? And you're not dead.'

Graeme enunciated the next words with exaggerated clearness. 'I – Didn't – Kill – Him. There's blokes in the force want to see me go down, so they're not backing me up, that's what this inquiry's all about. And that's the truth, so take it or leave it, pal.' Graeme fell silent. He fiddled with the glass ashtray, slowly rotating it on the tabletop between his thumb and fingers while his eyes wandered around the room. Waiting.

Relief blossomed inside Roo. It sounded true. Graeme had belted Stanley around but didn't kill him. He could live with that. It made sense. Of course he'd bashed him, but bashing was … it wasn't nothing, it sucked, yeah, but so what. Get locked up you expected it. Like him and the slopes, them's the breaks, eh. No good fucken whingeing about it. Roo began to relax. And as for Jimmy and that bullshit about them hanging him, well, Jimmy was a well-known lying dog who'd wind him up for the fun of it. Roo wouldn't forget Jimmy in a hurry. He'd meant what he said in the watchhouse. He gave his father a sideways glance.

'But, well, what killed Stanley then?'

Graeme was left breathless for a split second. He believed him!

'That's what the fucken coroner's supposed to find out, and the jury's out on that one still. Ah, look' – his confidence growing by the second – 'will you look at the facts. He was pissed out of his brain, he was smoking dope and probably popping pills too. He hit his head at least twice that day, hit it hard before he even saw the inside of a cell. For all I know he was drinking bloody metho in the park. You know, it's not a good look. It was just fucken my bad luck he decided to drop that night; he could have died any time. And if that's not good enough for ya,' Graeme told him, 'I dunno what to say, except you know where the door is. I'm sick of this. If you don't believe me …' He gave the smallest of indifferent shrugs and stared at Roo, blown out that he – Graeme Madden, copper for fifteen going on sixteen years – had been put on trial yet again, when it was Roo who was the crim

216

that just got out of lockup. How did he do it?

Turning and facing the window, Roo slowly nodded his assent to the streaming cars which thrust their way along the black snake of the freeway. He saw Stanley, slack with grog, fall and hit his head on the gutter. He saw his eyes roll up in his head momentarily, and a bloodburst begin to unwind in the boy's brain. He saw Graeme toss him into the paddy-wagon, unknowingly adding to his fate. He imagined Stanley in his cell, briefly conscious, and then pain searing through his head, and darkness falling onto that thin face.

A terrible burden fell away from him.

'No,' he said in wonder to the turbulent night outside, 'I believe you.'

Chapter Eighteen

Several days passed, and Roo cautiously investigated what it meant to have a home. It definitely had its attractions. There was always plenty of food in the fridge, for one thing, not to mention the wide-screen TV and a video shop on the corner. He had access to a phone and he rang Newcastle with Graeme's permission on Hayley's birthday. Graeme even reckoned that if he made an *effort* and got a *job,* he'd pay to hook them up to Foxtel, and Roo was still thinking about that one, turning the world sideways to do so. Work. Like a straight. He'd seen one of Graeme's payslips when he was reluctantly doing the washing one time ('You can do the housework to pay for your board till you start making some real money,' said in a tone of magnanimity that hid Graeme's hatred of woman's work), and the staggering amount of money you got for showing up five days a week had left him reeling. Made a bloke think again about getting a job; it might be worth it after all. Roo had known fellas in John Oxley do armed robs and come away with less, the dumb try-hard cunts.

His life was different in this new place called home – different but for the most part satisfactory. And after a while Roo even reached tentative fingertips out towards the idea of *father*. Certainly Graeme considered himself that. It was easy for him, Roo mused with a tinge of bitterness. No problem – kid shows up, he's the kid you adopted out, no problem, he's yer son. So he's a bit of a crim, but he's a champion runner too, so that evens it out. Sweet. Bit harder on this end but. You find the old man you've looked for, well maybe not actually looked for, but thought about lookin for, anyway, wondered about as you lay in bed and looked through bars a thousand million times, wondering where is he, where's the bastard now, is he alive or dead? Why'd they give ya away, why didn't they want ya, what's wrong with ya? What's the matter with ya? Not so easy to rock up and start hugging him like nothing happened, eh? Roo held a good part of himself back on those rare occasions when he used the words *Father, Family, Dad*.

Most of the time Graeme was blustery with good humour towards his son, chaffing him about his running, fairly silent about his crimes. Sometimes Roo could see him straining not to snap. ('Pick ya towels up off the floor when ya finished with them, eh Roo?' 'Don't leave empty smoke packets around the house, son, they won't pick themselves up.') While they were doing stuff, or the TV was showing them another world to separate their different lives, the two men were fine. Sometimes though, the inquiry would bring Graeme back to Circ-e Street grim-faced and tense, and on those nights Roo stayed out of his way till he'd had a few beers. But whether they were doing the grocery shopping, or cacking themselves at *Australia 's Funniest Home Videos,* or boasting to each other that 'they would! they really would!' do what the bloke on *Who Dares Wins* challenged, one thing didn't ever change.

They never mentioned Stanley.

Roo soaped the last of his yellow fading bruises – arms, ribs, upper thigh – under the hot jetting streams of Graeme's shower. He shampooed his hair, and found that the last of the scabs from the possum scratches had softened and disappeared. His scalp was smooth under his probing fingertips. Even the lump given to him by the Asians had shrunk to a minor raised spot, no longer tender. He tested his leg and found it didn't hurt to put all his weight on it, bent. That meant it was almost time to go back to training.

He groaned to himself. The coach had given him time off on the basis of tendonitis after the state titles and his two weeks' grace were drawing to an end. Good timing, Roo told himself sourly. If you're gonna get bashed up, do it in the Easter holidays. At least he didn't have to make up some bullshit for the coach about why he could hardly move for two days. For the first time since it happened, Roo wondered if he should have gone to the hospital, had a head scan or something, but it was too late now anyway. It'd be right. The headaches were gone.

He stepped out and dried himself on a fluffy white towel which he carefully remembered to pick up and hang on the railing. Then Roo wandered nude down the hall to the spare room, in no hurry to get dressed. Suddenly energised by the shower, he took off sprinting to the end of the house, his dick swinging wildly from side to side as he ran. He touched the end wall and sprinted back to the lounge, where he puffed for breath in front of the picture window. He lowered himself onto the carpet and did twenty-five fast push-ups, then rolled onto his muscular back, heaving. The flogging he got at the shop hadn't done him any lasting damage. Lucky, Graeme had said, and Roo felt it. Lucky to be out of stir, lucky not to have been badly broken, lucky to have a home and a father who ... who what? Who cared?

Lying there on the lounge room floor as he got his wind back, Roo remembered that he was young, and strong, and that he could manage his life. Had the curse lifted? Maybe Darryl had been right about the Buddhist shit, 'bout doing nothin and it'd be okay.

It'll be okay, he said aloud to himself, testing the sanity of this unlikely proposition. A faint smile broke across his face. *It'll be okay.* Yeah. Maybe it would at that.

That afternoon Graeme's Commodore turned into the drive just before six-thirty. He's early, thought Roo as he saw Wimpy welcoming the man with a waggling stumpy tail.

'Shouldn't you be at training?' Graeme greeted the lad as he came in the door. 'You could always go and watch ya know.'

Roo made a face. 'Tomorrow.'

It was sweet. Wiseman had told Coach he was in the team less than half an hour after the race so there was no need to stress out about it. His father was in a good mood, so Roo risked asking: 'How'd it go today?'

Graeme's mouth twisted up on one side, and he shook his head. When he spoke, he had prisoner's eyes. 'Dunno, really. You think it's alright, and then … they pull something else out, or someone says something and it comes out wrong on your side. You should come along and check it out, you know. But we won't really know what's going on till Thursday. Bill come over to me at my desk this arv and says, "Well mate, it's not over till the fat lady sings," so whether that's good or bad, you tell me. What did you do with yourself today?'

'Went down the job place,' said Roo. It was true. Centrelink was onto him about his benefit, now, as well as Graeme. Anyone'd think he was taking money out of starving babies mouths by being on the fucken dole.

'Find anything?'

'Oh, not much. They wanted some people up in Gladstone, fish cleaners and that for this new fish canning place, but they wanted you to have Year Twelve.'

'To fucken clean fish?' Graeme couldn't believe it. 'Ah, you don't wanna go to Gladstone, anyway,' he stated casually. 'It's a dump.'

'Oh, I dunno. It might be alright, me and Leena used to talk about going up to North Queensland to her relations' place. Coconut trees. Bikini girls and all that.' Roo grinned and Graeme's heart grew heavy. If Roo left and Faith didn't come back soon …

He argued the case. 'Yeah, and a billion Jap tourists

jabbering away at you. Why don't you settle down a bit, just hang around Brisbane? You'll find a job here if you really want one, there's always jobs if ya want work.' What the kid needed, he thought, was another girlfriend to settle him down. Shouldn't be hard, a good-looking kid like that. Should have birds crawling all over him.

'Yeah ... oh, I dunno what I'll do. I've got the Australian titles to worry about first.' Roo was offhand. Who gave a fuck? Why was Graeme always on his case about work? A million bloody Australians outta work and he acted like he was the only one.

'Well, why don't ya stick around till the inquiry's over anyway? No point moving in if you're just gonna take off again straightaway,' Graeme said, frowning. 'Make this your fixed address and organise yourself a job, try and make something out of your life. That's the way to stay outta jail, you know. It's true, the devil makes work for idle hands.'

Roo lifted his eyebrows and drew a breath in. It shit him when Graeme tried to run his life; on the other hand it was the first time Graeme had come right out and actually asked Roo to stay. *He really wants me here,* thought Roo.

'I'm not going back to jail,' he declared with great certainty. 'Fuck that. Just I, ah, thought you'd be getting sick of me by now, eh.' The light tone belied the effort the words cost him, the risk of them. Here's the knife, Dad, do your worst.

'Happy to have ya here, mate.' Graeme blinked as he spoke, and he instantly turned away, unnecessarily shuffling newspapers and magazines into even neater piles. 'And don't worry about Faith, she'll be sweet too,' he added, hoping it was true.

'Oh. Well, maybe I'll stick around for a bit longer,' said the young man in surprise.

Graeme smiled ruefully at him and swallowed the lump in his throat. 'Attaboy. Hang around for the next week. Then if the Internal Investigations clear me we'll be set, and if they don't I may as well go and knock meself anyway, eh, so you won't have to worry about me.' He forced a half-grin as he went to get changed.

He emerged from the bedroom wearing shorts and running shoes. 'How about a jog around the block? I need to take Wimpy for a run before she starts eating the local grommets.'

Roo laughed at the man jogging on the spot. Check the old man in his ancient Easts singlet and crappy white Reeboks, what a shamejob.

'What's so funny?' Graeme protested. 'I might be your father but I'm still bloody fitter than most forty-year-olds around the place.' He examined his gut carefully for evidence of flab.

'Yeah, yeah, yeah.' Roo replied, switching on the TV and splaying his legs in their skin-tight new black jeans they'd bought up at Garden City. God Graeme was funny sometimes. Always trying to go one better than him about stuff. Booze, fights, running. He had to be badder than any other bastard around. Bit like Jimmy really. Mostly Roo just humoured the man, but Graeme was still puffed up, challenging him.

Graeme pushed against the wall, stretching his

Achilles tendons. 'Go on. I reckon I could keep up with ya over, oh, four hundred metres.'

'Oh, dream, old man!' said his son incredulously. 'I beat Dave Bedouri on an off day once.'

'So ... whaddya scared of?' said Graeme recklessly, ignoring Roo's reference to the former state champion, 'I bet ... I bet you ...' He trailed off as he realised Roo had nothing of value to bet except the new clothes he'd bought him himself. Not much sport in taking that back, as if he really wanted a pair of suede skateboarding shoes, or a Public Enemy T-shirt anyway.

The young man looked over at his father. 'Okay, let's make this interesting,' he said. 'I bet you a fortnight's washing up that you can't keep up with me from the front gate to the shops. That's about four hundred.' He got to his bare feet and went out onto the veranda. There's a sucker born every day. Shoulda said a month.

'What, dressed like that?' Graeme queried. Roo wore jeans and a denim jacket.

'It's not the clothes, it's what's in em.' Roo quoted his coach. 'I've done the hard yards, mate – have you?'

Graeme just snorted and led Wimpy out onto the deserted footpath. The concrete was cold under Roo's bare toes, and he jumped from foot to foot. Wimpy pawed the air with her front legs, yowling with excitement.

'Wanna headstart?' Roo offered, finding a seam of kindness in himself.

'Do you?' Graeme shot back. The kid snorted.

'Ready?'

Roo nodded in disbelief. He had to be *dreaming*.

'Set, go!'

The two of them spurted down the hill. Roo let the older man think he was doing okay – and he was, really, for an old guy – until they were close enough to read the number plates of the cars parked next to the shops. Then he gave Graeme a vicious grin and accelerated. Wimpy bounded along beside him, stretched into a long flat blur of dog.

'You're right,' he said deadpan when the man arrived, 'I shoulda got changed. These jeans slow me down something shockin, eh.'

Graeme grunted at him, blowing hard, then went inside the shop, and came out with a packet of fags and some groceries they didn't particularly need. The little smartarse was too good. Graeme wasn't sure if he was proud or pissed off to be beaten so soundly. His son, Brisbane's answer to Ben Jonson.

'You reckon you're pretty fit, do ya?' he asked when he went back outside to the boy and the dog. Roo bounced on the spot, then lifted his knees fast, speeding on the spot. Skin agleam with sweat, he was the picture of good health and fitness. He was exuberant, pumped by the run.

'You said it, man!'

'Well if you're so fit you can carry this stuff back to the house then. Spare a poor old bloke the effort.' Handing over tins of baked beans, soup, dog food. Roo moaned melodramatically as he felt the weight of the bags.

'Oh man, what did ya last fucken slave die of?' he moaned.

Graeme smirked as he took Wimpy's lead out of his hand and headed to the park.

'Insubordination.'

★

The next morning Graeme pulled the sleeves of his dark blue suit down over his shirt cuffs. The bloody thing felt like a straightjacket. He undid three buttons and frowned at the expanse of white shirt that billowed out in front of him. Alarmed, he checked in the mirror. It was okay, he told himself, he wasn't fat but ... he buttoned the jacket up again, and – again – found it to be uncomfortably tight. Even – he wriggled his shoulders – even the arms were too tight. So it wasn't that he was *fat,* he'd just put on size. All over. He was eighty-five kilos, but solid kilos, hard kilos. That was different to fat, wasn't it? He tensed his mouth in dissatisfaction as he got undressed and, casting a longing look at his uniform, put on his cheaper grey suit instead. Well, he reasoned, the navy suit was, how old? He couldn't remember when Faith had brought it home, but he'd worn it to Scooby's wedding, which made it at least five years old, if not more. No wonder it was a bit tight under the armpits. Once he had his other suit on Graeme relaxed. Not bad. He smoothed his hair and felt his chin. Not bad for an old guy. Then he had a sudden idea that made him smile.

'Hey Roo!' Kid preferred being called that, he said. His son's head appeared around the door. 'You still coming?'

'Ye-eah.' Now that he had Graeme to get him past the gatekeeper.

'Try this on for size.' He threw the blue suit at the lad.

Roo caught it with an expression as incredulous as it was alarmed. 'What?'

'Go on. Try looking respectable for a change.'

Roo held the jacket up to the light. It was dark navy

blue, almost black. He pursed his lips and held his head to one side. Suits were stiffsville, only … Will Smith wore one in *Men In Black* and he was one cool nigga. He tilted his head the other way, uncertain. John Travolta wore a suit in *Get Shorty*. John Lee Hooker wore a suit. He frowned uncertainly.

'Go on!' Graeme urged. 'That's a good suit. It cost three hundred bucks, and that was years ago. If it fits, you can wear it to Court, too. Save yourself a bit of time.'

Bemused, Roo disappeared into his room. He carefully took out all but one gold earring. He put on a plain black t-shirt. The trousers were loose around the waist, but notching his belt in a couple of holes solved that. His hair was newly cropped, his shoulder muscles stood out under the tee, and his hard butt was tight in the long pants that fell in satisfactorily loose folds to the floor. He spun in front of the mirror, being a Bee Gee without knowing.

He slipped his arms into the jacket and drew it up onto his shoulders, buttoning it easily. It fitted him like a glove. He stared at the mirror. Bulk excellent. It wasn't him. It was … it was Graeme Madden's son, that's who it was. The son he really wanted, the one who'd never done time, who'd finished school, who had a job and a girlfriend and a life. Roo checked himself from side to side, worrying that he looked too straight. Finally, he put another earring into the same ear. There. Perfect.

When he showed himself to Graeme in the loungeroom, they both burst out laughing. Graeme looked at Roo's feet.

'Want a pair of shoes?' Cop shoes.

He flinched. 'Nah. My skating shoes'll do.' Black suede ones from the surfie shop in town.

Graeme nodded. 'Better get cracking, eh? I don't want to be late.' It was getting near the end of the inquiry, and each day he was coming home a little tenser, and a little later.

They drove into town. At the foot of the staircase this time the young cop didn't blink as Graeme waved his pass in the air. The dickhead didn't even recognise him, Roo realised in amazement. Straight clothes – they were like a fucken magic carpet. As he walked up the stairs to the inquiry with his father, Roo felt this new and important lesson sinking into his brain.

Chapter Nineteen

Outside the room where the inquiry was being held, Graeme told Roo to wait until everyone else was let in, then sit in the audience. It would take between one and two hours, he said, then they should be able to go to lunch in the cafeteria.

'I've gotta go and talk to the lawyers now, okay. You'll be alright here, won't ya?' he said.

'Yeah.' Roo felt invincible – and invisible – in his new clothes. He looked around the waiting area with its dark carpet and hired pot plants. A smoke would have been good, but that'd mean hoiking downstairs again and he wasn't confident enough to take on the young pig by himself, so he stayed put.

The area swarmed with lawyers, cops and other well-dressed people he didn't recognise. Maybe some of them were the journalists who wrote that stuff in the papers. Roo enjoyed wearing the suit among this lot, blending in. No one gave him a second glance.

Then, to his horror, he saw Mum King heading up the stairs. The Murri woman he'd seen the first time he tried to gatecrash was walking behind her, still carrying her briefcase, and Darryl and Leena followed. How'd *they* get in?

Roo was speechless with terror. What could he say to them? That he was here to see his father up for Stanley's murder? If they thought they hated him now ... O God O God! He bolted to the men's, where at the worst all he'd have to deal with was Darryl. *Jesus*. Jesus Christ! If it wasn't so terrible, he thought, it'd be funny. Sometimes it felt like his destiny in life was to crouch on bloody toilet seats hiding from people – only this time he was in a fucking three-hundred-dollar suit. Roo put his face in his hands, trying not to become hysterical as he wondered what the hell to do next.

He knew it'd been a mistake to leave his bag at home. If he brought it with him, he'd have his watch and know the time, and when it was safe to leave unseen. It had to have been half an hour, he thought, if not more. The thing was, he didn't know if that was enough time for the inquiry stiffs to get organised and start inquiring. They seemed to take their time about all this stuff – Stanley died nearly six weeks ago, after all.

Roo shifted his weight, leaning back on the white porcelain of the cistern with his legs braced against the door in front of him. Seeing the Kings, if only briefly, had shaken him. Leena, swollen in front but still glowing with that dark prettiness and kick-arse attitude that had first caught his eye when she visited Stanley in John Oxley. She'd done her hair different now, cut it kind of shorter and bleached the hank in front. She was a good-looking female alright. Roo was briefly stirred to lust as he thought of her, but his speeding mind quickly passed onto Darryl. Big, broad, calm Darryl with his second-hand bookshop philosophies and his way of looking at you that made you shame to lie to him, and made you want to be a better mate than you had been. Roo sucked at his bottom lip, wishing there was some way to go back to the way it had been. De-pregnify Leena. Resurrect Stanley. Make Darryl see the pressures he'd been under when they blued. Have all the Kings there watching and screaming, yahooing for joy when he won at the state titles, instead of suffering Graeme's rigid congratulations. Was it really too late? Would they listen if he went crawling back? There was no way to know.

Roo startled. Was Graeme in the dock right now, while he was sitting on the loo wasting his time rewriting the past? Was he standing there hanging his head and wondering where the cheer squad was? Anxious that Graeme shouldn't think he was a piker, Roo got up and looked out into the room. Empty. He checked his look in the mirror, surprised once again by his appearance in the suit. He admired himself as he thought about leaving the building, or perhaps trying to find the cafeteria Graeme had mentioned. He sighed. This one time when doing nothing would definitely not make everything alright. He had to decide between the risk of seeing Graeme's famous bloody inquiry, or taking the soft option and avoiding Leena's mob. Roo trembled with the stress of deciding which way to jump.

He felt blindly in the suit's inside pockets, and came

across a pen in one and in the other a pair of cheap sunglasses. He weighed them in his hand for a moment, then put the glasses on. He looked in the mirror. Wearing shades inside – especially ugly, old-fashioned shades like these, refugees from 1989 – was ridiculous, but it would make him anonymous. No one would recognise him, no one except Graeme anyway.

Roo thought about it for a minute, and then took out both his remaining earrings and put them carefully with the others in his wallet. He looked in the mirror a final time. You'd never pick him for someone who'd been in Herschel Street watchhouse last week, that was for fucken sure. He knew the Kings had never seen him in a suit – he'd never worn a suit before in his life. His hair was shorter than it had been for ages, almost crewcut, and the earring holes that ran up both his ear lobes were only visible if you were up really close. Roo licked his lips, positive he was unidentifiable, and went to the inquiry room.

He saw that the morning's proceedings were in full swing already, and the audience had their attention on the Murri woman standing at the front desk. She was arguing the toss with the thickset man who looked like he was in charge of things – Roo admired her guts, wishing that he'd had her on his side the times he'd been put away, instead of the weak Legal Aid pricks he'd always had pleading guilty to save themselves a bit of work.

Graeme, his face whiter than Roo had ever seen it (or that could have been the fluoro lights) was sitting to one side next to another woman, a younger migloo one, paying careful attention to what the Murri lawyer was saying. Other men in suits were taking notes or simply watching. From where Roo had quietly sat down at the very back of the room, he could see the Kings three rows away, or the back of their heads anyway. They were straining to hear what was going on; Leena's body language spoke of irritable incomprehension, Darryl and Mum's crossed arms of cynical understanding.

Roo felt his insides, already jumping since he'd come into the building, tense even further as he went into the courtroom again. He wasn't the only one, either. From ten metres away he could smell the fear coming off Graeme, and it filled him with wonder that a big man, a cop, could sit there so afraid. He was white-faced and he was sweating. Roo couldn't think about it properly for a moment. Graeme being both things. A cop. Afraid. They didn't go together in his mind, and confusion for Roo was a shortcut to violence. He found himself angry at the judge in the front of the room who was hassling his father. Why didn't the prick lay off? Then he remembered again what it was all for – Stanley. Stanley was dead. While he sat and observed, Roo's sympathies seesawed irrationally between the Kings and Graeme. He scratched at his neck. Maybe they were both right – but it seemed impossible to feel bad on both their behalfs, just as it had been impossible not to believe Graeme when he looked straight at him the other night and said he was set up.

'... find it an unlikely and unconvincing scenario, frankly.' The black woman finished. Mum nodded her approval vigorously, and Leena looked like she was about to start clapping when Darryl put a hand on her arm, staying her. The bloke out the front made a note then asked the lawyer to take a seat. She walked forcefully back to her chair, knowing she'd done a good job, with a hostile glance at Graeme, who stared at the front wall, pale and oblivious. Even as he admired the woman, Roo began sweating in sympathy with his father. He knew just what it was like to sit and hear your faults discussed in public and have your life absolutely in someone else's control.

The man at the front gestured impatiently, and a suit sitting with Graeme got rapidly to his feet.

'Nothing further to add,' he said. 'Except that these events have been very well detailed in my client's statement, and are consistent with both the first and now the second coroner's report. The, ah, Energex report also clearly shows the time of the power failure to be between 6.15 and 6.47 pm, which contradicts what I can only describe as the weak and unsubstantiated argument the inquiry has just had afflicted on us.'

'Very well,' said no-neck unemotionally. 'In that case this inquiry will adjourn until next,' – he paused and shuffled his papers – 'until next Monday at 2 pm to consider the evidence before it.' The man glared at the small audience. 'While these matters are not, of course, sub judice, I would ask all parties involved to use an element of discretion as far as the media are concerned. There has been a disproportionate amount of unhelpful attention given to these events already, none of which has aided the course of this inquiry.'

'I bet you would,' Mum King muttered as she got to her feet. 'Don't want no spotlight on ya little mate, do ya? Discretion!' She snorted aggressively as she went to consult the Murri lawyer.

Everyone in the room shuffled to their feet, and Roo melted away to the cafeteria. Graeme would understand – he'd have to. As he walked briskly away up the corridor to the head of the stairs, Leena narrowed her eyes at his disappearing back. She'd recognise Roo's profile anywhere. Dressed to the nines, too. She felt a sharp twinge of jealousy for Roo's handsomeness that was now available to all and sundry. For a moment she went to call out to him, find out where he was staying, have a bit of a yak and see where he was with it all. The presence of her mother and cousinbrother stopped her, though, made her shame to chase him after the way he acted. She smoothed the material over her bulging abdomen, jarred up a bit by Roo's disappearance. Nice, though, that he came to the inquiry thing. Kind of paying his respects to Stanley, in a way.

'That Roo?' asked Mum, gazing in the same direction as she was.

'Mmm.' A non-committal sound.

'Want me to go get him?' she offered.

Shaleena shook her head. 'He knows where I am,' she said, putting a sour edge to her words that wasn't matched by what she felt inside.

'Fair enough,' Mum shrugged. 'It's your – life.' She had almost said funeral. Darryl gave Leena a measured glance; as was usual, he was seeing a great deal more than he said.

CHAPTER TWENTY

Saturday morning. Graeme dried his hands efficiently on the chequered tea towel that hung off the front of the stove and wandered out to the lounge.

'You know much about cars?' he asked Roo, who was in front of the TV, sorting through videos to find out what they'd watched last night as they got on the piss, and what they hadn't yet seen. He tossed aside *Beavis and Butt-Head* to keep; the other night they'd cracked right up over it.

What a pair of deadshits, eh. Graeme reckoned he'd arrested them both at least a million times in the past decade. He'd loved it, and now Roo couldn't wear his Metallica T-shirt for fear of sarcastic comment.

'WHAT?' Roo yelled.

Slightly hungover, Graeme walked over to him, seized the remote and turned the TV down. The Spice Girls continued to wail and shake their moneymakers at the world.

'Do you know anything about car engines?'

Roo put his arms up in the arrest position, pulled his shirt up over the back of his head, and turned into a paranoid high-pitched Beavis on speed. 'Are you threatening me?'

'Yeah,' said Graeme, grinning, 'I am. Do you know anything about cars?.

'Oh … not that much. Little bit. Why? What's wrong?' Roo looked up at the wide screen and was immediately transfixed by Scary Spice. He grew an instant erection.

'The car's due for a grease and oil change, that's all, and I—'

'Oh, I can do that,' Roo said in a crushing tone that suggested anyone who couldn't, should be in a sheltered workshop. 'You got the tools?'

'There's some … Faith got me a kit a couple of Christmases ago. It's downstairs. I guess they're still all there.' Graeme was dubious; he wished he was better with them, but cars weren't his department.

Roo knew the kit he was talking about; it was missing a Jap screwdriver. 'No worries. You'll need the oil, but.'

'Engine oil?' Graeme was trying to sound capable.

'Yeah … of course.' Roo fixed him with one eye. 'Four litres. Got any grease?'

'I'll go down to Target and get some. Anything else? Are you sure you can do it alright, I don't want the car fucked up.'

Roo rolled his eyes with terrible weariness. 'I've helped strip a racing Torana down and rebuilt it, I reckon I can do a bloody grease and oil change.'

'Whatever you reckon,' Graeme said, radiating mistrust.

'I am the Great Comholio!' Roo was being Beavis again.

'You wanna come down the shops?' Graeme asked him as he slipped his deck shoes on.

'Nah, I'm gonna have a shower, wake meself up. You go.'

'We need anything else?' Graeme asked.

Roo gave it a nanosecond's thought. There was enough pies 'n stuff for lunch. 'Nuh.'

Graeme went to get the keys. Roo sighed with relief when he drove down the street, and then went to masturbate undisturbed in the blissful solitude of the bathroom, where all four – or why not five? – Spice Girls were wet, naked and panting to service him.

Roo hauled himself awkwardly out from under the Commodore and Graeme handed him a petrol-soaked rag. The dog nosed at his feet, curious as to what he was after under there. 'No cats, Wimpy,' Roo said, heaving himself to his feet. 'Bad luck.'

'You look like a black and white minstrel,' Graeme joked, as his son dabbed at the greasy streaks on his arms and face. Roo ignored this, as he ignored every statement of Graeme's that had even the slightest hint of racism. The man seemed oblivious to the meaning of the English language sometimes. He talked about American blacks and other dark people as if it bore no relation to his own life or, more to the point, to Roo's black friends or to Stanley. He just didn't fucken get it, Roo had come to realise. He didn't get the … the connection. To him, Roo was white and that was that. The world was a simple place, literally black and white for Senior

Sergeant Graeme Walter Madden. There were goodies and baddies and he was the guy in the middle, protecting the one from the other. Roo didn't bother arguing. He could tell it was no use. Do nothing and it'll be alright. 'Well, there you go, she's done. Any other little jobs around the place for me?' Roo said drily.

'Leaves in the gutter,' said Graeme. 'Oh, whippersnip the garden beds, fix the palings under the house, wash the car, wash the dog—'

'Fuck off.' Roo was sore from lying on the concrete for most of an hour using the wrong-size screwdriver. 'The most strenuous thing I'm interested in for the next couple of hours is twisting the top off a few beers.'

'Sorry, mate. We're out,' said Graeme, not sounding sorry and not offering to leap to Roo's help by trotting straight down to the bottle shop either.

'Shit, we're not!' he exclaimed, stopping his clean-up and looking aghast. 'Last time I looked, which was at breakfast.'

They had a six-pack each last night, surely the kid remembered? Anyone'd think it grew on trees.

Roo heaved an indignant sigh at the world. This was bloody great. 'Not even any hotties?'

Graeme shook his head, growing irritable at Roo's transparent attempts to get him to buy more grog. Christ, he went through enough of the stuff. They were drinking three cartons a week between them. Faith'd have a fit if she was here.

Roo was silent. Any decent red-blooded Aussie male would offer to shout him a drink, seeing as he'd just saved Graeme about sixty bloody bucks on the car, if not more.

He waited with growing frustration, too angry to let it go but afraid to ask for what he wanted. He hated being poor, he thought bitterly; he'd commit armed rob one of these days if things didn't start to look up soon. Why should he always go without the stuff other people had? Those other lucky bastards that had real families, who never had to go through the shit that dogged him. 'If you noticed at breakfast,' he finally said to Graeme, trying to sound calm, 'you could've at least picked a sixpack up when ya went past the pub.'

'I asked ya if we needed anything,' was Graeme's short reply.

A host of answers to that swarmed on the tip of Roo's tongue (I thought ya meant food; you'd already seen we were outta beer; why didn't you think of it yourself?) but he said nothing. He sulkily cleaned himself up, and decided in the shower to go and get charged after training with his little remaining dole money. He'd play pool that night, and party on. Minus Graeme.

After lunch, Graeme fell asleep in front of the TV and Roo gently took the phone into the kitchen. Expecting another huge drama, he rang Leena. Darryl answered, and this time to Roo's relief he didn't hang up on him.

'Oh, she's gorn up the shops, eh.'

'Can you give her a message?' Heart thumping away with unasked questions.

'Mmm. Spose.'

'Um, me number's 5883 0992. Tell her to ring at six tonight, willya?' He should be able to screen the incoming calls then, while Graeme made tea.

'Yeah, okay.' He repeated the number. A neutral pause. 'That's not Troy's number is it, eh?'

'Nah, he's still in SDL. I'm, ah, staying with this bloke you don't know at Mount Gravatt, eh,' said Roo hastily. That was all he needed.

'Oh, right, yeah I could tell it was out that way. How's it all going?' Darryl sounded happy, almost like old times, and Roo's brow wrinkled. Don't get all fucken friendly on me now, mate. The irony would be too much to stand.

'Yeah, not too bad. Look, I gotta bolt, eh. Just tell Leena to call me, willya? It's important, eh.'

'Yeah.'

Roo put the phone down. Too late to resurrect that one. His head told him he had to keep this new life apart from the old one or there'd be trouble. All sorts of trouble. But that still didn't stop him from wanting Leena to call, so he could talk to her, explain some stuff. If he could only manage things, he dreamed vaguely, organise it so the truth came out little bit by little bit, maybe she'd get used to it the way he had. The spray-painted roses would help, soften her up to his pleading. If things worked out, maybe eventually him and Leena could fuck off, go away together after the Australian Titles, and start afresh somewhere else, somewhere where no one had ever heard of Max the backdoor king, or Jimmy the Cunt or even Graeme let's-fuck-everyone-else's-lifeup Madden. Somewhere green and peaceful with no stress, no hassles. No history.

★

Graeme was still snoring in his armchair as Roo replaced the phone. The car keys lay in a metal jumble on the floor next to his empty tea cup and the unread newspaper. Roo picked them up silently and looked out at the Commodore in the drive. Bitchin' thing looked like it was speeding when it was standing still, eh. He gave a loud experimental cough. Graeme didn't budge; the man looked like he'd died.

Three minutes later Roo was coasting backwards out the drive with his training gear in his bag. When he fired the big V8 it was two hundred metres down the hill, and Graeme still didn't stir.

Roo expected the track to be empty now that the States were over, but there was a few people around. Jesse, the one they all called the Polynesian Princess was there with his discus, and so was John and a flat-faced bloke Roo didn't recognise, both jogging easy laps as they talked about the state titles. A couple of hurdlers from the local high school were doing their thing on the other side of the track. John waved and Jesse came over to where Roo stood on the rim of the rubberised circle.

'Hi there, muscles,' Jesse wore a muted shade of purple mascara.

'Hey, man.' They gave each other a high five. 'Is Coach around?'

'Ah, he was earlier on … don't know where he went.' Jesse waved towards the basketball hall with a dark, manicured hand. 'You're only about an hour late.'

'Yeah, what else is new? How's it going? You still training?' Roo asked. Jesse had come third in the javelin, and so was probably out of a place in the team. There

243

was no way Roo'd be at the track if that had happened to him.

'Well, for those of us mortals who have to train our little black butts off, sweetheart, it's a never-ending fucking grind, isn't it? Not that you'd know.'

Roo played an imaginary violin and made accompanying sounds.

Jesse stared nonchalantly as John and the stranger swept past them at low speed.

'Contrary to popular opinion, I do have to turn up now and then,' Roo said.

'Yeah, can't go breaking our little coach's heart, now, can you?' Jesse smiled lazily.

'I'd better get down to it.' Roo said shortly, and went to get changed. Breaking hearts wasn't what he wanted to discuss with Jesse just then.

How did he get away with it, Roo wondered, as he pulled his Nikes on, lacing them tight across his insteps. Maybe because he gave out an unmistakable message of looming violence, mascara or not. Like the time – Roo started grinning – the time them fuckwits from the coast had thought it funny to start mincing around and talking about spearchuckers, just as Jesse lined up to throw. He'd turned slowly, clocking Roo there ready to jump in when he heard them start up. He walked straight over to the main offender, oblivious to the time ticking away, carefully placed the tip of his javelin under the dickhead's nose as he leaned in with his weight and explained that in his culture men were free to be as they choose. Dickhead had a sudden change of heart and trouble speaking. Jesse didn't win, in fact he was disqualified as soon as the officials recovered from the shock; but the others were all pretty quiet for the rest of the afternoon. Roo noticed a different attitude after that in his own club towards their pet Polynesian poofter and Jesse continued to do pretty much what he pleased, and when.

Roo warmed up that afternoon with a half dozen slow laps, keeping an eye open for Coach, who failed to materialise. Disappointed, Roo pushed himself around a couple more times, then stopped. It was his own fault for being late, of course. The hurdlers were taking their gear down; John was already in the shower. Jesse was still hurling objects through the air, but other than that Roo was pretty much on his lonesome. Run your own race, he thought. You've got the watch.

He trotted over to the starting line for a four hundred metre race, the one he would have really liked to star in, the glamour boy's distance, the one he used to win at school with no real effort. Roo breathed in and out quickly several times to supercharge his blood, then sprinted hard around the red circle of track, holding his left wrist high at the end and trying to make out the time as he slowed. It was shitty. Dave Bedouri could run faster than that, backwards, he told himself. Oh well, middle distance, middle distance. Can't put in what God left out.

Roo's curiosity was pricked by where the coach had got to. He abandoned his training and went over to the hall, where to his surprise he found the coach sitting drinking coffee with the unknown jogger. The short man with the flat face had changed and was now dressed in slacks and a collared shirt, with an expensive watch decorating his forearm. He was older than he'd seemed running beside John, his face more lined and beaten by the years. Roo hesitated to approach. The flat-face bloke didn't look like a copper, but in that get-up he could easily be a lawyer or something else to avoid. He was sitting relaxed with a leg crossed over his knee, happily observing the world with an air of mild preoccupation that suggested more important matters which he'd attend to shortly. In Roo's experience that look spelt power, and power only meant one thing in his book – trouble.

'Oh, g'day, Roo,' the coach said in his usual open friendly tone. 'This is someone I want you to meet. Phil Smith.'

'Hi.' Roo gave the guy a wary smile and reached into the side pocket of his bag for his smokes. Never heard of him. Maybe some runner from a million years ago. Coach was always dragging them out for the team to admire.

'From the AIS. Sit down.'

Roo fell weakly into a plastic chair, snatching his hand out of his bag as if it contained vipers. Blood roared in his ears. Why hadn't someone told him? Before he went running terrible lap times in front of the guy?

'I told Phil you probably wouldn't be here today,' Coach explained. 'He's just dropped in on his way up North. Looking for basketballers, isn't it,' he checked.

'And netballers.' Phil agreed.

Roo nodded, dumb with hope and fear.

'Dave Wiseman told me he saw you at the state titles,' the man said. 'Said you had quite a turn of speed.'

Roo shrugged, embarrassed.

'Have you ever thought about training full-time?'

Phil Smith asked, sipping his coffee as if he was asking Roo how his day had been.

'Ah, yeah. Kind of.' Well, he did train full-time, didn't he? What did the question really mean? Fuck. Why couldn't he ever understand what people said to him, why couldn't they speak English? Why did he always end up sounding in return like a Neanderthal? Roo wanted to scream with frustration.

He looked at Phil Smith's muscular neck with its glowing white collar, and thought: Conditions of Bail. He thought about the tats lurking underneath his sweatshirt, and about Sydney 2000. Canberra was fucken freezing, they reckoned. Gold medals and podiums glittered in front of his eyes. Roo thought: I'd do anything, mate. Anything at all. Tell me ta jump, I'll ask how high.

'Have you got a job?' Phil Smith asked him. 'Or are you studying?'

'Not really.' Roo was stricken. Housebreaking. Aggravated assault. Vehicle theft. Would that help? 'I've been looking for work lately.'

'Any particular field?'

'Um, gardening,' Roo blurted. 'Landscape gardening.'

Phil nodded and said, 'Well, mind you don't go dropping any bush rocks on your feet.'

Roo smiled, too afraid to laugh.

'I've got some forms to apply for scholarships,' Coach told him. 'We can have a talk about it later on. You're not going anywhere in the next few days are you?'

It was a dismissal as well as half a promise. Roo stood. 'Nah, I'll be here Monday arvo. Nicetameetchaphil.' He bounced over to the Commodore, and got home a

247

bare minute before Graeme snorted himself awake to the strains of the *Fishing Show.*

The King's phone rang and Roo relaxed. He'd thought the phone might be cut off, but Daz must have worked some overtime last week.

'Leena?'

'Yeah. That you Roo?' her voice surprised and wary, but pleased underneath.

'Yeah. How're ya going?'

'Not too bad. Where are ya?'

'Up at the fish 'n chip shop.'

They both paused. Leena turned the volume down on the Nintendo. What was he doing at the fish and chip shop?

'Small world,' said Leena, hiding her hopes.

'Can I come and see ya? I got something for ya.'

'Not another jumper, is it?' An opening, an acknowledgment of the gift. She didn't say no.

'Nah, I'm cleaned right outta jumpers.' Smiling. 'But I can get ya one if ya want.' Gammon.

'Well, come down here then if ya want to. Jimmy 'n the girls are at footy, but Mum's ere. She was arksing about ya the other day, too.'

'Is Daz there?'

'Nah, he went to Browns Plains to see Uncle Eddie. He's come down from the mission. Won't be back till later on. I was sposed to go with him but I got too slack, eh.'

'Okay, see ya in a minute then.' Roo hung up,

breathless and excited. Mum was asking about him, she reckoned. That had to be a good sign.

His chest was tight as he walked down the street and entered the yard.

'Anyone the-ere?' he called from the steps, holding the black roses behind his back. Funny to be standing like that when he used to just barge in, no worries.

Mum King appeared from the kitchen, one hand gloved in an oven mitt. A smell of roast meat filled the lounge. Where was Leena?

'Reuben Glover,' Mum's eyes were smiling. 'Come inside, lad, you're making the place look untidy.'

'Hello, Mum.' Roo kissed her on the cheek and went inside.

'Ar, look at ya now. Too skinny! Where ya been hidin? And what's that you've got?'

Roo produced the glossy black bouquet and announced his intentions. 'They're for Leena. If she'll have em.'

Mum peered at his handiwork, and then at the boy's face. Inside her, a huge knot of tension dissolved. He was back with em, she knew he was a good boy after all. That's if Leena …

'Black roses, what'll they think of next,' was all she said of his offering. Then she called out, 'Leena!' adding to Roo, 'She's in the shower. Make yaself a cuppa if ya like.'

'Ta, I will.' He would have said something about dinner smelling good, too, if he wasn't still jumpy as hell. Didn't want Mum to think he was being cheeky.

'How's the runnin goin, luv?'

'Good. Real good. I might be going to Canberra,

249

eh. To the Institute of Sport.' Roo glowed with this information. 'That's why I wanted to come see Leen.'

'Canberra? You takin off then?' Mum was disappointed and lay her cards on the table. 'I thought you was here to kiss and make up.'

'Dunno if I'll go down there … haven't made me mind up yet. And they haven't properly asked me either. I wanted to talk to Leen, too.'

Roo had just put the milk back in the fridge when Leena came into the room, her dark hair wet against her back. She's beautiful, Roo thought.

'Hey now,' she said nervously, noticing the bouquet.

'Hey.' He went over and kissed her on the mouth as he gave her the roses. 'These're fer you.'

'Ta.'

Had she kissed him back or not? Roo couldn't tell.

Mum carefully basted the roast, pretending not to be listening with both binung fully tuned.

'Gotcha cuppa? Come out the back then,' Leena said, wanting the limited privacy of the chairs under the gum tree.

'You wanna arks him to stay for tea?' Mum asked as they went through the kitchen door, a clear signal to Leena about what was expected.

Roo cracked a big smile at Mum. Leena snorted and kept walking. She wasn't about to take this fella back just to keep her Mum happy. It was her what had to put up with him.

'So what's all this then?' She gestured at Roo with the roses when they were both seated.

'I went to training yesterday,' he began, surprising

her, 'and there was this bloke there from the AIS.' He took a mouthful of tea. 'He asked me if I wanted to go and train down there, train full-time. For Sydney.'

'Yeah? What ya say?' Leena tried not to let her feelings show. If that's all he was here for …

'Told him I was interested. Nothing's definite yet, there's all these forms and shit first. And he doesn't know I'm on parole or nothin.'

'Oh. So …' she made a what-now gesture. 'Come to say yer goodbyes, have ya?

'No, not really. I love ya, Leena,' Roo burst out. 'And I wanna be with ya, and if I go to Canberra I want ya to come down with me. Coach reckons they put ya up in these flats, and I get paid to run, and there's a pool and stuff.' They could get away from Brisbane and all that had happened there. Leave Graeme and Jimmy and the ghost of Stanley and start afresh, where none of that mattered.

'What if it doesn't happen?' she asked. 'If ya don't get in?'

'But it will happen. I'll make sure it does. You should see how much I've been training. Hey? Whaddya reckon?'

'What about in the meantime?' Leena wanted to know. 'Do you wanta come back here, or what?'

Roo paused. He did and he didn't. Come back here and there was still all the shit to deal with. Stanley in the photo on the wall, Jimmy in the lounge. He was Graeme's son in Brisbane. Get away and he could be free.

'D'ya still love me?' he asked Leena softly, avoiding her question.

'Yeah,' she said in a slow voice, 'but it's gotta be different, Roo. Ya gotta think before ya do shit. Ya gotta calm down and stop doin crime, there's a baby to think about now. And anyway, I thought ya hated babies. I thought it was gonna fuck ya life up!' Her tone grew harder.

'I didn't … I didn't think about it. I didn't understand,' was all Roo could think to say. 'I thought … I got it wrong, Leen. I'm sorry, okay. Give us a chance, honey, come to Canberra with me.'

Leena looked at Roo, handsome Roo, wild Roo, badboy Roo, and wondered what he was really offering. Canberra meant nothing to her. 'Ya don't want to come back here, but.' She didn't understand. Was it Jimmy? Or her?

'I do wanta,' he said. 'But it's complicated. I can't explain properly. It's sorta got to do with Daz. Canberra'd be better. Get away and start again, just us two.'

Leena considered this strangeness. What did Daz have to do with it? Roo was a funny one alright. His eyes were shining as he waited for her answer.

'It's like …' he offered, 'it's like I've gotta clear it with him first.'

Leena nodded at that. That at least made a little bit of sense. Daz was the man of the house. That'd be alright, he still had time for Roo.

'Cold down there in Canberra, eh?' she said.

Roo nodded. Fucken oath it was.

Leena paused a long moment. 'Better get me another jumper then. And some fleecy pants.' She was grinning at him. 'And boots.'

His heart leapt high. 'And socks,' he added, kissing her.

'And scarves,' kissing him back.

'And parkas.'

'Come on, let's tell Mum.' Leena grabbed his hand.

'No!' Roo pulled back in alarm. 'Don't tell her yet.'

'What? Why not?'

'Let me talk to Daz first. There's stuff I gotta sort with him first. Okay?' He pleaded for time and trust. He had to let someone know about Graeme. There was absolution required, and Daz was the one to give it.

Leena stared.

'Please.'

She sighed. 'Okay. But Mum's gonna think it's weird as, man.'

'I know. I can't help it. I gotta talk to him first. And then Mum.'

'Ya stayin for tea?'

'Nah, I better not.' Roo stood and kissed her a final time. 'I love ya, girl. I'll ring ya tomorrow, okay?'

'Okay.' Leena was confused, but happily so. Darryl'd be sweet, she knew it.

Part Four

Arms Full of Fires

Chapter Twenty-one

Inside the Vulture Street pool hall, young men leaned with transparent intent against their phallic cues. Girls in tight satin pants and low-cut blouses flattened themselves on the tables, taking long shots that showed off their assets to their best advantage and making the young men's mouths water. Male and female, their blood itched with the promises of Saturday night.

With more obscure goals for that night (goals which, while they most definitely included sex, also went far beyond it), Roo sat and waited outside on the footpath, watching the straights going into the Indian restaurant. He watched them walk inside all stiff and polite to each other, knowing they'd come out an hour later un-notching their belts, belching hilarity, or teetering on sozzled legs. He was feeling pretty hot in Graeme's suit pants and his own black T-shirt. A couple of the straights even said g'day to him on their way up the street – now there was a fucken turn-up; he nodded coolly back. Every minute or so he'd remember Phil Smith – the AIS – and have to make an effort not to run screaming for joy up the street. But he couldn't. He had to wait for Leena.

The bouncer from the pub on the corner came wandering over after a while. Roo offered him a smoke.

The shaven-headed bruiser in the white polo shirt declined. 'I don't smoke, don't drink, and I don't eat red meat,' he said.

Roo gave him a strange look. With that gleaming bald head and footy-player's body he looked like a blueing machine.

'Not much of a life,' Roo said tentatively.

'You'll notice I didn't say anything about sex.' The bouncer grinned, then added, 'are you going upstairs?'

'Yeah, I'm just waiting for someone. How come you don't eat meat?' Roo didn't know any vegetarians. Or maybe Coach was one.

'I just look after my body, that's all, and too much meat fucks it up. Ya don't really need it. Look at gorillas – all they eat is bamboo and stuff. Listen, there's not gonna be any trouble tonight is there, son? I'm really not in the mood.'

Roo winced. He thought the guy was just being friendly. That fight was months ago anyway. 'Don't worry. I'm just playing pool, that's all. With friends.'

The bouncer nodded, looking at him cautiously. It had taken him a fair effort to eject Roo after the bikie's comment about Leena's colour and intelligence. A young Turk with something to back it up was exactly what his night didn't need. 'Yeah, well, I'm not worried. Just makes everyone's life easier if we all act civilised, eh?' The man tapped the side of his nose with his finger and went back to his post two doors down.

Roo mused on the word 'civilised'. Civil, he supposed it meant. Keep a civil tongue in ya head, Glover. Civilisations of the Tigris and Euphrates Rivers. Now we all civilised, colour bar and beer. Whitemen were the savages, Darryl said, look at em. Nuclear bombs and gas chambers and electric chairs and what they did to Murries. Do to Murries. Nigger nigger pull the trigger. Mum King never talked about the mission days, ah best forgot, best forgot. Daz watching TV, what the invaders did. *They call us savages.* Our old Law's in everything, Daz saying softly, everybloodything in the world, nothing left out, nothing without a place, no Kings, no Queens, no slaves, no servants. Nobody lost, everybody wanted – that's civilised. Try tellin them that. Huh?

Roo stood digesting all this as he wondered how late Leena was going to be. Now that the man had put the idea into his head, he felt like going in and having a charge, too. In the end it was twenty minutes before the Kings arrived, and Roo was upstairs being flogged by a pool shark. He swore as he missed his shot, then looked up and saw not only Leena but Darryl and another cousin, Wayne, standing there.

'Don't fucken show up when I'm playing good, do yez?' he snarled mock aggressively.

'Thought you said to meet ya tonight,' responded Leena laconically.

Roo grinned. Always the smart mouth on it, eh. 'Yeah, alright, I'm a gammon player. How ya goin mate?' He punched into Darryl's shoulder. Darryl let himself be hit, then pulled away, roughing Roo's head as he did so, and pretending to be pricked by its short hair. He shook his hand in the air. 'Ah! Ah! Not too bad, I guess, how's ya'self?'

'Sweet. 'Cept for this fucken game, eh.' He exaggerated his poor playing to show Darryl how meek and mild he was.

'You must be rich to be playing him, man.' Roo didn't deny it. He had some of Graeme's cash on him, ready for a big night. Had to celebrate, eh. The AIS! He was practically in the Olympic squad already.

'You playing or what?' asked Roo's opponent, in a tone that was a shade away from a racist sneer. He looked at the table. It was pretty bad; five of his balls left and the other guy already on the black. How'd he play so bad? He wasn't that crap a player, and he wasn't even charged yet.

'Hang on a minute,' Roo muttered to Leena and the others. He turned and, rattled by the thought that he could be sharing sex with Leena again within hours, took only moments to lose the game.

The shark scooped his money off the side of the table, bared his yellow teeth and disappeared without niceties. Roo sucked his almost empty stubby in consolation.

'Rack em up again, eh,' said Darryl to Roo, before turning to Wayne and Leena to ask what they wanted to drink. He took their orders and money and weaved his way through the crowd to the bar. They didn't have to wait long for him to come back with the glasses of grog chilling his fingers, almost sliding disastrously through them onto the wooden floorboards.

Roo fed two gold coins into the flat metal tray on the side of the pool table and the coloured balls fell into the end window of the table with a muted rumble. Darryl pushed a pot of beer at Roo.

'Ta.'

'Doubles, eh. Mugs away.' Darryl said, slurping the white top off his pot. Leena stowed her handbag on a narrow wooden shelf and took a rum and coke off her cousin. Roo chalked the end of his cue, rubbing it into the tiny square of blue dust that was strung to the table's end.

'Alright. You 'n me gainst them, eh, Leena?' Roo's voice belied his nervousness. She grunted assent and moved around to his side. He took aim, pumped the cue in his hand once, twice, then broke. The balls exploded across the maroon velvet of the table but none sank.

'Ah, you suck, man!' But Leena was only teasing him.

Other than some ritualised enquiries, plus swearing as balls failed to do what they were supposed to, the game that followed was silent.

When it ended Leena had to sit down. Backache, she said. She was nearly four months gone and feeling it too.

Wayne soon discovered a game of his own at another table, and left Roo and Darryl to play each other. He didn't want to be around if things went wrong.

Leena waved her fag in the air in a futile attempt to dispel its smoke. She had some news, if Roo was interested.

'What sorta news?' he asked, as he searched for the black plastic triangle.

'Bout this one.' She crossed her legs, and tapped the foot on top in the air in time to Jimmy Barnes screaming 'Working Class Man'. Her hands rested on her swollen front.

Roo took the triangle off the assembled balls. 'Uh huh. Go on.'

Darryl broke the pack open, sinking the large yellow ball.

'It's a boy they reckon.' Leena spoke in snatches, as if it was an effort to interrupt her breathing. 'Had a wotsaname, scan, up at the hospital. They took the pictures and it all looks like shit ta me, but they reckoned they seen his lil' buddoo there, eh.' She cracked up laughing.

Roo paused at this statement, wanting to coo and gurgle, to touch the stomach and talk to the lump. With Daz there, though, there was nothing he could do.

'So, ya happy?' he temporised inadequately.

Leena gave him a measured low-lidded look. She had desperately wanted a girl. 'Yeah. Fucken ecstatic. Whaddya reckon?' She gave a derogatory sniff and took herself off to the toilets. Roo ground his teeth at her back.

'So, Roo—' Darryl finally said as he missed on the large green. 'Shit, ya little green mongrel. So, what's going on? What's happening, man?'

Roo propped his cue upright against his toe and tossed the skinny end from hand to hand. He shrugged. 'Oh, fucked if I know. You tell me.'

'You talked to Leena, eh?' Darryl prodded. 'Bout what ya gonna do?'

'We, ah, had a bit of a yarn, yeah.' Roo sipped at his drink.

'What's she wanna do?' asked Darryl.

'She reckons when she seen me in town that day she realised she wanted me to come back home, eh,' Roo said softly in disbelief. 'Get back together.'

'Are ya gonna?' Darryl asked. This was news to him, but hardly surprising. Leena'd been sooking, crying her eyes out ever since Roo took off. Funny, eh? Think she'd be better off without him the way they blued allatime. It was hard but, splittin up. Darryl made a face, thinking of his own ex.

'That depends.'

Leena's cousinbrother narrowed his eyes at that, but said, 'Well, I won't stop ya, man. It's her life.'

'I know.' Roo took his shot and missed. 'It's not that. It's just ...' He stopped and sighed. 'It's um ... sorta complicated, see. The – ah – situation.'

Though of course Darryl couldn't see, not knowing what the hell he was talking about.

'What, cos of Max?' Darryl asked, frowning and wishing Roo would just bloody get over the guy's fling with Leena last Christmas. It was ancient history and he was here playing pool while Max was doing time with the big boys in Sir David Longlands.

Roo shook his head irritably. 'Nah, nah, not that. I can't really explain it, mate. It's more to do with Stanley. See ...' Roo's head fell backwards in despair. He had now or never to sort this shit out, but was it Darryl he had to convince, or Leena? Or even himself? *Well, my father's a cop and he's the one that pinched Stanley, and bashed him, and so when Stanley died ...*

'Stanley?' Darryl crowed. 'What's Stanley got to do with it?'

Everything, thought Roo. If only ya knew, my brother, if only. You'd try'n take me head off with that cue. 'Stanley and Jimmy,' he said. 'Look, I tell ya what. If you win this game, I'll tell ya all about it, okay. If ya lose, I get to decide when I tell ya.'

Darryl thought about this proposition for a moment but was unconvinced. 'Nah, fuck ya. Tell me now.' His curiosity was multiplying as Roo got more and more uptight.

'I can't,' Roo protested as he took a fag out of Darryl's pack that was lying on the bench.

'Why the fuck not?' Chucking him his lighter.

'Because ... because I told Leena I'd keep it a secret.'

'Bullshit.' Darryl wasn't swallowing that one, worse luck. 'You must think I'm a bit fucken myall, do ya?'

Roo shut his eyes tight, then opened them again. He lit the cigarette. Bugger the national tides, one smoke wouldn't hurt. 'Okay. But just remember one thing—'

Darryl waited impatiently while Roo took that first drag and then balanced the smoke on the edge of the ashtray. Roo looked at the felt-tipped table as he spoke, his hands spread on the polished wooden sides taking most of his weight. His muscular arms were stretched under the focused billiards light. The hair on his forearms glowed golden, forming, with the smoke, a gentle halo for his tattoos.

'—I'm the same Roo I always was,' he said with deliberate slowness. 'Okay?' He looked up, begging Darryl to listen to him, really listen. 'You know how when Stanley used to get locked up, or Jimmy, you'd tell Leena, *don't be so shame, that's not you, that's them – just cos they your mob don't mean it's up to you to always feel shame for what they do.*'

264

'Ye-eah.' Darryl didn't understand what Roo was getting at. 'But Leena's never been locked up, and you were long before we ever met ya. Ah, man, we don't give a shit about—'

'No, you dunno what I mean!' Roo muttered hopelessly. 'I just mean, I'm me, alright, I'm Roo, I'm not who other people say I am, or what my … my father is.'

'Your father?' Roo didn't have a father. What the fuck was he talking about? Then the penny dropped ever so slowly.

'Your shot.' Roo showed him the table with the cigarette.

Darryl lined the shot up. 'What's this about your father?'

Roo waited as he put the ball away. 'You know I'm adopted, eh. Well, to cut a long story short, I found him. And he's, he's a booliman.' Roo licked his lips. 'A, ah, Queensland copper.'

Gobsmacked, Darryl found a sudden sourness entering his mouth. Leena's baby had a booliman for a grandfather? Nice one, Roo. He felt a shudder of revulsion seize him, overlain with a fragment of pity. 'When did ya find this out? Where'd you find him?' he asked, then had another revelation that laid his pity to rest. 'Is this this fella you're staying with at Mount Gravatt, is it?'

Shame, Roo nodded.

Darryl didn't look up at him for ages. He sank the purple, the orange and then the black. Living with a cop. Roo. A booliman's son. How could he? How *could* he? After Stanley? Fucken hell. What a mess. Good thing Leena didn't know. Or Mum. 'Game.'

Darryl straightened, and saw Roo – tattooed, scarred, jawjutting, scowlmouthed – standing there miserable but trying not to show it. Hardly the picture of the Establishment. He's right, really, Darryl thought slowly, it's not his fault. He can't help it, can he? A thin veneer of anger wavered in him and disappeared. The poor little cunt.

'He's a mig I spose?' Darryl checked, just in case.

'Yeah. Me mum was a wog, apparently.'

'Oh. What's he think about you being … you know? About your record and that?'

Roo smiled weakly and shrugged. 'Oh, he gets on me case a bit sometimes. Usually we just don't talk about it. He's always on at me to get a job though. Fuck that.' He blew aside a stream of smoke.

'What about your Mum?' Darryl asked curiously.

'I haven't been able to find her yet. She left Brisbane years ago. Maltese, she was.'

'What's that when it's at home?'

'Sorta like Italian. Or something. It's near Africa, but. This island.' Roo added hopefully.

'Oh yeah.' Darryl was still staring like he'd never met him before.

'But, like, it's not my fault he's a pig,' Roo pleaded. 'I never even met him till a coupla months ago! But do ya see what I mean? That's why I can't …' He trailed off in despair.

'Yeah, shit happens, eh. But why'd ya have to go live with him?' Darryl asked. 'Can't you just …' Why jump into bed with the enemy? Bad enough them Murries that signed themselves up to a losing battle, without going around with a migloo copper. Put his teeth on edge to think about it.

'I got nowhere else to go, eh.' It was close to the truth. It was the truth. In a silken-smooth transfer of blame, he added, 'I rung ya up that day, I wanted youse to help me get a place with the Hostels instead, but ya hung up on me.'

Darryl put his cue away and drained his glass. It was difficult to know what to think about this. When Roo said pig, Darryl saw a blue uniform, and a man gesturing with a cruel baton towards Stanley's thin slumped body on a wheeled hospital bed, asking him to confirm who it was. Who it had been.

'And you know, even if he is a booliman, he's my father,' Roo appealed. 'I stayed in the bloody *park* when I first found out,' he added self-righteously. 'Down Musgrave. But it was fucken freezin and I didn't want to get pneumonia cos of me running, so I've been crashing at his place for the last ... little bit.' Make it sound temporary, less important than it is. Like you've found a bed and not a – a what?

'So, now you want to come back home, eh?'

It was hard to read Darryl's thoughts as he looked blankly at the table. Roo didn't like the sound of that. It sounded like he was crawling, desperate, a try-hard with nothing going for him. 'Well, maybe,' he prevaricated. 'I dunno. I might be going to Canberra, to the AIS to train ... Leena knows already. But—'

'Well,' Darryl interrupted matter-of-factly, lighting a fag of his own. 'I spose if you want to come back, and if she already knows ... I guess Leena'd be better off, eh?

Like I said, I won't stop ya. Not if you're gonna do the right thing by her.'

'That's not all. There's something else,' Roo said in a low voice.

Darryl sighed. 'Jimmy, I spose. What about him? Just fucken ignore him.' Jimmy, the bane of my fucken life, thought Darryl.

If only it was that simple, Roo thought, but took the easy option of pretending that, yes, that was the issue. 'It's, I gotta ... gotta ... I've gotta, oh Jesus, it's just so complicated. I'm gonna fucken kill him, thassall. The next time I see him, I won't be able to stop meself, Darryl, I'm gonna fucken ...' Roo was talking faster and faster.

'Settle down, mate, settle down,' Darryl soothed the lad. 'Ya not gonna kill anyone. See what hanging around with a pig does for ya?' He was only half-joking. 'Look, I'll have a word with him, okay, tell him to lay off ya. And if you hafta flog him up before he'll shut up, well ... that's his problem. Alright?'

Roo was doubtful about this prescription for domestic bliss, but gave in. 'Yeah, alright. But, um, that's not all. It, ah ...'

But Darryl was sick of arguing. In a life filled with problems and drama he didn't need to look for more. 'Listen, Roo, whatever it is, we can sort it out, okay? You better go see Leena, eh? Give her the good news. And mind ya get your moot outta that fella's place quick smart before you change ya mind. You don't owe him nothin. But if ya with us, ya with us, you know. No sittin on the fence being a whitefella,' he warned.

Roo wavered on the brink of this precipice. It would

be so easy to lie just one more time and go home to the Kings. What did they call it – *sins of omission*. He could just sort of forget to mention that it was Graeme who …

'I want to,' he said abruptly, surprised at saving himself. 'But I can't, I just can't. And I can't explain, either, not here. Not now. You'd throw it up in me face.'

Darryl was taken aback. He shrugged. 'Suit yaself. But what are we doing here then if you'd rather live …'

'I can't explain,' Roo repeated angrily from inside this sudden cage.

'Can't explain what?' Leena asked him, appearing with another round of drinks. The sight of her swollen front finished him. He threw his cue onto the table.

'*Nothing!* Fucken nothing at all! I'm sorry, okay, Leena! I'm really sorry!' Roo cried out and ran down the stairs.

'Go after 'im!' Leena said impatiently.

Darryl sighed. He told her to find Wayne and wait, and then went outside. He shoulda known that anything with Roo involved wasn't gonna be easy.

They sat in the public bar of the pub on the comer. Well on the way to being drunk, Roo had become surly and reluctant to talk, but Darryl chipped away at his resistance.

'You don't understand,' Roo scowled. 'Just forget it. Fucken leave me alone.'

Darryl looked over the busy road to the red bricks of the hospital. 'Remember that day with the wheelchair?' He smiled as he remembered.

Roo shrugged this off with a grunt.

'We seen you at the inquiry, Roo,' Darryl insisted, taking this as evidence of his good faith.

Roo laughed mirthlessly.

Darryl went on, 'Ya wouldn'ta been there if ya didn't care about us, about Stanley. We know that, okay. You don't have to worry so much, ya fucken uptight white. Just come back home and it'll be okay.'

Roo glared drunkenly at him. 'It's fucken 'brother' now innit? Wasn't brother when I had too much on me plate and had to get out for a bit, was it? Wasn't "you don't have to worry" then, was it, eh? Feels like yufla just fucken welcome me with open arms when it fucken suits yez, and fuck me off when it don't.' He turned from the messy human world to the wondrous simplicity of his fourth cold beer.

Darryl hunched on the barstool and methodically tore a coaster into neat centimetre-wide strips, wondering if he should waste his time arguing. Instinct told him, more than Roo's words did, that there was a deep vein of untapped shit running in this matter, bad business. It reminded him of that time Brianna-Leigh went spare, slashed herself up in Wilson, saying she hated everyone, the whole family, the fucken world could go and fuck 'emselves in the arse for all she cared. And how they had to dig to find the bastard at the bottom of that, a cousin no less. But who'd fucked Roo over? And did he, Darryl, have the strength to deal with it, the energy? God only knew being a whipping-boy for angry migs wasn't his chosen occupation. Darryl gazed at his glass. What would Uncle Eddie do? Clear bubbles of carbon dioxide floated to the surface and popped. He took a mouthful of the bitter fluid, and wiped his lips. 'Well, alright, let's talk about Stanley then,' he said, recalling what Roo had told him upstairs.

Roo drank deeply and waved to the barmaid for a fresh drink. He wanted to charge on till he couldn't stand up tonight. Till nothing could hurt him no more. He was fucken gonna, too. Against this magnificent quest, Darryl was merely an insect buzzing in his peripheral vision.

'Stanley's fucken dead. What's the use of talkin about him?' Roo said, gulping his fresh beer.

'Ah, what's yer problem?' Darryl asked, disgusted. 'We know you aren't ... just cos yer migloo doesn't make ya ... it's not your fault he got killed.' The words stuck in Darryl's throat but he forced them into the air. 'Christ, I know that, Roo. We miss him ya know, but we don't blame you for it.' It was his own fault, for tempting fate with that stupid fucken hat and jacket. He was to blame. And if he hadn't gone and ...

It's not your fault. The phrased circled inside Roo's mind. It's not your fault. But it is, Graeme's face reminded him, it is it is it is. Tis not. Tis so. Tis not.

'That copper,' he slurred into his fresh drink. 'The copper they're investigating, he reckons he didn't do nothin.'

Darryl was silent.

'He reckons it was like the coroner said, that it was, ah, wotsaname, misadventure from that punchup Stanley had in the park, eh?' Throw that one in the ring and see how it fared, Roo thought. See how quick he fucks off now.

271

'And you believe that?' Darryl asked in amazement.

'I don't fucken know!' cried Roo, snapping. 'I dunno what to fucken believe, alright?! Fucken liars everywhere, lies, lies, lies! He was charged up, wasn't he?' Roo rounded on Darryl aggressively. 'He was fucken pissed, eh? Who knows what happened? Who says they hung him? Fucken Jimmy the cunt, that's who. He's just a lying dog.'

'Forget Jimmy,' Darryl said quickly, not liking to hear him abused in that way, even though Roo was spot on the money. 'I never said they hung him, no one said that. Anyway' – rather bewildered – 'I don't see what it's got to do with you'n Leena. Just ...' Darryl hesitated. He couldn't say *don't worry about it*.

He couldn't say *forget it*. But then – 'Why not leave it up to us, eh?' he finally said. 'Don't concern yaself with it – think of it as our business. Your business is taking care of Leena and bubba, mate.'

Roo raised his head. 'Serious?'

'Yeah, serious,' Darryl replied. 'Come home.'

'They reckon it was cos of that storm,' Roo said miserably. 'It was just bad luck, really. Cos he was scared of the dark, eh, the extra stress on him, after he hit his head, eh? How's that for luck? He had to get grabbed then, during a fucken storm that lasted for half-a-fucken hour.'

'Mate,' Darryl said heavily, sensing Roo about to capitulate, 'I told ya, don't worry about it. It's not your problem, okay? But if that's what's worrying you, let me tell ya something, he wasn't all that scared of the dark no more. Remember that Elder I was talking about, at the funeral? Well he told me 'n Stanley that them spirits that run round at night, they're the same ones as in the day, eh. And after he found out about that, Stanley was okay at night, it didn't worry him no more. So he wasn't worried, and he woulda died anyway, storm or no storm, see.'

Roo gazed blurrily at the centimetre of golden beer left in his glass, trying to absorb this chunk of information. He was sodden with alcohol and couldn't think straight. It was Darryl's reasonable tone of voice more than anything that made the tears well in his dark eyes.

'Ah, stop it. Come on,' said Darryl, getting up with a decisive push off the bar. 'Come back upstairs for Christ's sake. Come and have a bit of fun with us and forget about all that for now. Wayne's got some yandy at home too, for later on. Make ya feel better, mate.' And with that Darryl took Roo by his limp unprotesting arm, and guided him upstairs, back to the family.

CHAPTER TWENTY-TWO

Somwhere between running away from the pool hall and being led, lamblike, back upstairs by Darryl, Roo had managed to lose the eighteen dollars in his right pocket. Wobbling at the bar, he felt the smooth material lining of his pocket in disbelief and pulled out three coins. A twenty-cent piece and two one-dollars. Two bucks twenty … ah, geez, no! 'How much?' he asked the bar guy.

'Six eighty-five,' the man repeated.

'I've lost my money,' Roo said hopelessly. The man raised his eyebrows, devoid of sympathy, and took the three drinks back. A couple of minutes later Roo was back at the table with Darryl and Leena, clutching a single pathetic pot of Fourex.

'What's this?' Leena asked impatiently. 'Fucken Freedom from Alcohol Week is it?'

'I've lost me bungoo. I had it there in me pocket, and it's fallen out somewhere.'

Leena rolled her eyes. *Men*. Bungoo was scarce enough without going and losing it. 'Man the Hunter,' she said sarcastically.

Roo flared. Bloody cheeky thing. 'It's not my fault!' he told her. 'I just fucken lost it somewhere. Or maybe someone pinched it.' Probably that's what happened, eh? Someone ripped me off when I was at the bar, and I didn't feel it.

'Will youse two can it?' Darryl broke in. 'I've got a bit, how 'bout you, Leena?'

'I'm out – pension week next week.' The five in her bra was taxi fare; she wasn't about to walk home with her back like it was, fuck that. She scanned the floor for dropped coins, but it was clean.

'Well, I've got ...' Darryl counted out what was in his wallet. 'Two bucks fifty left.' He shoved it towards Roo who went and got back one of the drinks he'd originally wanted, as he planned how he'd flog a bottle of Kahlua from the bottleshop to sweeten Leena up.

Darryl broke the balls apart and the fellas played again. The games were lasting longer now they were a bit pissed. It was heaps better value cos you enjoyed it just as much, only you got to play for about twenty minutes each game steada five, eh? Roo was relaxed, sinking balls kerthunk, kerthunk into the side pocket. The side pocket. The end pocket. He won that game, and the following one which was – sadly – a dry one. The fuzziest edge of grog was beginning to leave him already.

'One more?' Darryl asked him with a knowing grin.

Roo wondered how they'd play with no dough. Darryl looked quickly around and saw the upstairs management busy doling out cues and balls to people who'd just come in from the movies in town. He stood in front of the coin slot, fiddling with something for a minute. He grimaced.

Then the new lot of balls hurtled down into the window.

'Howdja do that?' Roo was impressed.

Darryl showed him a metal disc attached to a piece of fine copper wire.

'Bullshit!' It was too deadly. Darryl was real smart, eh?

'Nah, true. But ya gotta be careful, cos sometimes it gets stuck, eh.' Darryl put the device back in his shirt pocket.

Seeing Darryl outwit the migloo management that charged an arm and a leg for their cue hire cheered Roo up a bit. He managed to sweet-talk Leena even as he lost the game. Then through a cloud of dissipating ethyl alcohol he vaguely remembered: 'Hey, where's Wayne gone? Didn't you say he had—'

They were just in time to bludge the last buds of Wayne's stash off him at his place at Paddo. Not that he had a lot of choice – he was a cousin, and there were three of them, after all, and only one of him.

Chapter Twenty-three

Roo fidgeted as Sunday morning insisted on coming in through the missing plank of Wayne's back door. He was lying in a beam of sunshine, with Leena sound asleep next to him on the mattress, on her side, with a great lump of child attached where it never used to be. When she got undressed last night it was heaps bigger than it looked, eh. Put him off a bit, actually, he felt as if he was fucking with Max standing there watching. That and the grog ... she'd had to help him out for the first time ever.

Chilled air was blowing on his face. He sat up, spread the doona gently over his woman's shoulders, rolled onto his feet and then went for a piss in Wayne's loo. The kitchen clock told him that it was only eight-twenty. He couldn't hear anyone else up and about. Living at Graeme's musta got him useta jumping up at the crack of dawn, he thought. He dressed, then padded around the small house, checking it out. Two bedrooms, full of tangled brown arms and legs. A double bed in one of them, holding Wayne and his woman, Marie, and a small toddler between them, all fast asleep. Empty stubbies and chip packets and a packet of Tally-Ho papers lying on the loungeroom floor in front of the TV. A scribbled-on *Trading Post* open at Bargains Under Twenty Dollars. Roo grinned at this. The *Murri Financial Review,* Daz called it, and he was right.

Roo wandered on into the kitchen, with its three-quarter empty fridge, and even emptier cupboard. This was Mother Hubbard country, truegod. A kitchen with a three-quarters empty fridge; an even emptier cupboard. Ravenous from last night's munchies, Roo helped himself to the few remaining Weet-Bix in the box. He ran the kitchen tap until the hot water came through and gave them a good soaking. Then spooning happily, he went back to Leena.

'Hey, Leen!' He shook her by the shoulder, curious enough to risk one of her early mornings. 'Leen!'

She turned over and grunted at him, unimpressed.

'Leena—'

'What!' she muttered into her pillow made from a rolled-up coat.

'Have you ever been to Canberra?' he asked.

'Arrghhh ...' and in another moment she was back asleep again. Roo frowned and sat back on his heels, licking the Weet-Bix crumbs off his spoon before it set like concrete.

Late that afternoon Roo stepped off the bus and walked alone up the hill towards Graeme's house. He didn't know what he was going to tell his father now. Leena was expecting him home in an hour, home for good.

And Graeme had more or less wanted him to live with *him* for a million years, and he was the man holding the bail papers. Roo burned in anticipation of trouble.

He could handle it, he could look after himself. He just didn't know where it was going to come from, that was all, and the waiting made him jumpy and irritable.

Do nothing and it'll be alright, he suggested to himself. Himself was cranky after the big smoking night last night, and ventured to disagree. It was a minute later that he stood in front of the Italianate veranda. The two concrete strips that made up the drive were empty – well that was something anyway. Roo breathed in relief. He could just leave Graeme a note saying he was moving out and that he'd be in touch, eh. And once the inquiry was finished and once Leena knew the whole score, they'd work something out. Anyway, he could worry about that later.

Roo shoved down the unanswerable nagging questions that being with the Kings again had raised. He opened the gate and let a grateful Wimpy off her chain. Roo went to his room and crammed his gear into his sports bag. It no longer held all his possessions. He looked at the things Graeme had bought him up at Garden City, and at the stuff that was old. He'd have to leave some of it behind – he chose his old training shorts that were nearly dead, and a T-shirt with a ripped neck. Everything else fitted in when he squashed it hard. Then he sat on the bed and looked at the room with its bland decorations – a picture of tropical fish and palm trees, a Queensland Police Union Calendar, stickers from the 1993 State of Origin, a desiccated-looking basket of artificial fruit.

Not much of a place, not much warmth to it, but it was a roof over his head, eh.

Graeme had done his inadequate best to make him feel at home. Just it was a waste of time. Roo realised now – had always known inside – that the only home he'd ever have would be around Murries. He musta been born white by accident, he theorised, or maybe he got swapped at birth, ha ha. Sorry Graeme, bad luck.

Standing up and looking out at the gum tree in the backyard for a final goodbye, Roo started to go through the events of last night, what he could remember. It doesn't all fit, he thought uneasily, giving in to the questions tormenting him. Something's wrong. Just a detail, somewhere. He shook his head, but the thought wouldn't go away. Don't be a dickhead, he told himself, just bloody get crackin 'n get gorn. Leena's waiting for ya. Darryl and Mum King and the twins are waiting too. (As for Jimmy, well ...)

His brain spun in tight circles, trying to figure out what was tickling it. Then he heard a vehicle pull up outside. It wasn't the Commodore – what was it? Curious, he went out onto the front patio. It was a removal van, a three tonner with Graeme waving at him from the passenger window and grinning like his face'd split – first time for everything. Roo shifted uneasily. What now?

When the driver and Graeme swung open the big aluminium doors at the back, Roo groaned aloud. The stupid bastard. The *dickhead*. He felt like he used to when Hayley's mum would look hungrily in jewellers' windows and then meaningfully over at him. Guilty. Angry. Afraid. But most of all, trapped. He kicked his bulging sports bag out of sight behind the bar fridge, and faked the pleasure Graeme was looking for.

While his old man went back to Albion to get the Commodore, Roo stayed unwillingly downstairs and played by himself on the brand-new, two-thousand dollar slate-topped pool table his father had bought. For Roo to play on after work, he said, haha, very funny. *Facts,* thought Roo, still nagged by unease – by the conviction that someone was lying somewhere. But was it Jimmy or Graeme? In his mistrust, he seesawed between the two of them. *Facts.* Work it out, and then fuck off back home to Leena. Simple.

He racked the balls for another quick solo game to soothe his agitated nerves. *Facts.* Stanley mouthed off in the park that night, okay. No problem. That's exactly what Stanley'd do, cos the dumb cunt had no discipline, eh.

Roo broke the pack open with the white ball. Graeme slapped him around at Herschel Street cos he spewed up in the van. No problem. He'd have done it himself, maybe. Well, no, he wouldn't have, but he could see why a copper would. What'd Graeme say that night? *I clouted him across the ear a coupla times and got him in the chest once. I was aiming for his face.*

Okay. Fair enough. Roo started sinking balls. The orange. A miss on the blue. Miss on the purple. Sinks the purple. So Stanley's in that cell, that same padded cell as me and he's pissed. The blue ball fell whisper-softly into the side pocket.

281

He's pissed and there's a storm on and there's lightning, and he's shitting himself cos he's been smoking and he's paranoid and it's dark. He's alone.

Roo knocked the red ball down, and the yellow.

He's been hit. He's hurting, maybe dying. He can't think straight. He's not so sick he can't write his name on the wall in wobbly letters. Unless it was earlier this year. Whatever.

Roo missed on the green.

He's scared. Graeme's clouted him hard. He's hurt bad. He's hit his head earlier on already, twice. *That's not all.* What then? It's dark and he's yelling for help. Roo sank the green and missed on the black. It's dark. But he ain't scared of the dark no more, Darryl reckons. That old fella from the Cape told him it was okay. Was that true? Yep, Daz didn't lie, so okay, he could see that. Stuff like that, talking to Elders and that, mattered to Stanley anyway, more than to the rest of em. He was the – what'd you call it? – the spiritual one. The one into didge and the rest of it, always seeing things. Ghosts and shit. Roo shivered. Okay, so he's in the cell, and he's scared of lockup but maybe not of the dark no more. What did Jimmy say? *They come in and wet that goonah paper and plaited it up …* Roo missed on the black ball again. Hang on, go back a bit. It's dark but he's not yelling for help cos he's not scared of the dark. He's yelling for help because …

Roo shut his eyes tight, picturing the cell he'd been in. The flat metal bed. The padding of the walls. The lack of a communication buzzer. The busted light switch. The bucket that made such a noise when he clanged it. His eyes burst open and he looked at the wall of Graeme's garage. It was marked with the intricate electronics of the lighting and security system.

Getting warmer.

The buzzer in the cell's fucked. Stanley's dying. The light switch is broken. He's dying there. He's yelling out. He's screaming for help. He's real scared now. Things are busting up inside him. He can tell he's dying.

Getting hot.

The black ball bounced off the hard new cushion, and just missed the bottom hole. It spun itself rapidly into the middle of the table and stopped. The yellow garage light was reflected in its smooth black shiny surface. Graeme had lights in every room, more lights than he'd ever seen in a place. Ya wouldn't catch him with a busted light switch, Roo thought. Then he froze.

The first night he'd come to Graeme's, he'd seen the house lit up from the bottom of the street, like a fairy palace. His father kept the kitchen and outside lights on 'for security'. Graeme wouldn't put the bins out after sunset. The night Graeme bailed him out of Herschel Street, he went back to the watchhouse for a torch, a torch that turned out to be broken. Graeme was edgy and nervous going to the car park in the dark. The light switch in the cell was broken. The power was out the night Stanley died. Graeme's house was always lit up. Three weeks after Stanley died, the watchhouse torch was broken. Stanley was scared, knew he was dying. *The watchhouse torch was broken.* Roo hit the black ball into the bottom pocket harder than he'd ever hit anything in his life.

★

He left Circle Street feeling as though between him and the world was an invisible wall shutting out all sound, all sensation. Silence roared in his ears. He'd never felt that way except when running. Blank as a bomb-blast victim, he walked down to the shop, and beyond. He walked for hours in long spiralling paths that led nowhere, somewhere and nowhere again. He shook his head at his conclusions, but each time he shook it, more facts fell into place, and tiny pieces of pain assembled themselves into greater wholes. As the afternoon wore on, a terrible anger began to grow inside the boy.

More time passed. His feet padded on and on until Roo looked up to find himself standing at dusk outside Shaleena's home. Park Street, Woolloongabba. It was with a kind of dreamy disconnected pleasure that he noticed Jimmy sitting in the loungeroom with his sister, watching a video. Leena struggled to her feet and noticed Roo standing there. Her expression changed, and she came to the front door, where Roo stood on the low concrete steps.

'You'd be late for yer own fucken funeral, Roo.' She complained mildly, looking down at him and then nervously behind her at Jimmy. 'Eh Darryl!' she shouted out as a precaution. 'Look what the cat dragged in.'

'Sorry.' Roo smiled at her. He wasn't really all there. The person who was there was shaking. Lies. Always lies.

Sorry Leena. Sorry Stanley. Sorry Mum. Sorry Darryl. Sorry, sorry, sorry. It wasn't him, Roo thought with an electric flash of anger, that was gonna be sorry this time. Then he noticed Jimmy noticing him standing in the doorway. 'Whaddya doing here, ya white cunt?'

the black man said, splayed loose-limbed in a purple corduroy beanbag. He was sober. It wouldn't be a shamejob to fight him. *Perfect.*

Roo wasn't wasting any time. He glanced briefly at Leena and said, knowing full well what Jimmy's reaction would be, 'Come here and find out if ya wanna know, ya arsehole, or else keep ya fucken racist trap shut. You best get back inside, Leena.' He gently pushed her back into the hall as Jimmy stormed out of the lounge.

Leena gasped and slammed the wooden door in her cousin's path. Jimmy turned and with a fluid motion knocked her to the floor, then wrenched the door open. Roo stood on the front lawn, his shirt off, barefoot. Roo saw that Leena was on the ground and he leapt towards the house.

'Did you hit her?' he yelled at Jimmy. 'Did you do that to her?'

Leena looked up and nodded that yes, he had. Roo made a wordless sound of rage. Jimmy's day of reckoning had been a long time coming, his blood roared, and now it was here at last. Sweet.

Directly behind Jimmy came Darryl and Mum King, running. Mum shrieked with anger – these fellas! fighting! on her front lawn! the shame! – and told Darryl to ring their uncles, to stop them, to do something.

To her horror, he shook his head. She raced in and got an undefended slap on Roo's jaw before her oldest son seized her by the upper arms and walked her backwards to the steps.

'They gotta do it, Mum,' he cautioned her, holding tightly.

'There's bad blood there, gotta sort it out, just let em at it, Mum. There's nothing we can do.' His fists bunched themselves into sharp angles, but Darryl didn't move from where he stood beside the bottom step, protecting his mother.

She held her hands to her mouth as Jimmy and Roo snarlingly told each other how many times and with what extravagant measures they were about to be killed.

Then Darryl released Mum and stepped up to Jimmy. He said in a voice of absolute authority: 'Stop it, bruz. Stop right now, or I'll have ya meself.' Then he turned to his mother. 'It's gotta be, Mum,' he repeated.

A small crowd of neighbours gathered on the footpath, none game enough to intervene. Small boys' eyes grew large as Jimmy ripped a star picket out of the garden and weighed it in his right hand. Crumbs of brown earth fell from its pointed end onto the grass.

With her son and son-in-law both standing bare-chested in front of her house, Mum suddenly noticed the crowd. 'What youse all lookin at?' she cried. 'Piss off! This isn't bloody free entertainment for you lot. Gorn!'

'I'll call the police,' offered a teenage girl in response.

Mum's answer was swift and brutal. 'Fuck da police!' she snarled. 'Now get!'

The spectators moved away in slow bunches, and then Mum spoke again to the boys. 'The two of you ain't got the sense God gave to trees. If yez are gonna do this, do it right for Chrissake. Get out the back!'

Jimmy and Roo still stared each other down. Darryl stepped in then, and shepherded them through the side gate, separating them, as Mum went to check on Leena.

Once they were standing behind the house, Darryl spoke to Jimmy. 'Listen up now, Jimmy. Roo's coming back here to live, bruz. We've sorted it out, and he's gonna look after Leen properly now, face up to his responsibilities. So you can take it or leave it.'

The hate in Jimmy's eyes was answer enough. To him Roo would always be white first. He could never belong.

'He hit her,' said Roo, grimly warning Darryl, 'I'm gonna kill him.'

Mum came savagely down the back steps, bearing an aluminium softball bat in her right hand.

'No one's gonna kill anyone without my say-so,' she snapped.

'Now gimme that bloody thing.' She held her left palm out insistently for Jimmy's star picket. 'Give it.'

Seconds passed. Her palm lifted and then dropped by its own length. Its demand hung in the air between the three young men, crackling with authority.

Jimmy glared at Roo, then hurled the fencepost violently along the concrete of the garden path. It bucked and skidded, making a hideous scraping sound before coming to rest near the rusted wire gate. The star picket lay blackly across the concrete; it made a perfect right angle to the path. Seeing it there, Roo thought: step on a crack, break my grandmother's back. He wondered if Jimmy had meant to kill him with the bar, and whether he could have stopped him. Mum conferred briefly with Darryl, who walked over, picked the fencepost up and thrust it very deliberately into the soft dirt of the garden bed beside the gate, where it towered over Mum's marigolds.

'I've rung yer Uncle Eddie,' Mum informed Jimmy,' and he's on his way, so ya can knock orf and stay in the house till he gets here, right? Bloody fenceposts! What's the world comin to?'

Jimmy looked at Mum and Darryl standing firm together, glowered at the upright star picket, then, defeated, disappeared inside.

Still luminous with anger, Mum turned to face Roo. He jumped in before the barrage began: 'Is Leena okay? How's her—'

'Leena's gonna be alright,' she said shortly. 'Now get yaself under that tree till that old fella gets ere.' She pointed the way with the bat.

Roo raised his eyebrows – no ranting? no accusations? What was going on? He looked to Darryl for an explanation but 'Sit tight' was all that Darryl said before he escorted Mum away.

Roo went over and sat under the eucalypt, where he smoked, and wondered, and worried about uncles. Ten minutes later a cab pulled up, releasing Uncle Eddie along with two other men as lean and ancient as himself. All three wore the bush uniform of jeans, collared shirt and stained Akubra. One of them carried a very long, thin bundle wrapped with green canvas and tied with thin cord. The three Elders moved slowly, nodding and murmuring to each other until they reached the gate where Uncle Eddie came to an abrupt halt. The star picket turned his face into a creased black question mark.

Darryl quickly opened the gate and guided the men past it into the kitchen. When a cup of tea had been drunk and the situation explained, Uncle Eddie scratched at his grey beard.

'Better get em out the back then. You too, Mum.' Leena went to follow, but Mum insisted she stay inside. Wrong time, wrong place.

But Leena watched through the kitchen window anyway. Darryl collected Jimmy from the bedroom, and they duly assembled on the back lawn. Jimmy stood with his arms folded and his head down in front of Uncle Eddie.

Roo didn't know what to think when Mum beckoned him over towards the old men. Running was looking like a good option, but. He was just about ready to leg it over the back fence when Darryl saw his face, and quickly explained that the old men weren't there to take Jimmy's side, they were there to see justice done. Justice, thought Roo unhappily, I've had enough bloody justice in my life thanks very much. I'll be happy if I never see justice again. But Darryl was beside him, taking this turn of events in his stride, and so Roo trusted and was silent. Murri justice couldn't be much worse than the migloo sort, anyway. What doesn't kill us only makes us stronger, he thought, hoping not to disgrace himself. The man with the canvas bundle stood alert, waiting for instructions.

Uncle Eddie adjusted his hat onto the back of his head, and stood in front of the warring pair. He looked at each young man in turn with eyes that were blank of sympathy.

Roo fidgeted.

Jimmy swayed and kicked at the ground, and still the old man didn't speak.

'Which way?' he finally asked Jimmy. 'What you wanna go fighting with this whitefella for?'

'I hate him.' Jimmy spat the words at Roo.

'You hate yerself,' said Uncle Eddie sharply, 'now talk up.'

'He started it,' Jimmy accused. 'I was just ere mindin me own business and he come in and fucked everything up.'

'Which way him fuck everything up? House look alright to me. Mum bin look alright. Look to me like Leena the only one fucked up round ere, big bung eye blong you, uh?'

Jimmy looked at the ground some more as though it held the answer to his plight. 'He run out on me sister,' he muttered in the end.

Uncle grunted noncommittally. 'Run out on Leena?'

'Mmm.'

Uncle and the man with the bundle exchanged glances that Roo didn't like at all.

The interrogation continued. 'And that your business is it?'

Jimmy shrugged, a sulky lift of his bony shoulders.

Uncle grew sarcastic. 'This your business, uh? This your problem to run 'round and fix up, onetime? Ere comes Saint Jimmy, ere ta save the day? No need for Uncle Eddie, not now Jimmy's ere ta make things right.'

'It wasn't like that!' Jimmy burst out.

Uncle's eyes glittered like black ice; he went on as though Jimmy hadn't spoken. 'Or maybe this not your business at all. Maybe its ya mother's business, uh?' He paused.

Jimmy gave a tiny nod to the grass.

'And grown men's business?'

Another nod.

'Maybe you just gettin cheeky, playing at what you too fuckin stupid ta understand? Uh?'

'Yes,' Jimmy admitted in a whisper, no longer the big man.

Roo saw Jimmy's bottom lip begin to tremble, but he couldn't know that Jimmy was wishing Stanley was alive and with him. He needed his brother there with him to back him up in the face of this nightmare old man and his terrible questions.

'Too right it's my business. Up home they'd sort you right out. Yer blood'd be runnin fer nothin up there. You know fuck all, son.' He swung to face Roo, who was quaking beside Darryl.

Roo gazed at the thin old man who stood in front of him. There was no pretence about him. His strength came from Country, and he had no fear at all. Roo suddenly remembered something Darryl had said about Uncle Eddie, once after the funeral, about why he hadn't stayed in the church for the service. Darryl's explanation had been unusually terse and reluctant, as if he knew Roo wouldn't understand. Whiteman talk. Uncle Eddie stands in the Law. If Stanley'd lived he coulda bin a Lawman too, but he was too cheeky. Haveta be someone else now. So, Uncle Eddie's too sorry to stay in church, see? Darryl had never said who the 'someone else' was, and Roo didn't understand enough to ask. Maybe he's right, Roo thought with a heavy sense of shame bearing down on him. Maybe we do know fuck all.

Uncle Eddie broke the silence between them. 'So …
gonna face up to your responsibilities now, eh? Ya took
your sweet time 'bout it.'

'Yes.' Roo said to both statements.

'I dunno if I believe you.' Uncle stared at the white
face in front of him. 'You bin run out on that girl once
already. Maybe you'll do it again.'

'I won't.'

'You wanna be in this family?' Uncle Eddie probed.
'Or you wanna come and go as you please? Wanna run
away when it gets little bit hard, and come back when ya
need somewhere ta camp?'

Roo shot a resentful glance at Mum. Was that what
she'd told Uncle Eddie? It wasn't like that … was it? He
folded his arms against this idea.

'I, I wanna be here. With Leena and the baby. But
Jimmy …' Roo shook his head. It was no use.

'Jimmy what? Jimmy run your life? Or you run it?'

'I run it. But if he picks me, I ain't gonna stand back.
I'll—'

Uncle Eddie raised his hand at that, silencing Roo's
babble. 'Right. You two got bad blood Mum tells me.
Needs sortin out. He gestured to the two men and they
stepped into the inner circle.

Jimmy bunched his fists against the lot of them. If he
was gonna go down, he'd go down fighting.

'Vince can be backer for Jimmy. And Peter, you wanna
go backer for …'

'Reuben,' Roo answered, his stomach a tight knot of
fear as he waited for whatever was coming.

'Uncle,' Darryl interrupted, and whispered in the old

man's ear. What he said made Uncle Eddie tilt his hat backwards once more, and nod in approval. There was something to this young bloke alright. He wasn't silly, not by a long shot.

'Hold up there, Vince. Darryl wants ta go second fer his brother.'

Jimmy raised his head curiously at that, and when Darryl walked over to stand beside him, walked over in front of everyone, something long-forgotten fluttered in his chest.

'You don't wanna do this,' Jimmy told him. 'Whadda you know what I want, shitfabrains? Ya my brutha aren't ya?'

Jimmy turned away from Darryl, unable to speak. He tasted salt in the back of his mouth.

'And, ah, Jimmy,' Uncle's finger was up high, lecturing the lad and through him, the whole family. He spoke loudly so everyone could hear. 'This star picket business. You wanna fight weapon, boy?'

Jimmy shook his head frantically. A moment's pause, then Uncle's accusing arm fell to his side. The man carrying the spears shifted them to lean against his other shoulder.

'Good. You learnin.' With that, Uncle Eddie retreated to the chairs beneath the gum tree and rolled himself a smoke.

'What's going on?' asked Roo in weary confusion.

'Youse two can sort it out now,' Darryl said tightly. 'We're here to step in if anyone's gonna get hurt real bad. Peter's your backer. I'm backer for Jimmy. And then when it's over it'll be finished onetime between youse two, and youse can both live ere again. Alright?' The question was for both of them.

Jimmy nodded. Roo agreed and, with that, Darryl nudged Jimmy out into the open.

'Well, I'm here,' Roo said evenly, finding to his surprise that he at last had no fear.

'Whaddya waitin for?' Jimmy began by moving in and swinging at Roo's head, great glancing blows that were easily ducked and dodged.

Roo tapped him on the chin in return, darting in and quickly back out again. Then he split Jimmy's lip with a spinning back kick. Jimmy sank an uppercut into Roo's ribs that left him grunting in pain, then crossed it with a right that slid off Roo's eyebrows leaving a trail of bright red. Ninety seconds, and they were both blood-spattered, fuming in the dying evening light. A fire ran up Roo's side where Jimmy had cracked a rib. There goes my Nats he thought bitterly, as he lowered his left arm over his side to protect it from anymore damage. Ah, what's the use, you deserve it …

'You piece a white shit,' Jimmy charged him in a rugby-type move. 'Ya think ya can …' And it was on again as Roo's front kick missed. Their arms clashed, their legs, their foreheads and knuckles. Roo clinched Jimmy to him to save his rib; their blood flowed together, smearing over both their faces. When they broke, Jimmy informed Roo for the tenth time that he was about to be killed.

'Okay,' Roo heaved for breath. 'But first, I gotta tell ya something.' Get it over with. He was so sick of lies, so sick of em. People lied to ya and took your strength with their bullshit, well, no more. For a short time Roo left himself and wandered a dark path. He'd tell Jimmy the truth, once and for all, and then it'd be over, whatever happened. It'd be over fer good. If he died, he died. At least it'd be finished with, the horror and guilt of everything.

'When Stanley died—'

Jimmy's eyes gleamed. Mum made a choking sound. That name. Uncle Eddie stood up and listened harder.

'What?' Jimmy scowled.

'When he got killed,' Roo glanced at Darryl with a wild, full look, a kind of ultimatum, 'it was my father what killed him.'

Darryl took an unthinking step forward at that, then stopped himself. 'What?' he asked in disbelief. 'What'd ya say?'

'He's the cop. Graeme Madden. The one they're investigating,' Roo said simply and uncaringly to Darryl. His arms were loose by his sides. Nothing mattered anymore. 'He told me he didn't do it and I believed him, but now I know he's lying. He done it. He bashed Stanley, worse than he realised. And then he told me Stanley was scared of the dark, but it's him. It's him, he's the one what let him die cos he didn't have the guts to go in to where he was dyin'. He murdered him. I'm, I'm … sorry.' Having spoken, Roo heard the pathetic inadequacy of his words. He stood and waited for life to rain its vengeance down upon him.

Darryl drew a soft hand across his open mouth in astonishment. Then Jimmy let out an animal bellow of pain and rushed in. Earlier that afternoon, as he had wandered the southside streets, Roo had thought he wanted to die, had contemplated the leap off the bike path into the traffic of the South East Freeway. Now, although he remained stunned and heartsick, he quickly discovered that being punched in the side of the head by Jimmy James King had no appeal at all. Roo came back to life in his own defence, parrying Jimmy's punches, sliding away from kicks. He had no heart left anymore for hurting Stanley's brother, but he rolled and blocked to save himself. Jimmy attacked again and again; Roo weaved madly, and in the end nothing very serious connected.

Eventually Jimmy was too exhausted to go on. He fell back and Roo sank to one knee, seared by his rib and his awful tainted blood that made him an untouchable.

'That'll do man,' said Darryl, walking over between the two of them. 'Leave it. Or it'll be me next.'

Roo looked up at Darryl through a mask of blood, retching.

Darryl stared at the white boy with the eyes of a stranger, eyes loaded with questions.

'I'm sorry,' Roo repeated. 'I ...' But then what was there to say? He flung his hands apart and fell silent again.

'You're lying,' Darryl accused him, 'you're cracked.'

'No,' Roo answered, his lip curling down. 'He killed Stanley, truegod. There's no doubt in my mind. He done it, man. But ...' and his tone asked for forgiveness more bleakly than any words, '... he's not my father no more. He's just a murdering cunt and I never want to see him again. He's nothin to me.' Weak with pain, Roo stood up. He bit his lip to stop himself crying and slowly raised his fists to face height. He was ready for Darryl to start swinging at him. He deserved it – no one could blame Darryl. And Darryl would cream him, and then what?

They looked at each other wildly through the frame of Roo's fists. Darryl thought: this has happened before. I've stood here before and he's asked me for help. But it didn't matter. Nothing mattered anymore. He wasn't about to hurt him. Sweet Jesus it has to stop somewhere. It has to.

Oh man, save me from worse things. Help me, thought Roo. Help me or hit me, if ya don't I'm gonna die. I can't do this no more, I can't stand it. I'm weak. I'll die. It shoulda been me that died. 'He's not me father.' Roo said hopelessly, shaking his head. 'He's just ... nothin.'

Darryl reached out infinitely slowly with the fingers of his left hand, and pushed both of Roo's fists down. Roo shut his eyes, clenched his teeth and burst into loud racking sobs. In the background, Uncle Eddie nodded to himself. Yes. Good. He was the one, alright. Darryl would be the one.

'Alright,' said Darryl gently, 'alright'. In some way he didn't fully understand, the blood that was running down Roo's face and body made the whole business less shameful, made it somehow right. 'I know he's not, Roo. We all know. Just come inside and get cleaned up, eh. That goes for you too, Jimmy, come and get cleaned up.'

And that's exactly what they did.

Chapter Twenty-four

Two-twenty pm Monday, Police Media Room, Ground Floor. After fifteen minutes of legal gobbledegook that few in the audience could fathom, Bruce O'Connor stood in his dark suit in front of the roomful of people, many of them bearing cameras, and told them that the evidence presented to him did not in his view warrant further investigation nor the laying of criminal charges.

The matter, he said, had not been regarded as a possible homicide or a manslaughter from the beginning, and this investigation had proven that assumption to be absolutely correct. The young man in question was itinerant, profoundly alcoholic, had a personality disorder and a history of violence both to the public and to police. The measures taken by police officers on the night of his decease were determined to be regrettable but not excessive. The discrepancies in the Coroner's Report were of concern but did not lead him to recommend further disciplinary action. Senior Sergeant Graeme Madden was to attend a refresher course in arrest procedures, as per the latest review of the Police Service, which had advised such training for all personnel on a biannual basis. The inquiry was therefore closed. Questions from the media would be taken for five minutes.

Quivering with relief, Graeme answered queries from the tamer journalists, and then shrugged himself into a more restricted area of the building. He ran his hands down his face and blinked. It was finally over. Thank Christ. Jonesy, who had been with him on the night in question, came out and met his eyes.

'Glad that's over, I bet, pal,' he said, slapping Graeme's back.

'Fucken oath, mate. Fucken oath.' Grinning like a fool, Graeme shook his head with a grave expression to dignify his plight.

'They'll fucken crucify ya if ya lettem, that's for fucken sure,' Jonesy said.

'Yeah. I tell ya mate, it's been a fucken nightmare coupla months. Me wife's been away in Sydney, and … well, there's been all this family shit going down, too.' Graeme spoke in a tone of light complaint of his troubles.

'Mmm. Ah, well. TJS.' Jonesy shrugged, but sympathetically.

'It coulda been me up there as easy as you, eh?'

'Yeah, the job sux is right. Christ, to think I dreamed about being a cop as a kid. Ah, geez, for a while there I thought they were gonna charge me over it and I was gonna have to knock meself!' Graeme joked. He made the gesture of putting a gun to his temple and pulling the trigger. 'Peeyow!' he said slushily, vibrating his tongue at the back of his throat to make the bullet whizz.

'Yeah, join the club,' said his colleague, slapping him

on the back one last time before heading downstairs. 'Actually, I'll see ya at the club later on, I spose?'

'Yeah, I reckon. I'm gonna cut loose, mate.' Graeme stretched his fingers towards the ceiling. He felt like he could fly.

When the media had all disappeared, and he'd had the smoke he sorely needed, he returned to his desk to stow the paperwork. Graeme got a standing ovation from his colleagues, and that was something for cops to do, eh. He waved a hand at them to shut up.

'So, you're not going down for five to ten?' Bill shook his head with comic mournfulness. 'And we thought we'd finally got rid of ya, too.'

'Yeah, I love you too, pal.' Graeme was airy.

'I might not have to blow me brains out now, there's a tragedy for ya.' Bill laughed and shook Graeme's hand.

'Knowing your luck the fucken gun'd jam, mate,' he joked, 'and one've us'd hafta come and finish you off.'

Graeme grinned. Things were finally looking up. He noticed a fat yellow envelope sitting on the top of his desk. He eyed it, not expecting any parcels. 'What's this?' He prodded it, then picked it up. It was heavy for its size.

'Fat Controller stuck it there not long ago,' Ellen told him.

Graeme felt the parcel and recognition blossomed. He ripped it open. The police-issue pistol was hard and solid underneath his fingertips. So he was back in the fold, eh? Good-oh. Talk about taking temptation out of a bloke's path. The Fat Controller wasn't such a bad bloke after all. And certainly not a stupid one.

★

Roo successfully avoided Graeme's self-righteousness in front of the media and left the Police HQ with a bitter heart. He shuffled painfully across the road to the Transit Centre, checked the timetables, and then went straight to the phone booth. He had three calls to make before catching the bus back to Park Street. The connecting train he wanted left in an hour and a half. He could do it, just.

The first call he made was to Coach. Roo carefully explained about his busted rib, and how he'd have to miss the national titles. He was sorry, he said, but …

'What happened?' the man asked.

'It's a long story. But it's okay. Don't worry about me,' Roo assured him.

'Have you at least got somewhere to stay?' Coach asked in a worried voice. 'Cos if you don't—'

'I have,' Roo told him, 'or I will shortly. I'm gonna go to Cairns to me girlfriend's Uncles' place for a little while. Got some business to take care of. I'll be back. I'll be back to watch the Nationals in September. I just won't be able to run for a bit, that's all.'

'But what about those AIS forms we were gonna fill out?' urged Coach. 'Wiseman rang me the other day. He wanted to make sure you applied.'

Roo smiled at that. 'Yeah, I know. We'll do it when I get back, eh? I'll be good then.' Roo said this with great certainty. Things'll settle down with Leen. Do nothing and it'll be alright.

'Well, keep in touch, eh?' Coach planned to fill the forms in straightaway. Kid that could run like that.

'Yeah, okay,' Roo said. 'Oh, and Coach …'

'Mmm?'

'Thanks for everything, eh?' His eyes were moist as he rang off. Roo wiped his nose on his shirt and told himself what a weak prick he was. The second call was to Leena. 'If you're coming, I'll be there in ten minutes. The train's at five o'clock, so pack yer bags, honey.'

But he couldn't make the third call. Ten minutes came and went, and another ten. He rang Circle Street and got the beginning of the message but for the life of him (for the life of Stanley) he couldn't speak. He didn't know what to say. And yet something needed to be said. Blind Freddy could see that. He owed it to the Kings, to Stanley.

Roo went for a quick durrie, and then came back and looked at the public phone again. A way to say what he needed still eluded him. He dragged at his neck in frustration. Roo decided to go and buy the tickets him and Leena needed, then come back, make the call and bolt.

Having a plan settled him a little, and he went to the ticket counter full of confidence. 'How much is it for two economy returns to Cairns, mate?' he asked.

'Hundred and ninety-four each,' said the clerk, 'if you mean today. You're cutting it pretty fine.'

'Yep, today it is.' Roo counted out the money Mum had loaned him and put it together with his own and Leena's. It just covered the cost of the tickets, with a little left over for food. 'Here y'are.' He handed over the notes.

'To Cairns?'

'Yeah.'

'Luggage?'

'Just hand-held.'

'Names?'

'King, S. King and, ah …' Roo stopped dead at the question. Glover. Glover the lover. Who was that? A streetie, a crim. A kid in lock-up a long time ago. Or Madden. What Graeme said Stanley yelled: Come and suck me black cock, Madman. King. Martin Luther King, he thought. The march on Washington, that sea of faces in the poster Mum had. Rodney King and them LA riots. King.

Glover. Madden.

'The second name?' the clerk prompted.

Roo snapped out of his reverie. He noticed the time on the wall behind the clerk's head. Jesus, better get cracking. 'Oh, King fer both of em, that'll do. L.D. and R.W.'

'Here you are, departure lounge six in half an hour.'

'Ta.' Roo grabbed the tickets and knew the phone call couldn't wait any longer.

No cheap shots, he thought to himself, groaning inside as he fronted the phone booth again. Things were always complicated, always fucken impossible. With a sick feeling, he gritted his teeth. No excuses: Just do it. His legs trembled as he rang his father's work number. Roo couldn't believe what he was doing. He must be insane. Yer mad ya prick. He's a senior sergeant, fer Chrissake. Yer on parole.

'Faith?' You could hear the smile in Graeme's voice. Home free. The happy little chappy. Well, why wouldn't he be? Roo shivered. Soon put a stick in his spokes, the prick.

'It's me – Roo. I won't be coming back,' he told him baldly. 'And something else too, while I'm at it.'

Graham's smiley sounds faded away to confused ones, then built up to an angry outburst. Roo went on, oblivious.

'I … I've worked it out. Finally. About Stanley. Maybe I'm a bit bloody thick or something, or you're a bit too fucken good of a liar—'

Graeme tried to interrupt but Roo didn't let him. He was way past Graeme now, way past lying dogs of coppers and parents that didn't want you, or people what went off and died when you needed them. Reckless, the boy cast away the hope that had anchored him in Graeme's life for the past weeks.

'Shut-up! Just shut up … I told ya not to lie to me, didn't I? Anyway, I'm goin, you've had ya little inquiry thingo now, so no doubt you'll be right. I'm pissin off, ya won't be bothered by me again, mate.' Roo paused for a fraction of a second, and let a little extra acid into his voice before he added, 'I've gotta go and see a bloke about a busted torch.'

He waited just long enough to hear Graeme choke with surprise. Then he slammed the phone into its socket, picked up his bag and headed for the door.

Aware of the others still hovering in the office, Graeme carefully put the phone down. He groped in blind panic for his packet of smokes. Hastily, he scooped his sports bag up and told Ellen that he'd see them all at the club in five minutes. He climbed the three flights of stairs to the top of the building; once there he sat crouched on the wooden bench, high above the traffic and the abyss, his head whirling. His son's accusation echoed in his head. The broken torch. It was the luck of the Irish, wasn't it, the way things happened to fuck you up. It occurred to Graeme to call his wife, and then he suddenly realised that there would be no point. No point at all.

Dull with grief, Graeme smoked his cigarette and realised he was crying. Silent tears wet his face, and still nothing happened inside him to match the wetness. A minute later he slowly ground his smoke out on the concrete and allowed himself to think, finally, of the thin dead figure of Stanley King. It didn't seem to matter what he did, he couldn't get rid of it, that night, the stench, the screaming. You'd think when bastards were dead and gone, that'd be it, but no. Ghosts are real. People don't leave you alone, they're always there, always. The dark's full of them. Ghosts and strangers and fears.

The world's a funny place alright – in the daytime. The big man began to shudder where he sat. He stood up to try and get normal, snap out of it, but normal was gone. It had left the same time the boong did. It didn't exist. His life had turned into something he didn't understand anymore.

Graeme grasped the safety-mesh in his big hands, and rested his head against the cool metal. Below him he could see the tiny figures of people walking, standing and talking. Cars and buses. Life going on. No ghosts for those bastards. No bloody Stanley King haunting them. He stood gazing down, and then something odd, a small, marginal, insignificant hurt, brought him back to the present. In a kind of dream, Graeme Madden remembered the yellow envelope and suddenly understood that the irritating sharpness in his hip was the protruding metal hammer of his police-issue pistol.

It's done, Roo told himself. Fuck him. Friends like that. Family like that. No thanks pal. No more. No fucken way. As he strode exuberantly to the exit Roo marvelled at his newfound courage – I done it – and discovered with surprise that he was feeling almost … yeah, almost okay. Almost like he could like himself. Or something.

The winter sun was brilliant overhead in a windy, ice-blue sky. When he passed through the doors, a westerly was whipping off the mountains and chilling the entire city; it went straight through his cheap jumper. Shaky with cold and fear and hope, Roo squinted up from where he stood at the top of the Transit Centre escalators. The wind burned his face, but he was already up North.

I'll see ya in Cairns, mate, he told the blurry yellow disc in the sky that was giving light but no heat. Let's see if ya can do a better job of it up there. He rode down to ground level, stepped off the moving staircase and swung his training bag onto his back. Then the boy walked out from beneath the overhanging roof of the Transit Centre, out to the street, to the city, out to the big world where everything was waiting for him.